If it Falls

Naomi Young-Rodas

TSL Publications

Acknowledgments:

The Amnesty International Report on extrajudicial executions in Guatemala from which the extract at the end of the book is taken, can be found at: https://www.amnesty.org/download/Documents/16400 0/amr340031996en.pdf

The inspiration for the Don Postura story told to Benigno, came from *Our Word is Our Weapon* by Subcommandante Marcos, but is the author's own creation.

First published in Great Britain in 2020
By TSL Publications, Rickmansworth

ISBN: 978-1-913294-80-9

Prologue

Raphael is a sensitive man. He cries at concerts, he cries at films, but especially he cries at poetry. The great writings of his continent make him weep: Ernesto Cardinal, Pablo Neruda, Eduardo Galeano, Otto Rene Castillos. He would like to be able to write like that, but he can't write any more.

Some say there is nothing that doesn't move him. Others laugh at him, *machos* don't cry. Some say he's crazy. Crazy for love and grief for his *compañera* Lidia, gone *ya hace muchos años*, many years now; who died in pain, screaming out in the darkness of a mountain camp, while he held his hand over her mouth, frightened that her screams would attract enemy fire. You can see the scars on his hands where she bit him, almost to the bone, while the tears ran silently down his cheeks. That's when the tears began, and they haven't stopped since.

Raphael is a man lost in a world of words and nightmares. The nightmares come less frequently now, but still they come – always the same, pitch black, the blackness only revolutionaries hiding in the mountains know. Helicopters whirr overhead and in the distance, gunfire. In the glow of candlelight, sweat drips into his eyes and mixes *con las lagrimas*, the salt smarts. The pain begins in his hand; so unbearable he bites his own tongue to keep from crying out. But the ceaseless screaming is not his. He wakes bathed in perspiration, his hair soaked, bedclothes clinging to him like a straitjacket; he wakes before the silence that followed the screams, before the slap and the small weak cry of a newborn. There will be no more sleep.

Rising, he goes out to his small balcony, lights a hand-rolled cigarette and inhales, taking the smoke deep into his lungs. He keeps a supply already rolled; his hands shake too much to roll them at night. Sometimes they shake too much to light one. He stands on his balcony in the quiescent city. No one ventures out after midnight, not even the prostitutes. The night keeps the city's secrets, those who wish to know them will not return, but be lost to its darkness. Raphael stands and smokes and soaks up the silence into every pore until the screams are gone. He knows the silence is death and the screams are life, but the silence is easier to bear. Even in the city the air is cool at 4 a.m. The coolness dries the sweat on his skin, skittering shivers through his body. Despite everything he is still susceptible to sensation; too susceptible.

Back inside he sits at his meagre wooden desk. Lighting three candles, the eternal trinity, though he hates the dark, he can't stand too much light, he crosses himself out of habit. He still believes in God, reluctantly, but can no longer worship, his faith is gone. He kisses the black, miniature woven cross around his neck, never removed because of superstition rather than conviction. He gave Lidia the cross when they left for the mountains, much good it had done her, maybe he should have given her a *milagro*, a small silver charm of a body part, given to saints to protect the petitioner. But how could he have known to give her one in the shape of a baby. He only gave her his heart and it wasn't enough. He says the prayer he says every night – *que descansen en paz y yo tambien* – may they rest in peace and me also.

He writes bad poetry until dawn and the city begins to rise. He showers. The water is always cold, whatever the time of day, but he is lucky to have water, often there is none. He dresses in his work clothes, journalistic clothes, baggy linen trousers and a cotton shirt with the top buttons undone – a slightly crumpled look, which could be appealing, if it didn't show how little he cared. The revolutionary fatigues are long since abandoned.

He walks slowly to the corner where the Indian women make tortillas by hand, the warm corn smell almost tactile, and buys a small coin's worth that will last him all day. He returns home and makes coffee, the weak kind mixed with wheat. The best coffee goes for export or to fancy cafés he doesn't visit on principle. He adds plenty of sugar and eats tortillas with salt and *chimol*, so hot it sets his tongue aflame, the gulp of hot coffee adding to the burn. Tortillas are still his lamplight in the darkness, his blanket against the cold.

1

Raphael prepared to go to the office until he remembered it was Sunday. Every morning he went to the office of the newspaper, *Siglo Veintiuno,* to check messages and pick up assignments, though he rarely wrote or did research there. He mostly wrote editorials, a regular column on current affairs, the occasional in-depth report. He hadn't worked on the day-to-day reporting since he'd first started at the paper, back in the days when he'd just returned from the mountains. He'd been lucky to get the job. True, he'd been something of a name in journalism before he joined the guerrillas, but he'd changed that name since then. His old life had been disappeared; he'd had to make a new one, but he didn't want to, he wanted to curl up in a corner and die. However, fate was not so benevolent. Had he taken a risk going back to his profession? What if someone recognised him? What if someone recognised his style? But he'd never bumped into anyone he'd worked with before, and he'd been so changed that he might as well be a different person. He was a different person.

'Worked on a paper before have you? Any references?'

Oh yes, he'd had glowing references, but who knew where they were now? Who knew what his parents had done when they'd cleared out his apartment? He would have liked to have gone back and seen it, but those days were gone, best forgotten, best to concentrate on remembering who he was.

'I'll give you a six-month trial, but none of this wishy-washy stuff. There's no censorship at this paper. I want a proper column. If you're not up to it, I'll soon find someone else.'

Raphael was up to it. He didn't have much choice. And how hard could writing be, compared to death? How many years ago had that been? Too many. He'd worked hard those six months; proved himself. The publication of the collection of poems he'd written during the conflict had helped. He was invited to teach a class at the university, though he never felt very comfortable teaching others how to write when he could no longer write himself. Not poetry, not like he used to, though he couldn't stop trying. He could write his column in his sleep, but poetry, that required a soul, and Raphael had lost his. It was buried with Lidia. Somehow he bumbled through, was respected by his students on the strength of his one great work, but he hadn't published anything since.

Going home one night he heard recitation, words put to song.
'*Las lagrimas caen como gotas de rocio del nopal,*
lento y solo a veces.
El frio de las montañas se volvio en calor de fuego.
Las llamas se conviertieron en balas.'

His words. *Las lagrimas*, always the tears. So many words for crying and only one word for tears, those tiny rolls of salt-filled water that symbolised so much, weeping, wailing, sobbing, keening, he had heard them all, plaints, dirges, knells, elegies, but no requiems. There was no time for that when smoothing the earth over your loved one, waiting for the next bomb to drop. Running with a baby bundled on your back in a *rebozo*, bound like an Indian woman, whispering, telling the boy not to cry, singing 'hush now, hush now, the little light is shining,' while his whole body cried out to sing '*la llorona, llorona, llorona,*' the weeping woman. But there wasn't time for weeping, not even time for ashes to ashes.

Raphael felt like a fraud, because those poetic words no longer came. The students sang them, made his words the songbook for their lives, and the words were trapped within him. That night he went home and wrote his letter of resignation to the university, but he never got around to sending it.

Since it was Sunday, Raphael had time to kill. Later he was supposed to meet Lola, the new love in his life. No, love was the wrong word, lover perhaps. There had only ever been one love for Raphael. But there was something about Lola, something more than sex. Was it the way she tucked her hair behind her ear when she concentrated? The way she chewed her lip when she was nervous, all that energy fighting to get out. She was always restless, always on the move, the antipode to Raphael. He smiled as he remembered the first night they'd slept together. Worn out, Raphael was already drifting off while Lola moved around.

'What are you doing, fidget?'

'I need some water.'

She shuffled about, pulling the blanket up around her chin, then throwing it off dramatically. Her legs pushed against him and retreated. Raphael nestled his face into her neck, arm around her stomach pulling her close to him, loving the feel of her bare skin. She edged further and further away. The body that had been so intimate a few minutes before repelled his as it drew into itself.

He got used to it in time, though it never became a habit to spend the night together. Consciously or unconsciously, Lola demanded things her way and that wasn't always what he wanted. He wanted to be alone, but things weren't that simple. His life was merely an existence, and Lola was a complication he didn't need. Her very presence hinted that there was something more. Hinted that there might one day be love again. But didn't he know better than to hope for that? Didn't he know that happiness was always balanced by sadness? And yet Lola said his sadness was what endeared him to her most.

Watching *Los Olvidados*, the classic film by Buñuel, the first time they went to the cinema, she had taken his hand in the dark, seeing the emotion play on his face. For a minute he thought she understood, though it wasn't until much later that she knew about his life, and then only the headlines.

'Do you cry at Bond films, too,' she joked, taking his arm on the way out. He looked blankly at her. 'Hey, I'm sorry. I'm not making fun, honestly. It's sweet.'

'Sweet?'

'I like it.'

At the time he'd been too overwhelmed by her attention to take the comment to heart. Things were too new. *El organismo pide sal*, his friend Pedro used to say, it seemed his body needed loving, though his mind was reluctant to admit it.

Lola didn't cry at films and she didn't cry when they made love. Raphael sometimes wondered if anything touched her.

Raphael wandered aimlessly towards the main square. The streets hummed, brimming with life. Since the signing of the peace, though fear lived barely hidden below the surface and rippled through the nights, during the day a lively exuberance had returned, which could not be struck down. Indian women in their brightly coloured *traje* sold flowers. Their brightness mingled with the gaiety of their dress, giving a false sense of happiness. The majority were widows; they wore the widow's face of sorrow as they whispered in their secret tongues. Raphael had forgotten most of his Quiche, sometimes he caught a word or two he understood. He stopped and addressed an old lady, most of her teeth gone, bedraggled hair escaping from her headband.

'*Utz le ewach?*' 'How are you?' She smiled bashfully. So rarely did someone address her with respect, recognise her existence. He bought a bunch of the tiny bananas common to the area, telling her to keep the change. Eating one, he slid the rest into the leather satchel he always carried. Old men shuffled by carrying stacks of wood on their backs, supported by a band across their foreheads, bent with the weight. There were few young men. Boys begged to shine his shoes so that they could eat that day. Raphael was pleased to see one of the regular boys with a customer. He knelt, barefoot, before a tourist, one of the few dotted around the square that dared to experiment with the emerging peace to see the splendour of the country. Or maybe the man worked with the United Nations – MINUGUA, or was a Mormon – there were plenty of those in the capital. But no, he was too dishevelled for that, no tie, no name badge. This man was a tourist, a seeker of excitement and novelty, of memories to take home.

The boy told the tourist how his father was sick and now he had to clean more shoes. His accent was not from the city. Was it just a story to earn an extra tip, Raphael thought. When had he become so cynical?

Once he'd arrived in the *zocalo*, Raphael sat by the fountain – it still didn't work, though many years ago it had sent a beautiful cascade over the stone figures – and watched the crowds. There was the ubiquitous demonstration, placards and signs, the loud hailer rallying the faithful. Today saw the red and black flag of a union, and the speaker extolling the virtues of *La Frente*, the new coalition of left wing groups, even some ex-guerrillas, who hoped to make inroads into government; to vanquish the corrupt politicians and generals. Lola was not political, but she worked for the education project of *La Frente*. Part of their plan was to educate people about their rights and the importance of voting. This was hard when so many people couldn't read, even in their own language, let alone Spanish, and when so many had grown up with no idea what democracy was. Lola was good at it. He'd seen her once at a workshop and had been startled by her enthusiasm, an energy that seemed to extend to him only in the bedroom. He'd been surprised at her knowledge, the pedagogy of the oppressed in practice, when he'd never seen a book in her apartment.

The weekend workshop had been billed as a romantic get away, though he was the romantic, not Lola, and she'd proved it. 'Help me with this flip-chart.' 'Can you draw?' 'Oh, you're useless for everything! Sit in the back if you can't be helpful, or go and write a poem, write a poem about the future. The terror is over Rafa, we have to build the future.' The terror wasn't over for Raphael, he lived it constantly in his head. Build the future on what? There were no rocks for foundations, only blood-soaked sand that would soon be washed away. But he couldn't tell Lola that, she hadn't suffered, she didn't understand. He sat in the back and watched, watched her bring a glimmer of that future to the women's eyes. Lola, the great organiser of workshops, it sat uneasily with the image he'd formed of her, the recklessness, the abandon, clothes flung around in the morning rush to dress, bed left unmade, the endless searching for keys thrown down in a hurry. She never stopped, never stopped long enough to sense the sadness, and Raphael never moved quickly enough to push it away.

Raphael sat watching the sun sparkle on the side of the cathedral, the sky was a perfect blue. Next to him a girl rested, she mirrored the sky, dressed in the brilliant blues of the villages around Lake Atitlan. Dusk time cobalt, lapis and turquoise like the stones; tiny silver flecks glinted in the stripes of her skirt. She had slipped off her plastic sandals and rubbed one dusty foot over another. From her head she took the bundle of weavings she had been trying to sell. It was so large Raphael wondered how she had carried it. She was ten maybe, but small, skinny, the red cloth belt wound tight to

9

hold up her skirt. She turned towards him and smiled, looking him full in the face, no bashfulness, this was a well-travelled girl. Alone in the city? Making money to feed her family, far from her lake with its deceitful serenity and the smoke of frying fish. Her smile was electric, no hint of the tired feet and back, the loneliness, and the eyes … the eyes like Lidia's that had been so deep and full of love. Raphael smiled back, then turned away quickly.

He took out a notebook and began to make notes for an article, which soon became a poem scribbled in the margins. *El azul perfecto de los rebozos se convirtio en rojo de sangre* – the perfect blue turned into the red of blood. Maybe Lola was right, maybe it was time to stop dwelling on the past and write poems of hope. If only it were as simple as changing 'blood' to 'hope'.

It was a habit of his to jot down poems on scraps of paper and in the corners of other works. Sometimes he wrote over previous writing and could barely decipher the words. His notebook was stuffed with bits of paper, receipts and bus tickets, café napkins, pages torn from books. They summed up his existence, scraps and bits and pieces.

'Prof! Prof! Señor Raphael.'

He looked up into the eyes of one of his students, the one with blue eyes and Indian hair, one of the keen ones, full of promise. 'You don't have to call me Señor, Miguel.'

'I'm so glad I bumped into you. I have a new poem. Can I sit with you? Am I interrupting?'

'No, it's all right Miguel. I'm just sitting here watching the world.' That's what he did now; watch, not participate. Raphael put his notebook away and took the folded paper from Miguel. The poem was about Miguel's son. Raphael had never been able to write about his son, first because of pain, then anger. Would he have written something like this, full of wonder and joy? Why am I doing this, he thought. I can't write any better than my students can.

'It's good, Miguel,' he said, trying not to look at him, the lump in his throat making it hard to talk.

'But surely you have some comments? Look this part here, I was wondering if …'

'How about if I take it, and have a proper look? Do you have a copy?'

'Yes, oh, yes that would be good.'

They sat for a moment, Raphael wanting to leave, but feeling inadequate that he couldn't even give advice on a poem, when Miguel surprised him again.

'Um ... Prof, I was wondering, would you be godfather to my son?'

'What?'

'You know we had a baby. I'd like you to be his godfather.'

'I'm flattered Miguel, but I can't.' Raphael looked away, blinking to bring the world back into focus.

'But why not? It doesn't involve much. I talked to my wife. She'd like it too.'

'I'm not a good choice. I don't really believe in, I mean I don't go to church much any more.'

'It's not about religion! What better role model could he have?'

Raphael wanted to laugh, what worse role model could he have. What made this student think Raphael had anything useful to pass on to his son? 'Choose one of your friends Miguel. Someone who can spend time with the child.'

'But ...' seeing the determination in his face Miguel decided not to pursue it. 'Er, right, right, well, um, you'll get back to me on the poem, then? In class next week?'

'Yes, I'll make some notes. Miguel, I'm sorry, it's just ...'

'No, no, *esta bien*. Don't worry. My wife's cousin, I'm sure they'll be flattered to be asked.'

Raphael almost wished he could have told him the real reason, that it would be too much to bear watching someone else's son grow up, but he couldn't. No one, except Lola, even knew he'd had a son. In his mind he saw Benigno's smiling face, heard his laugh.

He's looking at me. Crouching in the dirt, just like an Indian, feet apart, knees bent, bottom tucked in, too coordinated for a child. He's playing with the truck I made him, he's fascinated by the rubber band, he can't work out how it makes the wheels go round. He turns the matchstick, sets it down, watches it roll away, giggles every time. It's stuck, stuck on a clump of grass in the mud, his face such confusion. 'Papi.' He wants me to go and help him. I'm cleaning my rifle, hands full; I have to fit the barrel back, 'just a minute, mijo.' I turn away from him, look at the gun, just for a second. I don't hear the bomb. I look up and he's gone. I think he's run away. I can't understand the smoke, people running, splashes of red, burnt charred metal, that smell, what's that awful smell – cordite, burning, acrid, then, then ...

'Noooooooooo Benigno!' Someone is holding me; my arms are pulling out of their sockets. I don't hear them, but I feel them saying, 'no, don't go, don't see.' I break away, I don't know how many arms hold me, but I'm stronger, my need is stronger, there's something burning a hole in my stomach, something like rage, grabbing my guts, my throat, I'm choking, I fall forward, taste dirt, mud grazes my cheek. I look up, there's a hand. A hand with a toy truck. I retch. They drag me away. I shout silently, I shout and shout, but nothing comes out. Later they tell me they'd begged me to be quiet, they had to smother my screams, so we wouldn't be found.

Raphael lit a cigarette. The match shaking as he let it drop and struck another. The Indian *compañeras* had prepared Benigno's body, covering him in the yellow flowers of the dead. Raphael couldn't even watch. He'd wanted a wake; wanted to watch over his son through the night. Watch him every second. If only I hadn't looked at my gun, he thought for the millionth time. If I'd gone to him when he'd called. If I'd watched him, if only I'd watched him.

'Cub'saj c'ux alak', Raphael mumbled to himself. They had whispered it over and over, while they'd dug the hole, while they'd covered him. 'Console yourself with patience.'

Raphael wiped his nose on his sleeve, looked at his watch. It was almost time to meet Lola. He got up and went in search of a bus, trying to lock the memories back inside. At Lola's tiny apartment he knocked their secret knock. Although he had a key, he liked her to open the door to him. She opened it and pulled him inside. She kissed him briefly.

'Come to the kitchen, I'm cooking.'

He smelt onions frying and pork on the edge of burning. He followed her in. 'I'm not hungry,' he said.

'What happened?' It was uncanny how she always knew when something was wrong.

'Nothing. Something reminded me of the past, that's all.'

'Ai Rafa, why do you never tell me?'

'What's gone is gone.'

'But it does you no good to keep it all inside. It's eating you alive.'

'Maybe I want it to.'

'But I don't,' she said. 'What about me?'

What about you, he thought. You'll be all right, you always are. 'You'll be fine with your other lover,' he said, wanting to taunt her. He couldn't tell her about remembering Benigno, but he wanted her to feel his pain.

'What other lover? I have no other.' She jumped to denial so quickly that it made him wonder.

'Don't lie to me Lola. I know.'

She took his hands and looked into his eyes. 'You don't know it, you feel it because you're a sad man and you have to make every pain your own and if that's not enough then you imagine them too, that's why I love you.'

'I don't need to imagine them Lola, unlike you.'

'What's that supposed to mean?'

'You know. I don't even know why you waste your time with the peasants, why don't you just marry a rich man like your mother?'

'What do you know about my mother?' she snapped.

'Nothing. I don't know anything about your family. We never go and see them. Do I embarrass you? I'm not good enough for you, eh?'

'That's not true Raf.' She stopped stirring, turned off the gas, and went over to him.

'There never seems to be any time, that's all. What's brought all this on?'

'Nothing.'

'Nothing, yes clearly it's nothing, when you come in here, having a go at me, claiming I'm having an affair.'

He didn't tell her he'd seen them. Though he hadn't seen the man's face, though they hadn't kissed, there was something about the way her eyes had shone, something about the way they'd touched, that told Raphael they were lovers.

'I'm sorry.'

'Come here,' she said. She put her arms around him and smoothed his hair like a child. Raphael let her lead him into the bedroom. He didn't have the energy to fight. There were enough problems in the world without that and maybe the truth was he just didn't care enough. He let her undress him, let her make all the moves, let himself be lost in her touch.

She laughed, 'See how I love you?'

He wanted to say, 'But you don't.' Instead he slept. Strangely he always slept in her bed, never a nightmare. It was dark when he woke. She sat next to him, naked, flicking through papers.

'What are you doing?'

'Looking at some notes for the conference tomorrow.'

Working, she was always working. He lay still, remembering the night he'd first seen them, weeks previously.

Walking home, he had noticed them come out of the cinema. It was pouring down, the early evening monsoon of rainy season. Raphael liked it. He had rolled up his trousers and walked freely through the inches of collected water, letting his Indian *huaraches* soak and get heavy, the cool water trickling over his toes, the slightly warmer squish of water and mud between the rubber of his sandals and the sole of his foot. His short-brimmed hat did little to prevent rain seeping through to his hair. Water ran down the back of his collar and mingled with the sweat on his back. He was daydreaming, lost in memories, watching his feet so that he didn't slip from the kerb into the even deeper water in the road, when he looked up to cross the street and saw them. More precisely, he saw Lola. She was the kind of woman who stood out. Her decisive walk, the way she held a room when she entered it, though she was slight, he could almost put his hands around her waist, but she seemed tall. Those eyes that penetrated; that watched every move.

They were paused under the awning of the cinema like a still from a film. It was a cinematographic moment, like Marilyn Monroe holding down her skirt, or Gene Kelly mid-swing on the lamppost in *Singing In The Rain*. They looked serious, as if the film they had just seen had been intense. The man's hand rested lightly on her elbow. An innocent enough gesture, but the gentleness of it conveyed an intimacy deeper than friendship. And there was the way she looked at him, that was love and passion and desire all in a few seconds. Raphael couldn't really see the man's face; only that he was young, with an impression of maturity and sensitivity, too subtle for Lola.

Then the moment was over. The young man struggled to put up an umbrella and Lola laughed, threw back her head and laughed richly, a laugh surely inspired by more than his struggling with the stubborn contraption. Finally, it was up, he took her arm and they rushed off into the rain. Raphael was not shocked. He felt like a voyeur, an unwanted guest, as though he had just caught them in bed. Yet he was strangely unmoved.

Raphael and Lola got up and ate, he in silence, she wanting to talk. On occasion she would join in his silence, but mostly she didn't understand that the most beautiful thing was to be with someone you didn't need to talk to. He and Lidia had sat for hours just looking at the stars, no words, no disharmony.

He wondered if Lola could have survived life in the mountains. She had enough passion for the struggle. She worked long, hard hours for *La Frente*, but she came at things from a different angle. She hadn't grown up poor. She was a city girl. In a different time and place she would have been a society woman hanging on the arm of a handsome rich man, more interested in doing her nails than in the political situation.

He looked at her. There was no doubt she was beautiful. The hazel eyes, the left one with its peculiar chunk of green, as though the paint brushes had been mixed up when they'd made her, the long dark hair. It was no surprise that other men chased her. No surprise if she gave in to them. He wondered what she saw in him, why she stayed. But then why did he stay?

Raphael chewed the pork slowly. It was a bad piece, tough, but they were lucky to have meat to eat and the spices Lola had added made it tasty. Sometimes Lola's impulsiveness scared him. He wondered if she ever thought about anything before she said or did it, but he knew she did. He saw her preparing workshops, and presentations, organising other people. He saw how carefully she orchestrated things, even seducing him. He felt sure she had

15

planned that, he just didn't know why. But it didn't take much for Raphael to become irrationally paranoid. Surely no one could blame him for that. How could he not be paranoid when he'd lost his wife? When his son had been taken from right in front of him? When he'd had to become someone else to return to the city? Someone had it in for him. They had files on him; he knew that, they must have. He knew what a bugged phone sounded like, the clicks and echoes.

'What are you staring at?'

'Huh?'

'What are you staring at, daydreamer?'

'Your beauty,' he said, not wanting to say anything deeper.

'Ah well, that I can understand!' she said, smiling coyly. Modesty was not a quality she possessed in excess. 'Pablo Collado is playing tonight. Shall we go and see him?'

His first inclination was to say no. That music was so beautiful it only made him sadder than ever, but he acquiesced. It would make her happy and make little difference to him.

'Yes, let's go,' he said and smiled.

She mistook his smile for happiness.

'We'll need to leave soon, so I can go to Mass on the way.'

'Why do you persist in that? You don't even believe in all that rigmarole.'

'It's you who doesn't believe.'

'But you're an educated woman, you surely don't think saying a Hail Mary will make everything all right.'

'I never said it makes everything all right. It makes me feel better.'

'It's a habit.' Raphael sighed.

'Maybe it is, but it wouldn't do you any harm to cultivate it.'

'Don't go there Lola, you know why.' They had had the conversation many times before.

'I know what? I know your wife died and that's all. Lots of people die, Raphael. You never tell me about it. You never tell me what it was like in the guerrillas.'

'I shouldn't have told you that much.' He felt like slapping her. What did she know about people dying? Whom had she ever lost?

'There you go, shutting me out as usual.'

Raphael sighed again. He didn't know what to say. He couldn't tell Lola about his other life. He wished he'd never told her anything about Lidia and Benigno. Those memories were sacred, not to be shared. 'Fine, whatever. Let's not fight about it. I'll wait for you outside the church or something.'

They sat in candlelight letting the music float over them. The haunting, spine chilling flute, summoning up the spirits of the mountains, the chill of a winter morning, the sorrow of death many times over. Raphael made no attempt to hide the tears that flowed down his face. Lola saw them and squeezed his hand. He wished Lidia could have heard this music. The only music she had ever heard was marimba and US pop music on the radio. They hadn't had time or money to go to concerts. Oh, but how they'd danced to the marimba! He could never get the rhythm right, the shuffling feet seemed too slow for the frenetic striking of the wooden bars, the comical tunes, the juxtaposition of the serious faces and the flying beaters. 'Move your feet, city boy,' Lidia stretched up to whisper in his ear. Maybe he shouldn't feel bad about Lola cheating on him, he two-timed her constantly with a ghost.

Lola drank beer. He sipped lemonade. He no longer drank, not on any principle but because he didn't think he'd be able to stop, and if he had to go on living he didn't want it to be in a drunken stupor.

Lola smiled at him, '*vas a quedar con migo?* Are you going to stay with me?'

Raphael rarely spent the night with her. He was torn between knowing that if he stayed he would sleep peacefully, and wondering how much he might write if he went home and had another bout of insomnia. Waking up with Lola always brought a pain that it wasn't Lidia. Somehow it wasn't real. For some reason, he usually left with a nervous sense that he'd never see her again. For reasons of self-preservation he avoided it. Tonight, he looked at her and nodded, suddenly and inexplicably grateful that it was him she wanted to be with.

Lola lay half across him, one arm around him, her breasts against his chest, a leg draped over his, her face close to him. It was strange

17

for her not to be on the other side of the bed. Her breath on his neck aroused him. He wanted to look at her but didn't want to wake her. She stirred and moved away slightly. He rolled her gently onto her back and began to kiss her breasts. She smiled in her sleep. Her lips opened slightly. He ran his hand down her body and between her legs. She moaned almost imperceptibly and opened her eyes. 'Well good morning to you, too!'

He smiled and they made love slowly.

While Raphael lay in bed, Lola jumped up and busied herself with making coffee, seeming to have immediately forgotten the sanctity of the moment, if she'd noticed it at all. He wiped the tears away, rose slowly, resisted the temptation to hold her and took the coffee from her in silence. It made a pleasant change that she had any time for him. She was always late, stuffing things into her bag, rushing out, saying, 'I'll call you,' and then not calling for days.

He sat at the table sipping coffee.

'Don't you have to rush off somewhere?'

'Trying to get rid of me now, are you? Have your wicked way with me, and then bye bye Lola!'

'That's not what I'm …'

'I know. I'm teasing. *Por Dios*, Raphael, lighten up a bit. The conference doesn't start until 10 a.m. But I have to leave soon to go and set up. Listen, why don't you come with me?' she asked. 'Or come to some of it. You should be there anyway, covering it for the paper. It's important you know. Rigoberta will be there, and Byron.'

'Yes, I suppose I should. I wonder why El Pelon didn't ask me to go.'

'Your editor has probably given it to some junior reporter. It needs someone decent on it.'

'And that would be me, would it?'

'Of course.' She gave him a peck on the cheek as she began gathering papers.'

'Let me look at the agenda. Hmm. I'd better go into the office first, but I could come to the first plenary at 11.30 a.m.'

2

Raphael sat at his desk at *Siglo Veintiuno*, looking out of the window, remembering his old life, while the newsroom bustled around him. Shutting all that out, he pulled a veil over his eyes and went back in time whenever he wanted. It was more real than present reality. He felt Lidia touch his face, so gentle and soft, so caring, so different from Lola's touch. Whenever Lola touched him it felt like a physical necessity, as if she needed the strength of his body. Not that he was a particularly strong man, physically; his strength came in his ability to withstand. There was no gentleness in Lola's touch, little warmth for him. In contrast he had felt surrounded by Lidia's love constantly, though she rarely touched him unless they were alone. He smiled to himself as he remembered them in a hammock, trying to make love.

'Ai I'm getting seasick! Get on top, *tonta*!'

'*No me dices tonta, pendejo!*' Lidia hits me playfully on the back for calling her stupid.

'Ouch, I was just kidding. Ah, I'm falling.' I swing a foot over quickly to the ground to support us, slip on mud without my boots, and nearly bring the whole hammock down. We break into uncontrollable giggles. Lidia is crying from trying not to laugh out loud. The hammock shakes so much I'm scared it will fall. 'This is hopeless. Why don't we lay on the ground?'

Lidia splutters, struggling to get words out. 'I'm not getting bugs in my chones for you, Raphael Sifuentes!' And she breaks down again.

'That's rich,' I say, 'from someone who bathes in the river. Goodness knows what bugs are in there.'

'Needs must.'

'Indeed.' We're serious again. We kiss. We kiss until the sun comes up, and the camp around us stirs, and the *compañeros* start laughing at the love bugs among them.

'Ah piss off, you lot,' I say throwing a wet sock at them. They laugh even harder.

'Oyes Rafa, what you smiling at? Daydreaming again? Do some work like the rest of us!' A colleague rushing past teased him. Raphael snapped back into reality and continued looking through the phone messages in his hand. He needed to talk to his editor about going to the ecumenical conference on the peace process, but El Pelon was not in his office. The reporters affectionately, though always behind his back, called him El Pelon because of his bald head. He was a rather harsh man, nearing retirement, with a dry sense of humour, but fair. Most people dreaded being called into his office, but Raphael rather liked him. While he waited for him to appear, Raphael typed up the end of his regular column and made some preparatory notes on the conference.

He was just going for some coffee when he caught the editor coming back from a meeting. 'Ah, can I have a word?'

'Hmm, I'm in a bit of a hurry here.' Hurry for what, Raphael thought, El Pelon was never in a hurry.

'But it's about something happening today.'

El Pelon gave him a 'carry on then' look.

'The peace conference with Rigoberta and MINUGUA. I'd like to go. We really should be doing someth ...'

'I'll decide what we should be doing something on, thank you Raphael. I already told Pedro to cover that. Have you finished the piece on the local election foul-up?'

'Yes, sir.'

'And the column?'

'Yes.'

'Humpgh, well I suppose there's no harm in you going too, then. Got some ulterior motive, have you? Fancy one of the organisers?'

'No, I just thought it would be interesting.'

'Pity. You could do with a bit of skirt, Raphael.' He winked at him. Raphael cringed inwardly. 'Go on then, get out of here. And make sure you call in regularly. I might need you for something else.'

Raphael gathered his things and rushed out. He was going to be late for the session. He debated getting a bus or walking. By the time he'd waited for a bus it would be just as quick to walk. What did Pelon mean, he could do with some skirt? Did he look like a sad old bachelor? Didn't he look like a man with a beautiful lover? He never mentioned Lola at work, but he was a bit offended that he came across as a man who was so obviously alone.

He was almost at the market just off the main square. If he cut through, he'd be at the back of the cathedral where the meeting was being held. He realised he was quite excited about the prospect of seeing Lola in action, of meeting some of her colleagues. He'd never met any of them. Didn't know any of her friends really, although there were names she referred to and expected him to know who she was talking about. Just as he didn't mention her at work, she kept him secret. Well, he didn't know that, maybe she did talk about him.

He hurried down the three steps into the covered market. It was hard to find a way through. People crowded the entranceway, selling lottery tickets and newspapers. A boy with a runny nose pulled on Raphael's sleeve wanting him to buy chewing gum. A blind cripple, with matted hair, held out a begging cup and mumbled incoherently. Inside, the market smelt of offal. At the stand selling tacos, the little scraps of pork fried in chilli mix until it turned red, Raphael could smell freshly chopped coriander and tortillas keeping hot on the edge of the hot plate. This vied with the mild, milky smell of *horchata* from the drink stand, and the rich aromas of mango and papaya, melding into a heady, overpowering mix. He squeezed past women waiting at the vegetable stand, their long, wide skirts blocking the path. It was a mistake to have come through here; he should have known he wouldn't be able to move quickly through the throngs of buyers and sellers.

The market was a maze. From the entrance, aisles of stalls spread out, deeper and deeper into its recesses, dried flowers and baskets, wooden boxes and carefully carved animals, religious artefacts, coloured candles and incense, T-shirts, jewellery and trinkets for tourists, though Raphael wondered how tourists ever found their way in to them. The scent of marigolds hit him as he edged his way around the flower stand and finally made it out into the open again.

At the door to the meeting rooms behind the cathedral, he flashed his press card, but was surprised how easily he was allowed in and given a packet of papers. The event was low key, no posters announcing it on the doors or walls at the entrance. He slipped into the main hall and found a seat in the back. There were not many empty seats and the air was stuffy, having been breathed in and out over and over. Raphael eased out of his jacket, sitting up straight as he did, trying to see where Lola might be, but he couldn't see her in the sea of heads focussed on the dais where the speakers sat. There was Rigoberta Menchu, the Nobel Peace Prize winner, and Byron Morales from the union, Rosalina Tuyuc and Nidia Gonzalez, and the chairman Raphael didn't recognise. They were already answering questions from the audience.

'What difference do you think the presence of MINUGUA will make, when so little has changed since the signing of the agreement on Indigenous rights?'

Good question, what difference indeed, thought Raphael. The actual war may have stopped. There might not be any bombing anymore, or burning of villages, but the government didn't care what the United Nations thought, or Amnesty International, or anyone else. The usual response was given. The presence of international observers would force the government to at least look as if it were prosecuting the perpetrators of war crimes and violence had dropped significantly since the start of the peace process.

Raphael listened, trying to think how he could overcome his cynicism and write something upbeat about the conference. He knew things were getting better; it just didn't make much difference to him anymore. He glanced through the materials he'd been given. What choice did people have? They had to keep struggling.

The session drew to a close and the lunch break was announced. Raphael got up and made his way to the front of the room looking for Lola. He found her in a cluster of people just to the right of the stage. She was talking intently to the chairman and taking notes. He sat down to wait for her and tried to gauge how many people were there. It was a good gathering, a wide spectrum of groups, religious, political, union people. Across the room he saw a man he was sure he recognised as an ex-guerrilla, but just then Lola come up to him.

'Hi, when did you get here?'

'Ah not long ago, I missed most of it, I'm afraid.'

'You can look at my notes later. Let me introduce you to some people.'

'Who's the man chairing the session?'

'Vitalino Paschual. He heads the coalition of protestant churches. He's well in with Rigoberta, too, one of her close advisors.'

'Really, and you know him?' Raphael was surprised that Lola knew such people, he'd always assumed she did training with common people, not that she knew the likes of Rigoberta. Raphael really didn't know Lola at all.

'He works with *La Frente*, too.'

'Hmm, a finger in many pies!'

Lola smiled at him disapprovingly. She really believed in this stuff. Raphael found that hard. He'd fought for everything he was against. He'd fought to make a future for his wife and her people, and it had failed. He couldn't summon up the enthusiasm anymore to even think he could make a difference.

They wandered around the room and Lola introduced him to people. People she worked with and various dignitaries. She kept looking at her watch; she was nervous. She filled a plate from the buffet, but only picked at the food, and soon set the plate down again, mostly uneaten.

'Listen I'd better get going, I have some things to organise before the next session. There's a press briefing this afternoon you might want to go to. I can brief you on the workshops later.'

'Yeah that sounds good. Do you want to meet afterwards for dinner or something?'

'I probably have to work. We'll see. I'll meet you back here later.'

Raphael went back to the table to get a couple more sandwiches. He looked up from the plate to see that man again. They looked at each other across the table, a bit longer than was polite, a look saying, 'I know who you are, and you know who I am, but neither of us is going to say anything.' Raphael nodded, almost imperceptibly and moved away. He sat down and took a bite of sandwich, chewing it forever before realising he didn't want it. The room was starting to fill up.

It was naïve to think he'd never meet anyone from his old life. But he hadn't thought about it. That had been a completely different world and now he was someone else. He shouldn't be here. No telling how many *compañeros* there might be around. But so what, they'd all do the same wouldn't they? The unwritten, unspoken code, we won't tell, we'll never tell, we'd never betray a brother.

He leant back in his chair. The room seemed to dim around him.

I'm running, tumbling over undergrowth, rain blinding me. Machine-gun fire, the rtt ttt ttt resounding in the trees, so I don't know where it's coming from. I smell it again, that stench of death, of wood smouldering, the metallic essence of blood. Urgent whispers, muffled cries, the panic, the smoke. My eyes are running from the smoky air around me. I cough. I see Lidia running in front of me, hair escaping from her cap, water weighing down her green jacket. Boom. The blast is close. Too close. I drop down. Lie against the ground. I hope Lidia is covered. The leaves tickle my face. We're going to die and I'm worrying I might sneeze. I put my face closer to the ground, into the wet leaf mulch and inhale the earth. I'd rather my last breath was of the Tierra Madre and not burnt flesh.

'Raphael. Raphael, *ayudame.*' I look up. I see nothing. 'Raphael,' barely a croak. I crouch now. Look around on all sides. There's a shape in the trees. It's Lucio. I creep over to him, close to the ground. He's leaning against a tree, holding his arm. Blood oozes out between his fingers.

'Come on,' I say. I put my arm around him and help him up. We stagger along the path. Open targets, but the gunfire is getting further away. We go slowly. He's heavy. He begins to drag his feet. His boots catch in branches. We trip and stumble.

'Leave me,' he says.

I can't leave him. 'Get on my back.'

'No *puedo.*'

I take his good arm and pull it over my shoulder so he's leaning against my back. He moans, then he must have fainted, because he's dead weight. I struggle on. I can't stop. I mumble over and over, something under my breath, anything para seguir. *'Keep going, keep going*, que estas en los cielos, *help me, help me.' I thank God he's one of the smaller ones, not much more than a boy, the company joker, the innocent flirt. And then we're there, with the others. Someone takes the weight from me, another pours water on my face. Lidia rushes up to me. 'Raphael what happened?' She's touching me all over. I wonder what's wrong, she doesn't touch me like that. Then she hits me, realising it's not my blood. 'Don't you scare me like that, you bastard. Don't you ...' I take her in my arms. 'I won't. I won't.'*

'Marco Rodriguez, *Prensa Libre*. What about the death threats against the judge in that case?'

Raphael looked around him. Had he been asleep? The memories were so real; sometimes he didn't know where he was. He would have liked to go out, get a coffee and smoke, but he was not in a seat near the door. He tried to concentrate and take notes, but the afternoon became a blur.

Eventually the session came to a close and Raphael went out to the main hall. Briefly he looked around for Lola, but he couldn't see her, so he went outside for a cigarette. There was a bit of a breeze that cooled his back. He realised his shirt was damp from perspiration. It was five o'clock. He should call his editor and check in, but he didn't feel like it. He threw the butt on the ground and went back inside. People were still milling around in the main hall. He was just about to look at his agenda, when he saw Lola. He eased his way through the crowd.

'Hi.'

'Oh hello.' She sounded surprised to see him.

'How's it going?'

'Yeah, good.'

'Do you want to go and get a drink or something?'

'I haven't really got time. There's a side meeting Vita wants me in, and then we'll be going to dinner.'

'OK. I'll make my own arrangements then.'

'Yeah, that would be easier. I'll see you tomorrow.'

She was already moving away, her mind on something else. Raphael leaned in to kiss her, but she just touched his arm lightly and walked off. It was as though she didn't really want to be seen with him, even though she'd introduced him to her colleagues earlier. It dawned on him that she hadn't introduced him as her boyfriend, only as Raphael, the journalist. Had she even said he was a friend? He didn't want to think about his relationship with Lola. What it meant or didn't mean. He didn't love her, so why bother?

Raphael wanted fresh air, a bit of time to clear his head. He was exhausted from his memories; from the fear of meeting people from the old days, and he needed to get his brain in gear to compose a piece about the conference.

On the way home he stopped at a street café for some soup. As Raphael sat looking out on the close of the workday, people hurrying home as dusk fell, he thought about the first time he'd met Lola. He'd been in the habit of going to a small café near his office and sitting there at length drinking coffee and writing. Nobody minded him staying so long; it was not a well frequented, or salubrious place. He'd been deep in thought, doodling absent-mindedly, when a woman's voice said, 'May I join you?'

He had looked up to see the woman standing in front of him, her hands full of coffee cup, cake, papers and bags. Her eyes were the only steady things in the sea of calamity of all her belongings. Those eyes looking straight at him, into him. Raphael smiled to himself remembering how she'd given the impression of being some kind of film star with myriad packages from an afternoon's shopping.

She had seemed impatient. Raphael had glanced around and seen that there were plenty of free tables. He'd wondered why she wanted to sit with him, but mumbled, 'certainly,' and began moving his papers. She was still standing, holding everything, obviously expecting him to do something. He took her cup, saying, 'here, let me help you', as he set it on the table. Finally, she sat down. She settled things around her and sighed deeply. He wanted to keep writing, but it would seem rude since she'd chosen to sit with him.

'Do I know you?' he said, for something to say.

'No, but I'd like to know you.'

Such a forthright statement from a woman shocked him. He couldn't believe why a woman so pretty would be remotely inter-ested in him. 'Why?'

'You look interesting.'

He laughed.

'And you're rather good looking.'

'Oh, come on, now I know you're teasing me.'

'No, you have a lived-in look, like a lot has happened to you. I find that attractive.' She smiled with her eyes.

'Oh yes, a lot has happened,' he said.

'Tell me,' she said, biting into her cake.

'I don't even know your name.'

'Lola.'

'Ah, the woman of sorrows.'

'Not so sorrowful.'

'Maybe you bring sorrow.'

'How could I possibly?!' She almost fluttered her eyelids, blatantly flirtatious.

He should have known then that she was shallow and immodest, but it was too late, he was hooked.

'So. tell me your name at least,' she said.

'Raphael.'

'Unusual,' she said it casually, as though she'd already known his name.

From the moment she had walked up to his table Raphael had the feeling that she'd searched him out somehow. Maybe had even been following him; had already known who he was. He still had that feeling two years later. He couldn't believe that she found him attractive. He should have been worried; in those closing days of the war the enemy came in all shapes, and often in very dainty packaging. But he was past caring. He had nothing left to lose.

Raphael ate his soup quickly and left. It was almost dark, but the sky had a strange yellow glow that anticipated a storm. Just as he reached his apartment, the first drops of rain began to fall. By the time he was upstairs it was pouring. Kicking off his shoes he dragged a chair to the doorway of the balcony to sit and watch the rain. The torrent soon soaked his trouser bottoms and bare feet. Some of the worries of the day slipped away with the water. The rain reminded of his time as a *guerrillero*. It always seemed to be raining in the jungle, soaking them in seconds. That's how he remembered it anyway, except for the cool mornings waking up with Lidia. Being perpetually covered in mud, clothes clinging to him, weighing down his pack, slipping and sliding in the sludge and invariably falling over to the giggles of the *compañeras*.

There were other *ladinos* in the guerrillas, but mostly they were Indians, and they liked to make fun of him, though it was always good humoured.

'Don't they have mud in the city, Rafa?' Katalina sniggers as she watches me try to get up.

I slide again, preventing a complete collapse by grabbing a branch. 'Good camouflage,' I say, wiping mud on my face and then down my trousers. Giggles break out around me. 'It's a proven guerrilla tactic, as used by Che himself.' I try to keep a straight face while saying this but don't really pull it off.

Raphael marvelled at the kind of world that could turn someone like him into a fighter. He didn't think he had personally killed anyone, but he couldn't be sure. Certainly he had fired his weapon. And after Lidia's death he was filled with such anger and pain, he could have killed thousands with his bare hands. For every Indian woman and child who died in hunger or in pain he had wanted to kill a hundred soldiers. He'd wanted to blow up military installations and firebomb the presidential palace. For the sake of his son he'd swallowed his anger; had eaten it whole, and it consumed him slowly from the inside, day in, day out, a continual ache.

For his son he had given up being a combatant and moved to be with the communities in resistance, providing what mirage of protection he could. That life had been no less precarious, but it provided Benigno with a wet nurse and the illusion of stability. What a fragile mirage. The son who had turned Raphael's anger to sadness was dead too. But hadn't Benigno's death been inevitable? Why hadn't he moved back to the city with the boy? Back then, the city hadn't been much safer and they would have lost the only family he had, his family of *comadres*, the only people who knew how he felt because they too had known loss; they had seen horror up close. Here in the city everyone was anonymous and alone.

He saw Benigno's smiling eyes, deep and dark like his mother's, pleading with him for a bedtime story.

'Papi, papi, I can't sleep.'

'Climb into bed with me. I'll tell you a story.'

The boy thanks me in polite Quiche. I chuckle. A son who speaks Quiche. I hadn't foreseen that. But then I never expected to have to sleep in my boots with a gun at my side. I never thought that my son's eyes waiting eagerly for a story would be worth all the wealth and comfort in the world.

'Are you comfortable, *mijo*? Then I'll begin. Once upon a time there was a beetle. He lived in the mountains and he was lonely. We'll call him Don Postura because he always spoke his own mind and knew exactly what he wanted. So, Don P decided to go to the city to find a wife because he wanted a cosmopolitan woman, not a country bumpkin. He set out with a dozen tortillas (this is a great deal of food for a beetle), some water and some tobacco. It took him a very long time because beetles are quite small and the city was a long way away. On the journey he had many adventures, because that is the way of life, it is never easy and never turns out the way you think it will.

'First he found some people living in the mountains, fighting for freedom, and they said, "Mr Beetle, please join us." But he said, "No, I'm going to the city to find a wife." And they cursed him, "beetle *indecente*, you're a disgrace to your people." Then he met some children whose parents had disappeared, and they said, "Help us to make food, Mr Beetle. Our parents are gone, and we don't know what to do." But he said, "No, I'm going to the city to find a wife." The children threw stones at him and he had to run away. Then he came to a funeral and the people said, "Help us bury him." But Mr Beetle said, "Bury your own dead, I'm going to the city to find a wife." And the people cried.

'So finally, Don P arrives in the city, and as luck would have it (and because it is getting late for stories) he found a beautiful lady beetle almost immediately. He put on all his charm and invited her to dinner. Now, Don Postura was very poor, but he had a way with words and so he found them a table at a rather exclusive restaurant. At the end of the evening they kissed and he said, "Your place or mine," (Not that he had a place, but one could always be found, well in these enlightened times of civil war it doesn't do to waste time.) The lady hesitated, so Don P kissed her again and she turned into a butterfly and flew away.'

'But papi, where is the happy ending?'

'There is no happy ending. I know you're still young. But I can't lie to you, you might as well know the truth now, it will save trouble later. Now go to sleep.'

Benigno snuggles next to me, then raises his head. 'But papi, if I kiss a girl will she turn into a *mariposa*?'

I laugh. 'No, but you're far too young for that!'

3

Raphael was stiff from head to toe and cold. He'd fallen asleep in the wooden chair in the doorway. Feeling as if he hadn't slept at all, he stumbled inside to wash and change. The mirror showed his haggard face and he wondered whether he should shave off his short, soft beard, but it was part of his new disguise and a link to the past he wasn't ready to give up. Very few men had beards; most Indian men struggled to even grow stubble. In that sense perhaps it was not good as it drew attention to his face, but it was completely different to the clean-shaven look he had sported when he had lived in the city before and that was the point. But the man at the conference had known who he was, or if not who, then *what*.

He was thinner and looked older than his real age. The beard made him look academic. Distinguished, Lola called it. His family probably wouldn't recognise him, if they were still alive. He hadn't seen or heard from his parents or brother in over ten years. When he had joined the guerrillas, he hadn't told his parents, only his older brother.

'Why are you doing it, Raf?'

'For love.'

'For love?'

'Yes, they burned Lidia's village. We have to go.'

'Umpgh, that Indian.'

He hadn't expected such racism from his own flesh and blood. His brother said the word Indian as though he were disgusted to have the sound in his mouth. True, his family hadn't exactly been ecstatic when he had begun courting Lidia. His father had definitely tried to talk him out of it, but after the marriage it seemed they had at least tolerated it with good grace.

'It's not right what's going on, you know it's not,' said Raphael.

'Hey, I'm no government supporter, but those Indians are all communists.'

'Oh come on Benjamin, you don't believe that propaganda! And even if they are, does that make it all right to massacre innocent women and children? To burn villages?'

'They're not doing that.'

'They are, Ben, they are. How can you be so blinkered?'

'It's none of our business.'

The debate had raged for hours, neither side conceded.

'If you go, you're no longer my brother,' said Ben.

'If you don't support me, you're no longer mine.'

'You can't tell our parents.'

'There are enough disappeared in this city, one more will come as no surprise to anyone, not even my parents.'

And so Raphael had slipped away in the night with some cigarettes, a notebook and pen and little else. Gone away with the woman he loved, to the same country, yet worlds away. To a life that was unlike anything he had ever known, and he had been happy despite the fear. He only hoped his parents hadn't mourned the loss too much.

That first night in the mountains had been thrilling but silent. The black mountain air enveloped them. The *compañeros* he had just met whispered inaudibly or didn't speak at all. In the following months his ears grew accustomed to the whispers and gestures and he came to understand them, as he understood the various combinations of birdlike whistles that signalled danger.

We sit around a small fire. Things are quiet tonight, and the leaders have decided it's safe to light a fire. We'll have to kick dirt over it if we hear helicopters. A small bottle of corn liquor is passed around, acquired especially for us, for our first night. It's almost like an initiation rite, a second honeymoon, although the first was only a weekend in Antigua. I take a sip. It's strong. I feel it burn all the way down to my gut. Lidia's eyes are full of pride. I think she didn't believe I'd do this, though she'd never say that.

31

We lie on the ground. A blanket is draped between low trees forming a cover over us, but I can still see the sky. I count stars. Lidia lies against me. She's already asleep. I didn't think it would be so quiet. Then in the distance I see lightning, and here a boom of thunder. Only it's not thunder. The night performs its pyrotechnic show just for me, and it's hard to contemplate that under that lightning, death and destruction is being wrought. The glow of the bombs looks almost pretty against the blackness, lighting up the grey and purple clouds.

Having changed clothes, Raphael had a quick cup of coffee and left. The conference had another session and he wanted to be there at the beginning. The bus was packed, and he was lucky to find a spot to stand. Raphael loved the *barrio* buses with their saints or rosaries hanging from the mirror, exhortations to God to save them from the perils of the road next to silver silhouettes of big breasted naked woman, sometimes even a sign declaring how much the driver loved his mother. And the loud, vibrant salsa music, '*cumbia hasta luuunes*!' Dance the week away. The streets in the capital were in a better state than anywhere else, but still Raphael's head brushed the roof as the bus lurched through potholes. The buses were re-conditioned school buses from the United States and not designed for adults. Raphael, taller than most, found the buses particularly cramped. He loved to see the foreign tourists try to fit into the tiny seats, their knees rubbing against the metal, taking up the space of three Indians.

The driver was particularly enthusiastic, dedicated to his horn, eager to break through the gridlock, swearing in the benign fashion favoured by Guatemalans, '*a la gran …*', singing along with the radio. He was successful and Raphael was deposited in the square earlier than he'd hoped. He lit a cigarette and looked up to see Lola across the street, about to enter the hall. She was standing very close to a young man, maybe the same one he'd seen her with before. Raphael debated whether to go over and interrupt them, see exactly who the man was. He began to cross the street when Lola kissed the man on the cheek and he hurried away, turning to wave as he did.

Lola was just pushing the door open when Raphael reached her and put out a hand in front of her on the door.

'Ah Raphael. You startled me.'

'I bet I did. Who was that?'

'Who?'

'Oh come on, don't act all innocent. I just saw you kissing him.'

'That wasn't a kiss; it was a peck. He's just a friend.'

'Who? What friend? A colleague?'

'No, not a colleague. He's a musician. I've seen him play a couple of times.'

'And where was I?'

'How should I know where you were? We're not joined at the hip.'

Lola let go of the door and stepped back outside. 'Can you please not make a scene here. I work with these people. What's got into you, anyway?'

'I don't know.'

'Well, cut it out. He's just a friend. I love you.' She kissed Raphael. 'Come on. Are you coming in? I've got to get to the first session.'

'You go ahead. I'll be there in a minute.'

'All right, but I probably won't see you until it all finishes this afternoon.'

'OK.'

She now gave him a peck on the cheek and went inside.

Raphael smoked another cigarette and looked at the programme to see which sessions to attend.

Raphael left the conference at lunchtime. He expected the last session to be just the usual summing up, so he went back to the office and was relieved to find no messages from his editor. He spent the afternoon working on a piece about the conference, between wondering about Lola and her young man. Was he being over-sensitive? Perhaps they were just friends. Lola was a demonstrative woman. She liked to touch people. It was just a quick kiss on the cheek after all. And why was he bothered? He decided to go back and meet her, take her out for a nice meal, let things settle down a bit.

They sat in the Pan-American hotel looking over the menu.

'This is a bit posh. What's the occasion?'

'No occasion. I just thought I overreacted a bit about that bloke, and … I don't know, we don't go anywhere nice much.'

'I wouldn't say that, but I'm not complaining.'

'So how did the conference go?'

'Pretty good, I think.'

'But what can really change Lola? There are still people being killed left, right and centre.'

'The war's stopped. You've got a civilian president.'

'In the pay of the military.'

'Don't be such a cynic. With the United Nations here, they're going to have to be a bit more open.'

'Don't count on it.'

After dinner, Raphael walked Lola home. It was still early when they stood outside her door, but she seemed reluctant to invite him in.

'So, are you going to ask me in?' he said, leaning against the doorframe.

'I don't think so Raphael. It's been an exhausting couple of days. I just want to relax, have an early night.'

You usually want an early night with me, Raphael thought, but he didn't really mind. 'All right.'

'I'll call you.'

'Uh ha. Goodnight.'

That was a first, thought Raphael. He was always the one who didn't want to stay the night. Perhaps she was just waiting for him to leave so she could go out and meet the cheek pecker. Should he go back and see if she went out? 'Don't be stupid Raphael. You can't spy on your own girlfriend.'

He had to wonder why he was so bothered about the possibility, the unsubstantiated possibility, that she might have another lover. Honestly, what did he have to go on – a look and a hand on her arm outside a cinema a couple of months ago, and a peck on the cheek today? She still hadn't said who this friend was, though. What his name was. Why hadn't she talked about him before, if it was just an innocent friendship? Raphael had never been jealous before. He thought he didn't care that much. Maybe he needed some time away from Lola to decide what he wanted. Their relationship wasn't going anywhere. He couldn't see himself marrying her and that was selfish. He should let her go, let her find someone who would marry her and give her a family. Not that she'd ever mentioned wanting children.

'Ah Lidia, Lidia, why did you leave me? Everything's such a mess now.'

* * *

Raphael didn't see Lola for several days after the conference. She'd seemed different then, distant, and he wasn't convinced it was just her work and being busy with the event. Maybe he shouldn't have confronted her, implied again that she was having an affair. She didn't expect him to ignore it, did she? He hadn't slept with her since the night before the conference had started. That morning she'd been attentive, affectionate and then later she'd been so off-hand with him. Still, that was Lola – unpredictable. One day she'd be passionate, the next day involved in work, giving the impression that their relationship was just a fling, nothing important. They often didn't see each other for days, but this time it felt different.

He wished he didn't feel anything for her. It wasn't love, it wasn't like it had been with Lidia, but he couldn't seem to leave her alone. He also had a feeling she was bad news, a kind of premonition that something bad would happen. Not that he would get hurt, but that things wouldn't end well.

Raphael was just wondering if he should humiliate himself by calling her, when she called him, all cheerfulness and full of life, as if it had only been last night that they'd made love, as though there had been no silence in between. That annoyed him.

They were both astute and experienced enough to never talk openly on the phone, too many lives had been lost that way. They never used the real names of people or places. It was second nature to them to refer to everyone by nicknames. The whole business gave the arranging of dates a certain haphazardness and spontaneity. Lola usually suggested a time and place, and if he wasn't working on a deadline, Raphael usually agreed.

By natural inclination Raphael was very ordered, liking to know where everything was, nothing ever out of place. He liked his life that way. Even living in the mountains as a guerrilla, where it would have seemed that such order would be impossible, they had led a very disciplined existence. Their lives had depended on knowing where their equipment was and being able to pick it up in a second and run with it; in knowing exactly where they were; in knowing exactly what they were doing.

In anyone else he might have found such spontaneity and apparent randomness annoying, but in Lola it was strangely appealing. He found he liked not knowing when she might call him, if she might call him. So why was he bothered now that he hadn't heard from her? It was nothing particularly unusual.

'I'll see you at the academy at 7.30,' she said

'Fine, but make it 7.00.'

And so, they agreed to meet at the El Salvadoran restaurant across the street from the military academy at 7.15 p.m.

Raphael just managed to get a seat on the bus, or rather the corner of a seat next to two teenagers. In front of him sat an Indian woman, a thin red band of headdress caught up in her tangled hair, a vibrant coloured blouse slipping off her slender shoulder. Carefully created, it was now frayed and tattered, worn at the edges. Her bare feet were cracked and covered in dry mud. The woman had a baby slung across her back, two skinny bedraggled boys stood next to her. One of them was throwing up into a dirty rag, trying to hide his illness. Raphael could tell it was not just motion sickness; the boy had some rampant kind of disease that was wracking his tiny body. Other people on the bus were complaining, calling her a dirty Indian, urging her to take herself and her revolting children off the bus. She looked at the boy and slapped him, a short, sharp whack across the top of his head. Silent tears formed in his eyes. Raphael couldn't believe it. Why didn't she take him in her arms and comfort him like a mother should? He wanted to say something to her. But he realised in her own way she was trying to protect him, in the hope that by appeasing the crowd they might be able to stay on the bus until it was their place to alight. It didn't work. The other passengers were becoming more vociferous. At the next stop she hurried the boys off the bus and then stood plaintively at the side of the road as Raphael watched. He wanted to gag; he was repulsed by the cruelty of people. They looked like ordinary enough people, working people, not rich and racist, though clearly they were prejudiced. It was ingrained in them, even though they were only one step further up the ladder to her.

Raphael sat and thought about what caused such hatred. Why was his country imbued with it? His whole relationship with Lola seemed petty and pointless compared to such grand matters. Resentment began to rise in him, not because she was like the people around him, but because she took up his energy, fervour he could be using for something else, for something better. But he had no passion. He was tired, tired of having survived, tired of the interminable wait to be reunited with his family.

It was still early when he arrived at the restaurant. For a while he doodled on a napkin, jotting down ideas for a poem about the experience on the bus, sipping a soda, struggling with words to convey the inhumanity.

Lola's arrival roused him from his reverie. He looked up.

'You look sad,' she said sitting down.

'Isn't that what you love about me?' He replied sarcastically. He didn't want to fight with her; he loathed bickering, but an irresistible urge for conflict rose up in him, just as it had the last time they'd been together. Was he subconsciously hoping she'd get angry and leave him? A waiter came and they ordered *papusas*, the El Salvadoran staple Lola was so fond of, though Raphael had little appetite. The room was heavy with the smell of cheese and frying tortillas, it weighed down the air trying to smother the tension rising between them.

'It is,' she said, not taking the bait of his tone.

'I don't cultivate sadness for your amusement, you know.'

'I know. I never said it amused me. I like the fact you're so sensitive, that you have feelings. Most men don't, or at least they won't admit they do.'

The food arrived and they ate a little, trying to make small talk. Lola was back to her usual self. It was hard to believe she had not asked him to stay last time when she ran her foot up and down his leg under the table. She ate from his plate, taking pieces of his food, the way only intimates do. She let her hand brush against his at every opportunity. She pulled out all the tricks in her repertoire, but it only made Raphael more annoyed. Compared to the lives of people like the woman on the bus, Lola seemed like a spoilt schoolgirl, trying to win back the toy someone had snatched from her. She was ready to play now. She obviously assumed they would go back to her house, that they'd make love, as usual.

'Why haven't you called?' Raphael asked.

'Is that what's bothering you? It's only been a few days. I've been busy, that's all. You don't usually mind.'

Raphael shrugged. 'Busy doing what? Screwing someone else?'

'Raphael! What do you take me for? I thought we'd cleared that up. What's wrong with you?'

'Nothing,' he mumbled.

'Nothing? How can you say nothing's wrong when clearly something is.'

Raphael wanted to argue, but he didn't have the strength or the aptitude for it. 'You didn't tell me who he was. If it's all so innocent, why are you being so secretive about it?'

'I'm not. *Por Dios*, Raphael. I already told you, I met him at a concert. I see him now and then. There's nothing to it.'

'So, what's his name then?'

'Josue, all right? His name's Josue. Tell me what's wrong, *mi amor*,' she said reaching out to take his hand.

Raphael pulled it away.

'Fine. Keep your precious silence. But don't accuse me of things I haven't done.' With that Lola pushed away her barely eaten meal and left.

Raphael walked home through the darkening city. It was almost that time when it was no longer safe for anyone sane to be out. He should have caught a bus, but he couldn't stand its claustrophobia. He didn't want the heat and closeness of people, the clawing smell of humanity that at times in the past had so excited him. He wanted to feel free of it though he knew he wasn't. He was never free and couldn't see a time when he would be.

He swallowed his anger. He felt it burning down his gullet like *aguardiente*, felt it growing like a tumour deep within him. He hated himself. Instead of shouting like a man, instead of telling Lola how she angered and annoyed him; how the world angered him, he ingested the rage. Just as he had when Benigno had died. If he tried to explain, then tears formed in his eyes and the words wouldn't come out. He was a wimp, a *maricon*, he wasn't cut out for conflict.

Suddenly he hit the wall next to him. He didn't feel anything. He hit it again. Nothing. 'Why am I so useless?' They're gone. I can't change that. My life's a sham. I can't talk to Lola. I can't tell her about what it felt like to lose Lidia, about Benigno. I can't even feel anything anymore. To prove it, Raphael ran his knuckles down the wall, rubbing off the skin, but he felt nothing. He watched the blood ooze slowly from the cut. 'Why didn't they kill me, too?'

He could see Lidia's face, her dark eyes so alive and fiery in the calmness of her features, her long black hair wound up beneath a Che Guevara style cap that made him laugh every time he remembered it, her solid traditional-ness in her *huipil* and Indian skirt, so impractical for modern warfare; her combat boots sticking out from underneath it, and the ancient rifle slung over her shoulder, so incongruous. If he hadn't loved and admired her so, she would have been a perfect candidate for a cartoon strip, they all would. All that was lacking was a string of bullets across her chest and the Pancho Villa style moustache.

The typical colour of skirt for her region was bright red, but for the sake of camouflage she had changed it for one of dark green. But on the rare occasions when she washed her white *huipil* in a stream and laid it out on a rock to dry while she lay naked next to him, her dark breasts against his chest, he worried that the whole world would see its whiteness and find them.

He had looked upon Lidia's face and thought himself the happiest man alive, despite the hardships. The nights spent on the move, fleeing, or lying huddled in a hammock listening to the bombs, or if they were lucky, on a quiet night, looking at the stars, telling and re-telling the tales of how they had been formed, how the Cuatrocientos, the four-hundred boys, had ruled the skies and how Hunahpu and Ixbalanque had defeated them and later become the sun and moon. Lidia had passion and fight enough for both of them. He was nothing without her.

Raphael tried to drag himself back to the present and his ridiculous fight with Lola. He knew that sex would remove all trace of their argument sooner than anything else. He could go to her flat now and apologise and be fairly certain that they would end up in bed, but he felt that she wouldn't really want him to. Though it was clear she had wanted him physically, he thought her mind had been elsewhere. She was either completely into him, or she ignored him, there were no grey areas. He shouldn't complain, his mind was almost permanently elsewhere, but he expected more from her. In his mind, Lola hadn't suffered; she knew nothing of the hardships of war. She had been sheltered in the capital, in the confines of a well-to-do family while his life was being blown away. He resented her because she'd had an easy life and that made her an optimist. He'd lost his life and now he was a miserable old cynic, unable to move on, unable to love.

4

The *Siglo Veintiuno* office was buzzing with the news of the death of a reporter from *Prensa Libre*. The man's body had been found early that morning, in an alley, without his hands, a common trait of the paramilitary group *Mano Blanco*, long thought to have been eliminated, but still operating with impunity. Reporters had already been dispatched to gather the gruesome details. At least these days they were allowed the details. A few years ago he would have disappeared without a trace, no newspaper report, no name released. His killer would probably never be brought to justice, though everyone could guess who was responsible, but they could at least write about it, if they dared. His death was a warning to their profession – go so far and no further.

Raphael's editor, El Pelon, called him into his office. No doubt he would ask him to write an editorial piece, something scathing. Raphael knew what was required – the outcry against impunity, the lack of freedom of speech, the questioning of why people were still being killed after the peace had been signed, all up to a certain point and no further. No mention of the authorities, no suggestion that the military might be involved, no mention of paramilitary forces and definitely no linking of those forces with the government. When El Pelon had said there was no censorship, he hadn't meant for his reporters to be careless.

'Rosario Recinos. Did you know him?' asked El Pelon.

'No,' said Raphael.

'I've spoken to his editor. You're to go over there and look at his files, see what he was working on, talk to his colleagues.'

Raphael nodded and left. He felt numb walking out, blinking at the sunlight. This was nothing compared to the horrors he'd seen as a guerrilla, and journalists had been killed before; yet he felt shocked. He realised he'd stopped looking over his shoulder. He'd lost his feelings; shut down his capacity to feel pain: its only outlet being his uncontrollable tears at music and art. He was still paranoid, but that was a way of life, a suspicion of the authorities that would never go away. All these years and nothing had happened to him, so it wasn't going to. Even though he often wished he'd died with Benigno, he'd stopped believing his death was imminent. Raphael was glad now of the shock, the twinge of some sort of feeling, the return of fear.

It was not far to the office of *Prensa Libre*. Once there he stood outside and smoked a cigarette, savouring the nervousness in his stomach. Then he wound his mind into writing mode, stoking the embers of fiery rhetoric, getting angry about the murder.

Once inside, he found the editor who handed over Rosario's personnel file and the stories he'd been working on.

'Can I take these away with me?'

'I'd rather you didn't. There's a room over there you can use.'

'What was he like?' asked Raphael.

'An idealist. He still thought journalism was a noble profession. Young, a little gullible, but fairly streetwise,' replied the editor.

'A family man?'

'No, but he had a fiancée.'

The editor gestured for Raphael to move to the vacant room.

'May I see his desk?'

'Well, he shared it with some other guys, but yes.'

He led Raphael into the newsroom and pointed to a cluttered desk. 'That was Rosario's.' Raphael's eyes scanned it, looking for clues of a personal life. There was a small snapshot of a beautiful, but older woman pinned to the board used to divide this work-space from the others.

'The fiancée?'

'Yes.'

'Pretty woman.' She looked a little like Lola, he thought.

The rest of the board was covered with clippings and news stories. Under a pile of papers on the desk Raphael saw the corner of a book. He pulled it out. It was a battered copy of his own book of poetry.

'His?' he asked, inclining his head towards the book.

'Could be. I don't know. Like I said he shared a desk, and he shouldn't have been reading poetry at work anyway.'

'No,' Raphael concurred, though the man was beginning to irritate him.

'Don't go in for it myself. Do you know the fella?'

It amused Raphael that although El Pelon must have told this man his name, he had either forgotten it or made no connection to the name on the book.

'No, no I don't,' Raphael said and retreated into the empty room to read the files.

When Raphael glanced at the clock on the wall, he saw that he'd been reading for hours, but still there wasn't much to go on. Rosario had studied literature at university and this had been his first real job. His references were good and solid, but not exceptional. If Raphael had been born about fifteen years later this could have been his life, though without Lidia he doubted he would have had the necessary passion for journalism, more likely he would have been a mediocre professor writing mediocre poetry in his spare time, dreaming of the great Latin American epic he'd never write.

He sighed. The work files revealed little. No big breaking stories. The only hint of intrigue were some hand-written, barely legible notes in the margin of a year old clipping about the disappearance of highland village pastor, Manuel Chavez, who had been missing for two weeks. Villagers feared for his life following his denunciation of a local military commissioner for the kidnap of one of his parishioners.

Something jogged Raphael's memory; he went back to the journalist's cubicle and looked again at the board full of clippings. There, another small article, the pastor had been found in a shallow grave in a cornfield with thirty-three stab wounds ... international pressure called for the arrest of Colonel Lopez of Chimaltenango. International pressure? For a village pastor? Why? What made him so special? Even a year ago people were killed on a daily basis, gone unnoticed, no obituary, no funeral, much less an international outcry. Raphael had a feeling that there was something unusual about this story. Even though it was out of date, there was something left unravelled. It looked like Raphael would be going back to the highlands. Not to the hinterland of his guerrilla days, but far enough, into Indian land, into his *recuerdos* and nightmares. He felt a buzz he hadn't felt since the old days, a lump in his throat, a light feeling in his stomach, and the determination that he had to find the truth.

If Raphael were a different man, he wouldn't have to search for the truth. He could write editorial rhetoric with his eyes closed. He could write a piece on the young journalist with little effort and even less research and still have the authorities wishing he were the next person to be silenced by *Mano Blanco*, but that wasn't his style. Maybe this story had nothing to do with Rosario's murder. Another Indian dead in the highlands – that wasn't big news, it was barely news at all, but Raphael couldn't rest until he knew what had happened and why Rosario was so interested in the story. He slipped the clipping and some notes into his notebook and left the office.

He wanted to leave straight away, but he knew he had to talk to his editor and he felt the need to talk to Lola. Apprehension brewed in him, some feeling not yet fully surfaced. He felt bad that they'd argued. He wondered where his anger of the previous night, had come from. He didn't want to leave, even for a couple of days, with that being her last memory of him. He wanted to kiss her goodbye and say he was sorry. When he got back they were going to have to talk seriously about their relationship, but for now he wanted their parting on friendly terms.

El Pelon was not pleased. He wanted a quick response to the killing. The exact details were less important. Not to mention that he thought the murder of a village pastor some years ago had nothing to do with the handless corpse of a journalist in the capital. Silently Raphael had to agree with him, but there was still something about the story that bothered him.

'Go but be quick. I want something for the Sunday edition at the latest.'

Raphael began to complain that it wasn't enough time.

'Hire a car if you need to, put it on expenses, but get this done. We can't afford to sit on this; we need to respond while it's hot. By next week it will be old news.'

5

It was Thursday, already early afternoon. Raphael called from the office and hired a car. He didn't bother to go home; everything he needed was in his leather satchel. If necessary he could buy a cheap shirt somewhere, or be dirty for three days; it didn't matter, but he had to see Lola. Something irrational deep inside him told him he wouldn't see her again. It was probably just the leftover bad taste of their row, but there was no harm in wasting half an hour to try to find her.

He hoped to find her at the offices of *La Frente*, but she wasn't there. Her colleagues didn't seem to know where she was, but he recognised a woman from the peace conference.

'Excuse me, do you know where Lola is?'

'Who's asking?'

'Raphael, I'm a ...'

'Oh yeah, I remember, you were at the conference.'

'Right. Look, I'm kind of in a hurry. I have to leave town on business. I was hoping to catch Lola before I left.'

'She's probably doing a training somewhere. I haven't seen her today. Wait here, I'll go and check.'

'Thanks.'

Raphael looked around. He'd never been to Lola's office before. It was housed in an old building, long corridors with rooms off them, a gallery overlooking the patterned marble floor below. The ceiling was high, and the dark green plants dotted around complimented the pale green of the walls, giving the building an airy feeling. It was calming, but Raphael didn't feel calm. He sat down and tried to calm his nerves enough to write Lola a note. He didn't understand why he felt so strongly the need to see her. It wasn't a fear for himself, though it was clear to him that if Rosario had been killed over this story he could put himself in danger. No, he suddenly felt in every bone of his body that he wouldn't see Lola again.

While he waited, he started the note. 'I have to go away for a couple of days for work. I'm sorry, about … I'm just sorry. I wanted to see you. I wanted to hold you. I wanted to look into your eyes one more time. *Querida* I …' He wanted to write 'I love you' but somehow that didn't quite sound true enough. He left the sentence unfinished, the note unsigned.

The young woman came back. Raphael folded the paper over quickly and looked up at her.

'She's doing a training in El Barranco. Do you know it?'

'It's near the dump isn't it? One of the *barrios* they made out of rubbish?'

'Yes, they're doing really amazing things there. They've got a water supply now, and … ah but you don't want to know about that, do you? It's the Aguilar Community Centre. Just ask for it when you get there, it's well known, but there aren't any street names there. That's if you want to try. She should be there until 4 p.m. at least.'

Raphael looked at his watch, he really wanted to get away, make sure of getting to Chimaltenango before nightfall. He didn't have much time, but the centre was on the way out of town, not too far out of his way.

'I've written a note just in case. Do you have an envelope?'

She went to a side office and came back with one.

He put the note in and sealed it. 'Can I leave this with you? Will you see her when she gets back?'

'She might not come back to the office today, but yes, I'll give it to her when I see her.'

Raphael thanked her and hurried off to collect the rental car. It was a good time to leave the city, not too much traffic; even so, he took his life in his hands driving round the *periferico*. There was no room for hesitancy, it was go with the flow or be crushed. Fast moving drivers vied with buses and horse drawn rubbish carts. The strange ensemble was in constant flow; it couldn't be slowed by the entrance of a newcomer. He imagined it the same in other cities, Latin American ones at least. Once he had been to Mexico City: that had been the same, only ten times worse, a hundred times more vehicles, a blue cloud of swearing over each car blending with the smog. The Mexicans were consummate swearers. Raphael smiled at the memory of his friend Pedro reversing off the capital city's ring road, having missed a turn.

He had to look closely for the turn-off; if he missed it he could forget about looking for Lola by the time he had backtracked. He took the next exit, and wound down ever decreasing roads until he was on a dirt road. This would be the last street with a name; from then on it was no-man's land. It seemed vaguely familiar. Raphael had done an article on slum-dwellers a couple of years previously and had been to this part of the city, or one like it. Originally the people had lived literally in the rubbish dump, some unfortunate souls still did, but gradually the desperate human need to live and better oneself prevailed. Houses were built with adobe bricks rather than cardboard and corrugated metal, tracks became well worn, the dirt compacting into streets, enterprising souls siphoned off electricity from the nearest lamp-post, a dangerous and illegal process, but the police had better things to do than track down people stealing *la luz*. The city police were the final branch of the military, doing their dirty work when necessary, and looking for ways to line their own pockets the rest of the time. Last time Raphael had been there people were still carrying water from over a mile away and defecating in the streams made by rainwater. The air still hung with that slightly fetid and mouldy odour of human waste.

Dust rose up from dry road, making it difficult to see and Raphael wound up the window he'd opened because of the heat. Children ran alongside, thinking he must be a foreigner, or rich at least, driving such a fancy car. The road was petering out now. He turned a sharp bend to the right, then stopped, not sure where to go. He opened the window and the smaller, less shy children ran up to his window. He wished he had some sweets or something to give them. He called out to an older looking boy.

'Which way to El Barranco?'

'You're in it *señor.*' Some of the children sniggered at his ignorance.

'I mean the community centre.'

'Down that street to the left. All the way to the end and you'll be right at it. Tall building, three or four floors.'

'Thanks. Here.' Raphael held out his hand to the boy and deposited a handful of coins. 'Buy these kids some bread.'

The boy looked down at the ground, too embarrassed, to say 'thank you.'

In a few seconds Raphael pulled up in front of the centre. The building was still under construction and the hallway inside the door was bare. There was no reception area as he'd expected. He wandered down the corridor, which was completely empty, and started to think maybe he'd got the wrong place. Then he heard noises above him. He went up the stairs and found people waiting in the corridor.

'What are you waiting for?'

'The clinic. There's a children's clinic here twice a week.'

'Thanks.'

Raphael went down the hall to the door at the end, where a harried nurse was taking details from patients.

'You'll have to wait your turn.' She pointed down the hall to the end of the queue.

'No, no I'm not here for the clinic. I'm looking for someone who's supposed to be giving a training here.'

'That would be next floor up.'

Raphael went up to the next floor where there was a flip chart set up in the corner, but no Lola and no presentation. Two women sat in a corner sewing on machines. He went over to them.

'Excuse me, was there a training session here?'

'Yes. They've finished.'

'Oh no. I'm looking for the woman leading it. I was told she'd be here until 4 p.m.'

'Could be. The director took her on a tour.'

'A tour? Of the building?'

'No, of El Barranco. I don't think you'll find them. Could be anywhere.'

'Aaigh. Thank you.'

Raphael went back to his car. He really should be going; it was a good hour's drive at least to Chimaltenango. It would be pointless to start walking these paths looking for her. She would be around when he got back. They could make up then; talk, sort things out. Lola wasn't the kind of person to bear a grudge for long. It would do him good to have a couple of days out of the city, busy with other things.

He found his way back to the main road, then wound out of the city, a splendid ascent of bends and curves, the torturous passing of snail-like trucks, and the road became unique, or so he thought. Gazing out at the landscape, the slums, the city of trash, where the homeless eked out a survival, he hoped and prayed it was unique, because people lived there beneath the twirling vultures. In the seething mass of detritus moved humanity, sheltering under cardboard, sifting through filth, eating hotel leftovers and worse. Raphael had lived for four years in the mountains and *selva*, it was paradise compared to the hell of the trash mound. As he rose higher, he looked out on the hazy conurbation below him, a city that held almost as many secrets as the mountains he was headed to, but not as many unmarked graves.

Soon he was into the cool mountain air. It felt different, even inside the car. Smelt different. That mystical smell of mystery and old traditions, of damp wool and mist, the smell of cold. It was surprising how much cooler it was suddenly as the sun was preparing to set. In the shadow of the mountains it was already cold. Raphael still needed to pay attention to the dangerous bends and frequent potholes, hit one of those hard and he'd have a flat tyre to deal with, but with the lack of traffic his mind was able to wander on the reason for his journey; on the story.

This pastor had been unusual in at least one respect: he was Presbyterian. Raphael had never heard of the Presbyterians. He hoped they weren't one of those strange groups of right-wing evangelicals. He suspected not if the man had publicly denounced a kidnapping and had international support; although that could be a bad thing too – look at those damn Mormons – the new US imperialist terror!

His first visit would be to the Presbytery office. He had managed to glean that much before his hurried departure from the city, that and an address. He hoped there would be people around who knew details of the case, and that there were people still alive who remembered, he might be unlucky on that count.

Having arrived in the uninspiring town of Chimaltenango, Raphael parked in the square and went on foot to find the office. Like most towns, Chimaltenango was laid out in a grid pattern, however he had trouble finding the address and eventually had to ask for help. He was directed down an unpromising dirt track off a side street and almost went past the plain wooden door with the tiniest of name plaques. He rang the bell and waited for so long he was about to give up. Then the door was opened by a barefoot Indian woman in rather shabby traditional dress of a red skirt and white blouse embroidered with birds.

'*Sí?*' she said sparingly, but in a welcoming tone.

'I'd like to speak to someone in the Presbytery office.'

'Are they expecting you?'

'Er, no.'

'*Espera,*' she said turning, and then, 'what name?'

'Raphael Sifuentes.'

She closed the door and a few minutes later returned and ushered him in. He wasn't sure what he had expected; surely not fancy offices, but the poverty of the place surprised him. The door opened onto an open courtyard with a dirt floor, though it looked to have been scrupulously swept. In the further recesses was a large room also with a dirt floor, which was covered with pine and the aroma of it drifted to him. The smell brought back memories of how Indians use pine to sanctify and purify. Even in the war, whenever possible, they had sought out pine branches when they had to bury someone, or for the small celebrations they sometimes held, weddings, births, namings. They tried to continue their traditions despite the obstacles. He remembered how the Indian women had gone to a nearby village and persuaded a shaman to come and name Benigno. He'd been in too much shock to even think of such a thing.

The old man had come and stood over the meagre pine needles they'd collected, removed the red thread tied round Benigno's umbilical cord and blessed him in Spanish so thick with Indian accent that he was barely intelligible, but the shaman spoke Mam not Quiche. After, he mumbled some words in his own language for good measure and they toasted the boy's health with corn liquor. The shaman drank so enthusiastically he had to be carried back to his village. Raphael wondered what stories he had later told of guerrillas carrying him off in the night for a baptism, and the other villagers thinking it was a drunken dream.

But more than anything, the scent of pine made him think of death, of wakes, where the earthy, almost medicinal smell covered the aromas of decay. Had there been a wake here? Or a celebration?

The woman led him to a room on the left, which gave the semblance of an office with two desks and chairs, a bookshelf, a phone, a fax machine and a newish looking computer, which all seemed incongruous with the simple surroundings.

'*Don* Marco,' said the woman, nodding to a young and very lively looking man rising from his chair. He had the jet black, spiky hair Indian men are prone to and a faint shadow of a moustache. His eyes darted and smiled in his face and he was so short that Raphael wasn't sure if he'd completely stood up. He extended a hand towards Raphael.

'How can I help you?'

'I'm …' Raphael paused. He didn't want to say he was a journalist; it probably wouldn't help him. Most Indians, with good cause, had a healthy fear of the written word as it was nearly always used to spread lies about them. 'I'm looking into the murder of a friend. He was a journalist and the only thing of interest I found in his papers was a story about Manuel Chavez, the pastor killed here.'

Marco's face flinched at the mention of Manuel's name and he pointed to a poster on the wall, which Raphael hadn't previously noticed. It showed a serious man kneeling, hands on a Bible by the look of it. The legend said, 'Blessed are those who are persecuted for righteousness' sake, for theirs is the Kingdom of Heaven.' Below it was Manuel's name and the dates of his birth and death.

Raphael studied the poster for a minute then returned his gaze to the young man's face. 'Could you tell me what happened? Why was there international interest?'

Marco gave him a cautious look, then gestured with his head for Raphael to sit down. 'Manuel disappeared. He'd witnessed Pascual Serech, a member of the community, being kidnapped by the military, and he publicly denounced it. It was a death sentence. We tried to keep hope, but I think we knew we wouldn't find him alive, but still we had to find him. We looked everywhere. This Presbytery has links with the United States – a church partnership. A group visits most years and sends money, supports projects, and there are some US missionaries at our seminary on the coast. They put out the word about Manuel's disappearance. They thought international support might help. It has sometimes in the past.'

Raphael nodded.

'Anyway, after a of couple weeks, it came to light that maybe it was Manuel who'd been buried in an unmarked grave in the cemetery here. We arranged for an exhumation; and it was Manuel. He had been found in a shallow grave in the *milpa* with thirty-three stab wounds. They wouldn't even let us bury him properly.' Marco's voice began to break. He composed himself and continued. 'So, we couldn't let it rest and our friends from the USA helped. They started a big campaign. There were letters to the Embassies in Europe too. We had a pretty good idea who was responsible, but no proof. Not that proof would have done any good; no one could touch the military. They were talking about signing the peace, but people were still being killed, everyone lived in fear.'

'What happened?'

'Despite all our efforts the man was never brought to justice. Now we focus our energy on other matters.' Marco said, starting to shuffle some papers on the desk.

'Are there people I could talk to about it?'

'Probably not. People will tell you what a good man Manuel was, and how he lives on, but they are village people, reticent, they won't tell you much more. Like I said we focus on other things now. But, if you're interested, there is a vigil tomorrow for the first anniversary.'

'The pine?' asked Raphael inclining his head towards the other room.

'Yes. There'll be a march through the town and past the military base at 3 p.m. and then a memorial here. We weren't allowed a wake at the time; they said we had to bury the body straight away. They thought too many people would congregate and it would get ugly.'

'I'll bear that in mind.' It would probably be helpful, and he might learn more about what had happened, but Raphael wasn't sure he was ready for the memories such an event might induce.

'Has anyone come here recently asking about the case? A young man from the capital?'

'Not to my knowledge. It's old news to everyone but us. Our friends from the US are here for tomorrow's event, but I doubt anyone else outside the community will be interested. The military have hushed things up, closed ranks around the man, even though we were assured there was a warrant out for his arrest.'

'Who?'

Marco remained silent.

'Colonel Lopez?'

Marco raised an eyebrow. 'You know?'

'His name was mentioned in one of the newspaper clippings. So, is he still around?'

'He's been seen a few times in Chimaltenango, but mostly he's in hiding, maybe moved away. Who knows? They look after their own.'

'And what happened to the man who was originally kidnapped?'

'The military continued to hassle him. He moved away. He had two brothers. One was killed. The other one stayed, but he was beaten into silence, now he just tends his plot of land, he doesn't do civil rights work any more.'

'Did Manuel have a family?'

'Yes, a wife and children. She had to go into hiding, she kept getting death threats.'

'And now?'

'We help her financially as much as we can, but only one or two people know where she lives. I am not one of them.'

Raphael was starting to think this was a pointless exercise. He couldn't see how this case related to Rosario's murder. It didn't sound like he'd even been there. But it was the anniversary, which was perhaps more than a coincidence if Rosario had kept following the story. Maybe he'd planned to do a follow-up story on the march. Raphael made a mental note to ask Rosario's editor if he'd planned to visit Chimal.

He asked Marco a final question. 'Could you show me Manuel's grave?'

'It's a public cemetery, you can go and look. I need to get back to work now.'

'And the unmarked grave was here too?'

'Yes.' Marco looked at his watch, as though he had to be somewhere else. He had nothing more to say. 'Where it says ZXX on the wall.'

Raphael rose and thanked him, shaking his hand. 'Oh, and is there a decent place to stay here?'

'Try the Hotel Entrada.'

'Thanks.'

It was completely dark when Raphael left the office. He'd have to leave visiting the cemetery until the morning. If nothing else it might inspire him to write his article. He didn't have much else to go on and he hadn't yet decided whether it was worth delving any further into the criminal acts of Colonel Lopez or attending the memorial. As he walked towards the main street a military jeep trundled past him. It sent shivers down his spine.

We're crouching by the roadside about to cross when the military convoy of four jeeps and a tank goes by. I sink down quickly, face to the damp earth, afraid that they will see me. My heart beats strongly into the ground causing a rebound like an earthquake beneath my chest. Lidia grips my calf so hard my leg begins to fall asleep, but I can't move, barely dare breathe. I raise my head a fraction to watch the vehicles pass though I can hear them and feel the vibrations of their heavy wheels joining with my pulse in a relentless pounding through my veins, through the earth, through my whole body. My pulse is so loud surely the soldiers can hear it. Time stands still; it seems like an eternity until the last wheels skid past sending a cold shower of mud into my face. The feeling of time suspended, my lungs ache from not breathing, the relief that they're gone. We were lucky this time.

6

On the way back to his car he spotted the Hotel Entrada, with a big neon 'entrance' sign with an arrow, over the door. It looked reasonable and would serve his purpose. He went in and booked a room, then returned to the street to look for a place to eat before the unspoken curfew fell and drove him back to his hotel.

Raphael wandered around town, getting a feel for it. He thought he might have been there once before, but he was more familiar with the market towns of the highlands, Huehue, Xela, the Nebaj triangle and the villages and jungle beyond. Chimaltenango didn't have the sparkle or touristic appeal of those places. There was no bustling Indian market, it was drab and dusty and the architecture was boring and bland. There were no buildings that stood out. He made a note of the location of the cemetery, noticing that its entrance was exactly opposite the main police station, which looked like a barrack, and returning to the main street again, found a café that looked warm and inviting, serving roasted meats. He chose a table at the back and ordered a coke and *cabrito azado*.

While he waited he thought about what he'd been told. Could there possibly be any relation to the murder of the journalist? It didn't seem as though Rosario had investigated the case, at least not recently. Yes, there had been some international interest, but as Marco had explained, that was a perfectly natural response of foreigners who had a relationship with the church. In this country the murder of one more Indian by the military for whatever reason wasn't really news, and the Colonel was so unlikely ever to be brought to justice, he would have no reason to commit more murders to cover up that one, assuming he was the guilty party. But then again, the military acted with complete impunity; if the man had a taste for killing he wouldn't need a particular reason. Raphael kept running into dead ends. Should he go back to the city and talk to friends and family of Rosario? Or just write the piece and be done with it? They would probably never know why he'd been killed, just another name added to an already long list.

The food arrived and he found that he wasn't really hungry, but he went through the motions of sustaining himself. The goat meat was tough and had a strong flavour. The grilled scallions were sweet but couldn't be bitten in two and slithered down whole in an unpleasant manner. The baked potato sprinkled with chilli was the best feature and Raphael tackled that with more gusto. His thoughts turned to Lola, and his stomach gave a flutter. That irrational fear surfaced again. He wondered if she was also eating, if she was out with her other man, cooking for him, lying in his bed. More likely she was still working. He hoped that this unsettled feeling he had was just some foible of his regular bouts of paranoia.

He tried to imagine his life without her. It would continue, of that he had no doubt, probably much the same as before he'd met her. How much would he miss her if she weren't there? If she chose to be only with her other lover, would he mind? His pride would probably not be dented; he could be a proud man, but not about women. He was not a macho who would be floored by the desertion of the woman on his arm. He thought perhaps he wouldn't mind very much if he lost her, then felt guilty as though he didn't care for her at all. He did, but it wasn't love. Maybe it was time to end things with Lola. They'd had a good run, they'd had fun, but he didn't want to get more involved than that and he was afraid he was starting to.

Raphael had been pushing the food aimlessly around his plate and now made a concerted effort to eat, although congealed roast goat was not appetising. He glanced up and saw a man he thought he recognised entering the restaurant. Without staring he tried to study him. He was large, with poky eyes behind his glasses. Raphael thought he worked with Lola at *La Frente*. Hadn't he been the man chairing the peace conference? The man caught him staring and Raphael looked quickly back at his plate.

Raphael paid the bill and left. On his way out he stopped at the table of the man he'd seen come in. He looked up enquiringly at

Raphael. He was large enough to stand out in the general poverty induced thinness of the majority. His pencil thin moustache gave him a military look. He was probably Indian but passed for *ladino*. He was well dressed and slightly suspicious looking. He had an air of intrigue about him that Raphael couldn't quite place.

Raphael held out his hand. 'Don't I know you?'

The man looked surprised but said nothing.

'Don't you work for *La Frente*, in the capital?'

'What do you know of *La Frente*?'

'I'm a friend of Lola Rodriguez.'

'Then you should know better than to talk so openly.'

Raphael was a little surprised. He knew the rules of secrecy, the unspoken codes friends and acquaintances had between them, the things that couldn't be spoken about, but the existence of the *La Frente* was no secret. They'd just been big players in a conference on peace with the Nobel Peace Prize winner for goodness' sake. Raphael was in no doubt that the security forces already knew who worked for them and exactly what they did.

'Why don't you sit down, you're attracting attention.'

How would he attract attention? There were very few people in the café and the only one who looked at all suspicious was the man he was about to sit down with. Still Raphael pulled a chair from an adjoining table and sat down.

'What are you doing here?' asked the man.

'Huh?'

'I heard you were at the Presbytery office.'

'What?' Raphael was surprised that anyone would have already heard he was in town let alone which office he had been to.

'I'm Presbyterian, and yes, I work for *La Frente*, and I know Lola. But this place is not safe. It's not all that it seems.'

'A journalist in the city was killed. I'm ...'

'I know. That has nothing to do with what happened to Manuel.' The man gave Raphael a pointed look to emphasize that.

'No, I'm beginning to think that it doesn't,' replied Raphael.

'Manuel Chavez is old news. Go back to the city.'

Raphael started to speak but thought better of it. His intrigue was aroused now. He would go to the memorial for Manuel, see what 'old' news he really was or wasn't.

He left and walked back to the hotel. There he sat in the courtyard and smoked a cigarette. It was still early and he could hear the background hum of traffic, people working in the kitchen, guests coming and going, a group of foreigners chatting in the dining room. He felt a pang of desire for the silence of the capital though he knew that silence didn't come until after 11 p.m. No doubt by that time Chimaltenango would be equally silent. Raphael both loved and hated the long silent nights. He would like to be able to sleep, but he appreciated the enveloping solitude of the night. Though the silence brought fear, it allowed him to write uninterrupted except by his own thoughts and memories. The night-time calm was like the silencer on a gun, a stifling blanket. The forces of evil moved through it stealthily, like a shark gliding through the deep. The only sign of their presence would be a cadaver in an alley in the morning. A body missing hands, or with marks of torture; or no body at all, just an empty room, a husband who didn't come home, a shoe left on a stairwell where someone was caught trying to run.

Raphael thought about the conversation with the man in the café. Why had he tried to warn him off? Why had he urged him to go back to the city? Why should this place be more unsafe than anywhere else?

He sat for a long time running things through his mind and finding no answers. By now people had retired to their rooms and quiet was descending. Raphael went to his own room. It was a drab affair, with paint peeling near the ceiling and the bed saggy and limp, but it was clean. He wrote up some notes from his interview at the Presbytery office, the exchange at the café, and some general notes on Rosario, then he was overcome by exhaustion. He slipped off his shoes and lay down in his clothes.

As he lay there Raphael pictured himself snuggling under the blankets with Lidia. He liked to conjure up a happy memory of her before he slept; it was almost like having her there with him. All his memories of Lidia were happy. If they had ever quarrelled, he'd forgotten it. He blocked out the days they didn't speak because she was annoyed with him. He couldn't block out the horror of the war, but he could make her perfect in his memory and that was what he wanted.

He remembered the nights early in her pregnancy when he had gently stroked her belly, which showed little sign of her condition, incredulous that in those circumstances she could be pregnant. It was beyond inconvenient for a guerrilla in the highlands to be expecting. For that reason alone, they believed it was the will of God, meant to be, and neither of them ever considered trying to get rid of the child. As the time of her confinement drew nearer, they stayed at base camp; he doing whatever work was required – chopping wood, cleaning weapons, collecting water and supplies; she sewing, mending the uniforms of the group and making baby clothes. There had been a good chance that the baby would not survive, or would be born a weakling, given their poor diet, though Raphael tried to bring her meat and milk as often as he could, even stealing it sometimes, although he wouldn't steal from the poor. One night he had received a hefty kick in the knee trying to milk someone else's cow. It had swollen so much he could barely walk for two days. The *compañeros* laughed themselves silly that his only injury of the campaign had been sustained by a cow's hoof. He couldn't remember another occasion in his life when he had ever laughed so much. Lidia had to beg them to stop because the baby got so excited and wouldn't stop kicking. That was when they decided to call him Benigno if it were a boy. Raphael had never imagined that Lidia would be the one to not survive, that the baby would be strong and healthy and live up to his name in every way.

Raphael awoke in the darkness, sweating and gasping for air, but this was not his usual nightmare. It was not of Lidia, or Benigno, or the jungle nights, asleep fully clothed with his gun by his side. The image imprinted on his mind was of Lola bound and gagged. He sat up and fumbled for the lamp. He tried to take deep breaths to calm himself, but he felt his supper rising in his throat. He ran across the corridor to the bathroom and threw up. Back in his room he sipped water. It was 3 a.m.

He knew it was going to be a long time until daylight, but Raphael was in no frame of mind to pursue his usual nocturnal activity of writing poetry. He pulled out the battered copy of Rene Otto Castillo's poems that he always carried with him. That book had travelled everywhere with him, from the city to the mountains and back again. The author had been murdered, probably more for his guerrilla activities than his writing, though there had been a time when being caught with the book was probably a jailable offence.

When Raphael next opened his eyes, it was light. He went and showered, though the water was little more than a trickle. He was famished and remembered losing last night's meal. He ate a full breakfast of eggs, beans, *platanos* and tortillas, and headed out for the cemetery.

Outside the air was cool and fresh; it smelt like country air. The air up in the highlands always smelt different. The smell of Momostenango on a clear day, that smell of markets, wicker, livestock, chickens, the mingling of subtle scents from the vegetable stand, that indescribable scent of religious feeling, of sacredness because the old Mayan religion was strong in that place. It was palpable. The smell of the dawn was fresher in the mountains, clear, pure. You felt you could bathe in the dew and be cleansed of every sin. It was never like that in the jungle areas, there the trees kept in the smoke of the fires, where you always woke to the scent of wood cinders with a hint of copal. The moist ground emanated earthy aromas constantly, the unique blend of trees and plants that Raphael couldn't name, though he knew which ones were safe to eat, which bark could be used to make tea to soothe headaches.

Raphael drew the morning air into his lungs, like nectar, but this place, this story, brought back too many memories – violent and calm, beautiful and frightening, and the constant sadness in him crept like moss covering the bark of a tree. He walked swiftly to the cemetery and through the gates. Though he couldn't see it all, Raphael could tell that the cemetery was large. This could take hours; he had no idea where Manuel's grave was. To his right he spotted a small office and went over to it. It was plain and dark with a concrete floor and a wooden bench that acted as a counter, behind which sat an old man who blinked at him as though the light from the doorway bothered his cataracts. Raphael didn't really want to ask where Manuel's grave was and though the man should know he doubted that he would. He felt somewhat wary about asking where the unmarked graves lay too, but he did. The man remained completely placid, his face expressionless, and told him to follow the main path all the way to the end and he would find them.

The top part of the cemetery was given over to elaborate family tombs, some in marble with hovering angels. He wondered who had the money for such extravagance and what kind of people would want to entomb their loved ones in these palaces for the dead. Lidia had been buried near trees with no marker, not even a wooden cross. He would never be able to find it again. He wouldn't be able to visit her on *Dia de los Muertos*, sit by her side and reminisce, bring her flowers and her favourite foods. He was deprived of that part of his culture. It was the same every November, while others cleaned family graves and made preparations to commune with the departed, or built *altares* in their homes, he carried his grief deep inside him. He had nothing to build an altar with, no photo, nothing that belonged to her except the woven cross he wore. He had even less of Benigno. He hadn't kept any of the few makeshift toys he'd had, the bag of stones he'd played with. Without Benigno they reverted to the debris they had been, twigs and pebbles, a doll made out of a cornhusk. He hadn't been able to bear to hold them or even look at them. He'd burned them along with Benigno's paltry collection of clothes, ignoring the pleas that the smoke would attract military helicopters. He did it in anger and anguish, burning his hands, scorching his clothes, singeing his beard and the hairs in his nose. He had smelt the burning for days and no matter how many times he went to the stream he couldn't wash away the smell.

Raphael wondered what his parents did on the Day of the Dead. Since they had assumed him to be 'disappeared', had they bought a gravestone even though there was no body? Had they celebrated a mass for him? He had disappeared into the night and never returned, as dead to them as if he had passed away. But could his brother have gone through with a funeral, knowing he was still alive? He wouldn't put anything past his brother, and anyway Benjamin probably thought that if he wasn't dead then, as a guerrilla he soon would be. Raphael hoped that his parents had at least mourned, that they lit a candle before his photograph on 1st November. Maybe they were already in their graves too.

Raphael rarely thought about his family. He had no family. His family had been Lidia and Benigno and now they were gone. But he thought of his parents and brother as he walked down the hill, the graves gradually becoming simpler. He remembered his childhood years, playing games in the patio of their house.

'*Oyes tonto*, let's climb up onto the roof,' said Benjamin.

'Mother will kill us.'

'Oh are you scared, chicken?!'

'No, I'm not scared.'

'Go on then, *andele.*'

'You go first, you're the oldest.'

'Yes, but you're the smallest, you go. That way I'm here to catch you if you fall.'

His brother picked him up, pushing him up the wall until he found a foothold. Raphael smiled as he remembered hurrying up, not looking behind him to see if Benjamin was following, and then waving triumphantly from the top, as his brother waved back from the alley where he stood with his friends laughing at him. His older brother was always teasing him, always knew best, always had to have the last word. At least then it had been good-natured, the typical rivalry of brothers, the natural need of an older brother to show off and be superior.

In later years they had grown closer, sharing adolescent traumas and stories about girls they were attracted to. Then their paths began to diverge as Raphael became more radical and Benjamin more conservative. They had opposing opinions on the civil war, on justice. And when Raphael married an Indian woman, albeit a beautiful and intelligent one, that was the end of any sibling relationship.

Was his brother married now? Did Raphael have nephews or nieces? It didn't matter. If there were such children it would bring Raphael too much pain to see them. Benjamin deserved to die a lonely old bachelor, but that was not the way life worked out. The ironical sense of humour of the gods meant that Benjamin probably had a wife far better than he deserved and a whole house full of children.

The *campo santo* was still, no one was tending graves that morning. At the end of the path was a low wall, broken glass jutting out of its top, with numbers painted on it. And there was ZXX, an uninspiring earthen mound, now empty unless it had been re-used. Raphael stood in front of it soaking up the atmosphere, the stillness. There were many thousands of unmarked graves across the country. At least this man had ended up in a graveyard. Many had been dumped unceremoniously in gullies for wild animals to find. Or in side streets and rubbish dumpsters as a warning to others. But this had not been Manuel's first resting place. Marco had told him he'd been found in the *milpa*, to the Mayans even more sacred than consecrated ground, this man must have been close to God. But that hadn't prevented him being taken in the night and stabbed thirty-three times before they slit his throat. Where was God in this land where so many worshipped faithfully? Where was the sun in this place where the day-keepers rose daily to welcome it? Raphael fingered the cross beneath his shirt. God had forsaken them all.

He had a hunch that the proper grave of Manuel would be close by. The path made a left turn around the edge of the cemetery. He followed it and soon came to a wall of graves, slots one on top of the other, five or six high. He began to read the names and about half way down the wall he found it, Manuel Chavez 1952-1995, "Manuel lives, only his body lies here." Raphael knew they believed that, his family, his community, he knew only too well that they had to. He had to, as well, the alternative was too terrible. He may not understand God, but Raphael knew there had to be something more than this life. He had to hope he'd see Lidia and his son again.

It dawned on Raphael that he must have been standing in front of the grave for some time. He turned to leave and thought he saw someone watching him from behind a nearby obelisk. He looked closer but saw no one. He walked towards the monument, but there wasn't anyone there. Either they were experts in disappearing or it had been his imagination.

Raphael walked slowly back through the graves. He should go back to the city. El Pelon was probably right, there was no story here. There were only questions, unanswerable questions. Also there were his worries about Lola; he knew something was wrong. He was no psychic, he'd never been able to tell what was going to happen to himself or anyone else, if he had been maybe he could have saved his family, but he had never thrown up as he had in the night. The image of Lola bound and gagged kept coming back to him. He was used to waking up in fear; insomnia and Raphael were well acquainted, but he hadn't known panic like that for many years.

I'm woken by Lidia shaking me.

'Raphael, Raphael quickly, they're coming.'

This is the first time danger has really been close. I'm afraid, but I don't want to show it because Lidia looks so calm. I throw the blanket off, shove my feet in my boots. I fumble with the laces, all fingers and thumbs. My heart is racing, laces slippery with my own sweat. I tie them in a knot, push the length of it into my boot and hope it holds.

We follow others, down the bank of the ravine. I don't know which is worse, the thought of being shot or falling down the valley. I see flashing lights above me, hear the gunshots. I clench. I want to pee so badly I think I will. Then it goes from my mind as someone in front starts shooting. We edge up the bank and peep over the top. I lie with my gun facing the road, resting on the ground. I feel someone warm beside me. I can't move my head to see who it is. I'm frozen. Soldiers run past on the road. We open fire. Two or three fall, the rest keep running. Did I do that? Did I shoot one? My finger is on the trigger, gripping tight. I have to wait a few minutes before I relax enough to move my fingers. I don't want to see how many bullets are gone. I wait as long as possible before I clean my gun. I don't want to know that I might have killed a man.

At the cemetery gates another military jeep drove by and as it flashed out of sight Raphael saw police on the opposite corner watching him. More likely they were congregating in preparation for the march. He had no reason to think they were watching him; they were just standing on a street corner.

Somehow, he knew now he had to go to the memorial. He went back to the hotel and made arrangements to stay a further night, had lunch there and spent some time doing preliminary work on his article and daydreaming about Lola. The cemetery filled his head with thoughts of death that swirled around with his fears for Lola, making a bile-flavoured milkshake. If something happened to Lola would he mourn her like Lidia? Would she gradually become perfect in his eyes; all faults forgotten? Would he light candles before her photo and take flowers to her grave? Probably. Ritual was soothing, even if it had no meaning.

Raphael went round the hotel and into the main street. In the distance he could already see the march approaching. He stopped there to watch. Gradually a white banner with blue lettering came into view. '*Quien mato a Manuel Chavez?*' Who killed Manuel Chavez? Manuel Chavez, martyr for justice. The banner was carried by Indian women. Behind them was Marco with an older man and two Americans, and then a group of twenty to thirty community people.

As they congregated outside the police station, the sky grew dark and it began to rain, slowly at first, then in torrents. Raphael stood to the side of the main crowd so he could watch. The group stood impassively with their banners, oblivious to the water that ran down their faces, so that Raphael couldn't tell what were tears and what was rain, on his own face or anyone else's. They made no speeches or demonstrations; simply their presence was enough. Several policemen hovered outside the station and the surrounding streets looking worried. Manuel's face sagged on the sodden sheet, making the screen-print image even sadder. It would have been hard for Raphael to recognise that Manuel had been a good and humorous man when all the memorial images were so serious. Some indigenous people believed that the camera would capture their souls. The photo on the banner certainly hadn't captured Manuel's.

Back at the Presbytery office the smell of pine was pungent, enhanced by the humidity and the warmth of bodies. Raphael sat in the back and listened to the usual expressions of regret and calls for justice. Yet this was different. There was a feeling, something tangible, that these people knew who had killed Manuel and if the law didn't punish him, then their God surely would. And then it was voiced; Colonel Pedro Almendrez Lopez was the man who had killed Manuel. They all knew it, even the government knew it, but his buddies in the military would protect him. Lopez had killed Pascual Serech, Lopez had terrorised his brothers, and Lopez, with or without assistance, had taken Manuel, and stabbed him thirty-three times before slashing his throat. Lopez would do anything to evade justice. But justice would come, if not in this world then in the next. It was stirring stuff, but Raphael knew that retribution would only come in the next world and he was even doubtful of that. He slipped away before the speeches ended, before the community laid their brother to rest for a second time and the women intoned their tuneless laments.

As he walked back to the hotel Raphael heard the same singing in his head, but from many years ago. 'Console yourself with patience. Console yourself with patience.' But he could not.

7

Raphael left early next day for the city. At the main road, on an impulse, he turned away from the capital and headed north towards the Mexican border, though that was several hours away. He wanted to drive for a while, clear his mind, compose his article, but mainly he wanted to put off his return, put off hearing bad news about Lola, even though that was irrational. He should go back and put his mind at rest. Surely he would find her the same as before, in her apartment making coffee, laughing, making fun of him. Then he wouldn't be able to tell her about the fears he'd had for her; she would only tease him.

The road soon left the dusty outskirts of Chimaltenango and began to rise. The sun was already high and hot, he'd missed the cool mists of pre-dawn in which the day-keepers moved silently in the shadows preparing to greet the day, to welcome the sun and aid it through its trajectory across the sky. Their prayers would sustain the four pillars, which hold up the blue veil of the heavens stopping it crashing onto the heads of the people and destroying the world. But hadn't it already fallen? Hadn't the day turned into perpetual night with the coming of the military and the years of terror? Was a new morning finally dawning? Apparently not when the city still woke to handless corpses in its back streets. The article began to form in Raphael's mind, rich in allegory and Mayan tradition, using Indian mythology as a metaphor for murder and evil. His editor would hate it. The only people who might appreciate it would probably be too illiterate to read it.

He remembered the stories of the Pop Vuh, the creation myths of the Mayans. Once he had studied the book in depth while knowing little of its significance. With Lidia he had lived it vicariously; he had seen how the Mayans kept it in their hearts and lived by its principles.

In the time before people were created, when only gods walked the face of the earth, there were twin brothers Hunahpu and Ixbalanque out to avenge the death of their father by the evil Lords of Xibalba, the underworld. By trickery and cunning they passed through all the tortures of the houses of Xibalba. They played the lords at the sacred ball game of the Mayans and by obtaining the help of various animals, won the game and defeated the lords of evil. Then no matter what the evil ones did to Hunahpu and Ixbalanque, even though they ground their bones and sprinkled them in the river, they could not kill them. And Hunahpu and Ixbalanque honoured their parents – their father who had been killed, and they were raised to the sky and became the sun and the moon.

Then the gods created the first humans. They were not born of women, but the first four men were created by the gods out of corn. They had great wisdom and could see and know everything. Soon the gods decided that wasn't good; that men had been created by them and should not be equal to them, so they brought a veil across their eyes so they could only see what was close. The gods decided they should multiply so they created four wives for the men, and these were the ancestors of the Quiche people. But the people had lost their cunning and trickery; they could no longer overcome the powers of evil. Maybe the gods shouldn't have pulled the veil over their eyes.

The road was bordered on either side by *milpa*, the sacred corn plant, food of the gods and building block of humanity. The gods had tried before to make people of mud and then of wood, but the people of corn had been perfect, and their duty was to maintain the world, to urge on the sun in its daily journey and to prevent the sky from falling. The Indians had been faithful in their duties; the gods had failed in their protection, or was it the rich who had caused the downfall, the demigods who thought themselves all powerful because of the drop of conquistador blood coursing through their veins. Maybe it was just fate, maybe there was a pre-ordained map for the world that even the gods were powerless to stop. Just like the Indians, their gods were not as fearsome and almighty as the omnipotent white God. They made mistakes, they talked among themselves with an uncelestial democracy, they had a human face. It was as if they had been created in human form to keep the future generations mindful of their duties, of their partnership with the deities. Humanity wasn't made in the likeness of God, but the other way round. God was the creation of human imagination.

Raphael felt the blood move in his thigh. He saw the artery pulsing beneath the thin cotton of his trousers. The daykeepers, who kept the sacred Mayan calendar, could divine things by the movement of the blood, depending on which part of the body it moved in. This along with the reading of the stones, crystals and the vermilion seeds of the tzite tree drawn at random from the shaman's soft velvet bag; and the reading of the days, the Mayan version of the horoscope, determined your destiny in the coming days. Raphael wondered what the blood throbbing in his leg meant.

The road wound down to a dustier valley. Tiny paths led into the background where Raphael knew Indian villages lay, though there were no visible signs of life. These decimated villages stayed hidden, not trusting the alleged peace. Politicians were Hun-Came and Vucub-Came, the evil lords of Xibalba. No word from their lips could be believed. The burning may have stopped, but sons still vanished in the *milpa*. The civil patrols still manned their guard posts with their old wooden rifles taking whatever they wanted, whenever they wanted it.

Raphael longed to disappear into those villages though he didn't belong there any more than he belonged in the city. He was rootless, a mixed blood abandoned and forgotten by his family. His heart was with his Indian wife and son, floating in the ether of the after world. Lola didn't need him, she could manage perfectly without him, she only picked up people when she had a use for them.

It was late in the day when Raphael got back to the capital. He was just able to return the car to the rental place before it closed, then he took a bus to Lola's apartment. He would have preferred to call first, but there was no opportunity. With a certain trepidation he slowly climbed the steps to her apartment and knocked on the door. She didn't answer. He knocked again, though he knew that she would have opened it immediately if she was going to. He tried to look through the window, but it was pointless, the curtains were drawn. He left and walked briskly to his own apartment.

Raphael tried to convince himself that Lola was all right. She was probably still on her way home from the office, it was early enough, then he remembered it was Saturday, but it wasn't too out of the ordinary for Lola to work at the weekend. He needed to get on with his article; his fears about Lola would have to wait. They were just the work of his overactive imagination.

Back at home he set about writing by hand, as was his wont; he would go to the office in the morning and type it up in time for the late Sunday edition. The words flowed easily since he had mapped it all out in his ruminations while driving. There was no real substance to it, he knew no more now than he had before. As usual he became lost in his writing. It grew dark. Raphael paused to turn on a light without losing his train of thought and drank Coke without even realising he'd been to the kitchen to fetch a bottle. He ate nothing.

He re-read the piece several times and was satisfied with it. He was so practised he could write a standard column, almost exactly to the word, without having to cut, without embellishment.

Raphael went out onto the balcony and watched the night. What was the significance of the murder of the pastor Manuel Chavez? Was there any, or had it all been a wild goose chase? And what of the journalist Rosario – had he just been in the wrong place at the wrong time? Just an example to make sure the newspapers kept up their self-censorship? Or had Rosario been on to something hot about Lopez? Had he found some evidence to prove that he'd killed Manuel? The community seemed sure it was Colonel Lopez, after all he'd been seen kidnapping Pascual Serech. Had someone seen him kidnap Manuel too? Or was it all nothing – just an old newspaper clipping that Rosario had forgotten to take off his board?

And what of Lola? Where was she now? Lying alone thinking of him? Lying with her other lover? Lying in a street? There were too many questions to sleep.

He went in and lifted the phone intending to call Lola, but the instrument ended up cradled in his hand.

8

It was another bright sunny day that would be hot. Raphael's shirt was already starting to cling to his back like a lacklustre lover. There was a tightening in his stomach, a low hum of fear. He felt exhausted, strung out on coffee and cigarettes, haggard from lack of sleep, tormented by nightmares and worries. He craved rest. He needed to escape. Maybe he should take a few days off; he hadn't had any time off in months, go to the natural springs at Almolonga and soak for hours in the steamy volcanic water, then sleep. Go to the mountain village markets, see if the old daykeeper was still there, get the stones read, and see what his future held.

Raphael remembered his last visit to the old man in Momostenango, Teodoro Perez. The shaman had asked him his date of birth, 'Ah Tijax, the day of suffering, and you have suffered greatly my son.' Raphael had thought cynically that you didn't need to be much of a diviner to work that out, and that it applied to a great many people. 'People born on Tijax make good daykeepers.'

'But I'm not Mayan.'

'But your son is and he's of your blood.'

'What do you know of my son?'

'Only what your heart tells me. But why have you come to see me?'

'I want to know what I should do with my life.'

'You know the answer.'

'If I did I wouldn't be here.'

'You know the answer.'

Daykeepers were always so enigmatic. 'Count the days for me.'

The old man emptied his bundle onto the table, the red seeds and crystals spilling out, and said some words in Quiche over them, sifting the seeds from the stones, but Raphael left knowing no more than that he had the answers to his questions.

Raphael still didn't know the answers, but he felt the need to be pampered for a while. Lidia had been a strong independent woman, who didn't mind telling Raphael what to do when it suited her, but still she had cooked, cleaned and washed for him without question; made him his favourite food, washed his back and trimmed his hair, not out of tradition, but as an expression of love. He tried to imagine Lola looking after him like that and couldn't. She was too self-centred. Raphael pushed the thought of Lola away. There was a nagging disquiet at the back of this mind, but he didn't want to worry about her for the moment. He had his article to type up and submit. Once that was taken care of he'd find Lola, enjoy her company, try not to care about her infidelities. Then he would go away for a few days, relax, reassess his life. Maybe he should split from Lola, concentrate on his writing; try to bring out a new collection of poetry.

Raphael felt a little calmer. Making plans brought order and Raphael liked order. He pushed open the door of the newspaper building and went up to the second floor. The newsroom was quiet. Before he began work Raphael called Lola's office. The phone rang for a long time before an out of breath man answered.

'*Diga.*'

'I'm looking for Lola Rodriguez.'

'No one here today, except me. Don't you know it's Sunday?'

'Yes, but … Never mind. Thank you.'

Raphael felt a little foolish for having called, but there was no harm in trying. Lola did sometimes work on Sundays.

He was nearly finished typing when his editor poked his head out of his office and said, 'Raphael, let me see that when you're done.'

Raphael read through the piece one more time, saved it on file for the print run later that day, printed out a copy and went and knocked on the editor's door.

'So was the trip worth it?'

Raphael smiled. El Pelon had sandpaper-like humour and no patience for journalists who couldn't write well. He also liked to be right. Raphael was about to make his day. 'Well, it was like you said, I don't think that story had much to do with what happened to Rosario.'

'So been wasting my money have you?'

'I wouldn't say that sir, it was good to go and check and the trip gave me some ideas.'

'I can't afford to send my writers on road trips to get ideas, we're not in Hollywood, you know.'

'No sir. But speaking of which, I was thinking of taking a few days off. I haven't taken any time off this year.'

'Let me read this piece and then I'll let you know if you can have any time off.'

Raphael knew that was just talk, the editor couldn't refuse him a holiday. He'd fill out a form later. El Pelon put his glasses back on and picked up Raphael's work. That was his cue to leave and he took it.

Raphael went outside to smoke, though he could have done with a break from the nicotine, but he resisted a cup of coffee. The sun frazzled on his skin. He could almost smell the hair on his fore-arms burning. He inhaled deeply and blew out smoke. A woman walked down the street with her back to him. He thought it was Lola and started walking to catch her up, then he caught sight of her profile and realised she looked nothing like Lola. I must be going crazy, he thought. I have to stop this worrying and do something constructive.

He wanted to go to Lola's office even though the man on the phone had said no one was there, but that would be pointless. Why didn't he just go to her apartment? Why was he putting it off? As he walked in that direction, he passed the church Lola usually attended, though she often just popped into whatever church was closest. On a whim he entered. Church was one of the more likely places Lola would be at this time on a Sunday. He thought Lola usually went to Mass early, but to be honest he wasn't sure. They tended to avoid each other on Sundays so they wouldn't squabble about his lack of religion, and her blind allegiance to doctrine.

As he entered the church the frigid air hit his face and made him shiver. It was dark and he stood and let his eyes adjust. There was a Mass in progress, the second or third of the day. Raphael felt out of place. He knew what to do, but it was years since he'd been in a church. He dipped his fingers into the water in the stoup. The cool water felt refreshing as he made the sign of the cross. The air around him had a religious feeling, but it wasn't sanctified. It wasn't like the air in the mountains and the village chapels where Raphael had experienced his spirituality. He remembered the parish church in Santiago Atitlan with its plain wooden saints dressed in Indian clothes. They were the only spot of colour in the plain church, bare wooden pews and whitewashed walls, myriads of tiny candles stuck to the stone floor. No ornate silver and gold statues in glass cases, but simple wood figures on roughly carved wooden horses, dressed to the nines in local finery and gaudy Western fabrics. He remembered the eerie coolness around the memorial to Stanley Rothers, the American priest killed in 1981, when a good many of the villagers had also been killed by ransacking government soldiers.

Raphael edged forward, genuflected fleetingly and eased into the first available pew. He scanned the congregation for Lola, realising immediately that he probably wouldn't recognise her from the back of her head and that he wouldn't be able to speak to her unless he waited for the Mass to finish, but it would set his mind at rest if he saw her. The faint aroma of incense was soothing. As a boy Raphael had always loved the smell of church incense, but he loved even more the copal used by the Mayans. Its rich, tree sap smell so resonant of the divine. The words of the *Agnus Dei* floated over him, but they didn't register, and he didn't say them though he knew them by heart. Then he slipped out again, not bothering to bow before the altar.

Outside Raphael decided not to go to Lola's apartment yet. Most likely she wouldn't be there and then what? He'd go later. He needed to stop thinking that something had happened to her. It hadn't been *that* long since he'd seen her. And wasn't he wondering about calling it a day with their relationship anyway? There was no point rushing to see her when the upshot of that might be ending things.

Needing something to keep himself occupied, Raphael made his way to *Prensa Libre* to go over some of Rosario's articles on archive. It was too late to change his article, but for his own peace of mind maybe it would reveal something, and it would keep him busy until he went to see Lola.

At reception he asked for the archive room and showed his ID. He was shown to a small room in the basement. There was no computer database, even of more recent years, only microfiche versions of the last ten years and hard copies prior to that. Rosario had been working at the newspaper for only about four years, so Raphael decided to simply work backwards from his last article, looking for his name.

Since he didn't know what he was looking for he made a list of the date, subject, and a column for notes. Moving quickly through the main pages of the paper and ignoring all the advertisements, sports and business pages, he found that Rosario had covered the usual range of topics, though as expected the stories got smaller and less significant as Raphael went back in time to when he had started at the paper. In recent months there seemed to have been more stories about deaths and kidnappings, but not to the exclusion of more mundane news. Within a few hours he had been through three years' worth of papers, and articles by Rosario were becoming more infrequent and of little interest, the kind of stories the new boys got because no one else was interested in them.

Raphael stopped and turned off the machine to rest his eyes, it was a long time since he'd used microfiche for that length of time. Then he reviewed his list. There really didn't seem to be anything that looked unusual or formed a link. Clearly, he had been wasting his time. But then as he scanned down the column of notes, he noticed that the name Colonel Lopez appeared a number of times. Colonel Pedro Almendrez Lopez, his full name was listed in a few of the articles, more articles than he would have expected in the course of normal newspaper reporting, unless this Lopez was some kind of senior military figure or a serious criminal. Lopez was a very common name though, maybe it wasn't the same person in every story; but Almendrez was not so common, Raphael had never heard of it before, it was the maternal surname, but what sort of a name was that – after a nut!

Presumably it was the same Colonel Lopez who had been implicated in the death of Manuel Chavez otherwise Rosario wouldn't have noted it. Raphael switched the machine back on and began to flip through some of the stories. A Colonel Lopez of Chimaltenango did seem to appear in a number of them, either subtly implicated as the guilty party in a kidnapping or disappearance or making an official comment. Raphael wondered what Rosario's interest had been. And why so many of his stories were from the Chimaltenango area when he lived in the capital. Had he known someone there? Someone who had been killed or threatened? Or was he simply being a journalist following up a lead. Had he really found something substantial on Lopez? And could that have been why he was killed? Nothing in the files Raphael had access to implied that Rosario had any scoop worth being killed for. He wished he had access to Rosario's home, to see if there was more there. But that would only get him into trouble. El Pelon wouldn't be interested in an in-depth investigation of the young journalist, and if he'd been killed for something he'd found out about Lopez then Raphael really didn't want to find that information. Plus, if the man had enough pull to get Rosario killed, he surely was well connected enough to have his house searched and any incriminating information removed. Raphael would doubtless never know the truth, and he had enough worries of his own to put too much energy into the death of a reporter he'd never known, despite the tragic implications that had for his profession. Still, before he gave up on it entirely, he decided to go back to the offices of *Siglo* where there was a computer that could do a search based on a single name or topic. Out of curiosity he would put in Lopez and see if anything intriguing appeared.

Just as he was going out of the door, Raphael remembered that he had meant to ask if Rosario had been to Chimaltenango recently or had been intending to go. Raphael went back to the receptionist.

'Is the newsroom editor in?'

'I'd have to check. Who should I say …?'

'Raphael Sifuentes. *Siglo Veintinuno*,' he added remembering that the man hadn't been able to remember his name last time.

The receptionist mumbled into the phone, then handed Raphael the receiver.

'Hello.'

'Yes, I'm working on a piece on Rosario Recinos. I came in a couple of days ago, remember? I just wanted to ask if Rosario had been to Chimal recently, in the last two or three weeks say. No? And was he planning to?'

'Not as far as I know,' said the editor.

'Right, thanks.'

Strange. The thought that Rosario might have been onto something linking Lopez to the death of Manuel Chavez was a good reason for him turning up dead, but it seemed he hadn't been investigating the story, at least not recently, or not with his editor's knowledge anyway. Rosario might have wanted to keep things to himself if he thought he had a big story, but it didn't make sense for him not to have mentioned something to his own editor, unless he wanted to wait until he was sure of his information. No reporter liked to look stupid in front of his editor.

Back at his own paper, Raphael tried to narrow the search by putting in the title Colonel, and the other names along with the surname Lopez, and the place name, even so he came up with a surprising number of hits. Unfortunately, the database only contained stories from his *Siglo Veintiuno*, but clearly this Lopez had been busy. The references were listed chronologically. Raphael could immediately see that there were a large cluster of articles around the time of the disappearance and death of Manuel Chavez and then a steady number for a while which gradually petered out, although there was something as recent as six months ago. Raphael selected the latest article. It was a small piece from the back portion of the paper stating that Colonel P.A. Lopez of Chimaltenango would be retiring as a military commissioner. 'Lopez had been implicated in several cases of kidnapping in recent years and his name was mentioned in connection with the killing of local Pastor Rev. M Chavez. Both Colonel Lopez and military sources declined comment on whether his retirement was linked to these allegations.'

How very interesting, thought Raphael. Colonel Lopez retired. So what had happened to the warrant for his arrest that the Presbytery had been assured of? Just like Marco had said, his colleagues in the military were protecting him. His retirement would presumably ensure the Colonel protection from prosecution. Raphael flicked through a few of the other stories, but only found more vague references to Lopez's involvement in crimes, and unsubstantiated allegations.

9

Later that day, Raphael stood on the landing outside Lola's flat. Finally the moment he'd been putting off. He'd tried to keep himself busy all day, but now as he stood outside her door, he had to admit he was still worried. He fingered the key she'd given him, rolled it between his fingers wondering whether he should enter. There was no reason why he shouldn't. He was her lover, he had a key, he was entitled to be there, yet he felt like he was breaking in, invading her privacy.

But what if she were lying in there ill, too sick to call the office or a friend, too sick to call him for help. Raphael thrust the key into the lock, turned it and went in. He called out, no answer. The room had an empty smell, an unlived in mustiness. There was a cool, complete silence. He knew without looking that Lola wasn't there, but he went through the motions anyway. The door opened into the main room, with its kitchen area in the left-hand corner, the rest of the small space occupied by a rough wooden table and chairs, and the walls lined with vegetable packing cases that Lola used as bookshelves. Here and there, was a touch of femininity, an attempt at décor, candles in cheap pottery candleholders from the central market, carved animals from Nebaj and bright *huipiles* hung as wall hangings between the framed political posters.

He moved over towards the kitchen, there was a dirty plate in the sink, a pan where she'd heated up coffee on the stove, its dregs remaining, mould forming a skin on top. Lola was not the tidiest of women, but she was in the habit of washing up the day's dishes in the evening. Whatever morning she had last breakfasted here, she hadn't returned. He opened the fridge. No pungent smells emerged. In fact, it was strangely empty. Some cheese turning mushy from lack of use, tortillas hardened to a rock from not having been warmed up and eaten, coriander completely limp and starting to wither. No serious decay, but it was clear no one had been there for a few days. His stomach tightened and his mind began to race through all the possible scenarios. An accident? Kidnapping, assault, murder, disappearance – almost endless disgusting options that ran through his head, rather than the more likely and pleasant ones, such as visiting a relative, or a business trip. But for any of those wouldn't she have called, left a note at least? But then he hadn't been around to call, had he? But he'd only been gone a couple of days, and surely she would have informed her office if she had a reasonable excuse for absence.

All his fear and panic had materialised, come true almost as if he had willed it to happen. Perhaps she was with another man, the lover he suspected, driven by passion or love to abandon her home, to not call her colleagues. Raphael couldn't believe that. She had never done that for him. She was too conscientious, too committed to her work if nothing else. The most he could remember of their early passion was her leaving work early one day to be with him.

He walked into the bedroom. Uncharacteristically, the bed was made, the red blanket from Momo that she used as a cover seemed to be smoothed out more than she would ever smooth it. The room, the scene of so much passion, was too neat and tidy. Everything straightened up and regimented. He went to the bedside table and ran a finger across it, not a speck of dust, not like Lola, not like Lola at all. She kept the place clean, but never this tidy; she had more important things to do. And she always made the bed in the evening, too eager in the morning to get out into the world. One morning when he had started to make it, she had stopped him, 'let some air to it Rafa, leave it, there are big adventures to be had.' He heard her voice in his head like a ghost.

When he came to visit then she would make the bed, though in a hurried and haphazard way. Often she would fling herself back on it. 'Take me,' she would say with that flirtatious smile of hers. He opened the drawer of the bedside table. There was the book of his poetry, which he had given her for her last birthday. Opening the cover, he saw his own spindly writing. *'Muchos años mas, querida.'* Even then he had not managed to say, 'I love you'. His eyes began to fill. He blinked back the tears and continued to look in the drawer and found all his love-notes to her, all the poems written hurriedly and unromantically on scraps of paper, all bundled together with an elastic band. How so like Lola! Not a ribbon or scrap of fabric, but the nearest practical thing. But he was surprised that she had kept them at all, that she had kept them carefully and secretly in chronological order, by her bedside, next to where she had loved him. Perhaps he'd misjudged her; perhaps she cared for him more than he thought. He laid the bundle on the bed, intending to take it with him.

He looked over the rest of the room. It was the same, but not the same. Something was different; he couldn't put his finger on it. It didn't smell of Lola, he couldn't feel her. The tidiness, that was it, there was an uncharacteristic military precision to the layout. For the sake of thoroughness, he went into the tiny bathroom. It was sparse. Though she was vain Lola was not given to using a variety of beauty products. Her lipstick and mascara lay on a shelf above the sink, over which hung the mirror she used to beautify herself. He caught his reflection in it and started. Raphael barely recognised himself, looking much older than he felt himself to be. The sight of both toothbrushes together in one glass, his and hers, side by side, touching, made his eyes well again. Her shampoo stood in the window ledge of the shower, a thin piece of soap next to it. Even here it looked cleaner than he would have expected, but not surprisingly so.

He returned to the living room, not knowing what to do next. He supposed he should try and call her family. See if they knew anything, if perhaps she was staying with them. Probably it wasn't worth calling any of her friends. He felt sure that if he didn't know where she was neither would they. And to be honest he didn't know any of her friends. He could remember names of people she had spoken about, but he hadn't met many of them. He couldn't call any of them completely out of the blue and ask them if they knew where she was. The more he thought about it, the more he realised how little he knew about Lola. Their lives had never really meshed and commingled, they were two separate people living two separate lives who came together sometimes for sex, conversation, a meal together, friendship you might say, though they were not friends in Raphael's mind.

A friend was someone you trusted intrinsically, who you could rely on, who would lay down their life for you. Raphael had had friends in the mountains. None since. He had married his best friend. He suddenly realised how he missed those true friends and felt lonely. More alone than he had even felt after Lidia had died, when he was surrounded by friends to help him, though he hadn't appreciated their help at the time, had never really thanked them. Many now were beyond thanks. He felt the loneliness as a chill, a morning frost gripping him around the chest, making it painful to breathe.

Raphael tried to remember what, if anything, he knew about Lola's family, her father had died a number of years ago, he knew that. He thought her mother lived in the city, but he wasn't sure. Lola didn't talk about her much. And there was a sister too, slightly older, married with two young children whose names he couldn't remember. She did live in the city. Lola went to see her fairly often. She had said many times that he must go too but had never taken him. Andrea, yes that was her name. He should call Andrea.

He looked around for the small, worn leather book she kept her addresses in. He couldn't see it anywhere obvious. He scanned the shelves, looked through the few papers scattered on the table, but of course it wasn't there, she always kept it with her, in her bag. Raphael hadn't looked for her bag, not expecting it for one moment to be there, and with another scan of the room he confirmed that it wasn't. But there were notes on the small stool that held the phone. He grabbed up the pieces of paper and looked through them. Mostly they were phone messages, notes she had taken of meetings, numbers with no names, but at the bottom was a stiff piece of card with five names and numbers: Lupe, which meant nothing to him. Andrea, he hoped was the sister, Josue and Daniel, again he didn't recognise the names, and then his own name.

He dialled Andrea's number. There was no answer. He let it ring an unbearably long time, but no one picked up. Raphael slipped the piece of card into his jacket pocket. He would try calling again later. It occurred to him that the next logical thing to do would be to start calling hospitals to see if Lola had been admitted. Maybe there would even be a happy result, maybe she had collapsed somewhere with appendicitis and been rushed to a hospital without letting anyone know. It could happen. Things like that did happen; every day; in other places. In this land if someone disappeared suddenly without a trace, then they had disappeared for good. Raphael couldn't fight his pessimism and despair. He pulled out the phone book from under the stool and found the page listing hospitals. He even started to dial the number for the *Hospital General*, then he cradled the receiver. He couldn't do it. With no plan in mind he ripped out the list of hospitals and let the book slide to the floor.

Some time later Raphael was still sitting there with the list in his hand, in a semi-coma of despair and indecision. He had to get out of her house, walk around, decide what to do. Raphael went back into the bedroom and picked up the bundle of letters. Then he hesitated. He had given them to her, they were still her property, he had no right to take them. He would find her and then she would need them.

Once out into the street, he lit a cigarette, inhaled deeply and started to walk vaguely in the direction of his own house. He looked at the ground and tried to think, to think logically and rationally about what could have happened to Lola and what would be the best thing to do.

Engrossed in his own thoughts he didn't see the man in the shadows watching him, nor the fact that as soon as Raphael was a reasonable distance away, that shadowy figure climbed the steps and slipped silently and with apparent ease into Lola's flat.

As he walked, Raphael tried to go over things in his mind. He knew that Lola often didn't call him for days: that was not uncommon. Also, that he had not seen her since their ridiculous argument, but it was not her style to bear a grudge. He felt pretty confident that wouldn't have stopped her calling him, especially if she'd received his note. But had she? Had she been back to the office since then? She clearly hadn't been in her apartment for two or three days at least, and there was that strange feel to the apartment – the over cleanliness. It was obvious to Raphael that things didn't look good. He had to call the hospitals; that was the next logical step. Then a visit to the central morgue itself would undoubtedly be necessary, if only to eliminate that possibility. He ought perhaps to call the police, but Raphael had a natural distrust of the police or any uniformed authority and knew that more often than not the police were responsible for murders. He had to accept the possibility that Lola might never be found, though the powers that be seemed to have given up that particular form of oppression in favour of the more visible message of mutilated corpses.

Raphael prayed to whatever form of higher being he imagined was out there, to the old gods watching over them, to the ancestors, that Lola had not been tortured, or ... or God forbid, he couldn't even think what they might have done to her. He felt a slight burning sensation in his hand and looked down to see that the cigarette had burnt down to his fingertips without him having smoked it. He saw the scar on his hand where Lidia had bitten him, so long ago, where even in her pain she had tried to protect them by not letting her screams be heard. He lit another cigarette and looked up. Ironically, he was standing directly opposite the entrance to the Santa Maria Hospital. What a dismal place it looked. And strangely quiet. A couple of drunks slumped outside near the main entrance, but otherwise no one was coming or going. There were no ambulances screeching to a halt outside or relieved patients leaving on the arms of relatives. It was one of the capital's larger hospitals but tended to attract a slightly lower class of patient. If Lola had been ill and taken to a hospital, it was unlikely to be this one, especially as it wasn't anywhere near her work and not particularly near her house. Raphael had strayed quite some distance from her flat in his dreamlike ambulation. But in the past the Santa Maria had a reputation as a favourite place to drop off bodies. Since Raphael was there he may as well cross it off his list. Just go in and check that Lola hadn't been admitted.

He dropped his cigarette end and ground it into the pavement. Then he crossed the street, entered the hospital and went up to the main desk.

'Excuse me, could you tell me if a Dolores Rodriguez has been admitted?'

'And you would be?'

'A friend.'

'Hmmm, we don't usually give that kind of information to anyone but relatives. But you're the second person to ask.'

'The second one?'

'Yes, that young one over there.' She nodded to a young man sitting in the waiting area, his head between his hands, low between his knees in a stance of abject despondency.

'Wait here,' she said, 'I hope no more of her boyfriends show up.'

Raphael went and sat in the chair next to the young man. He wanted to talk to him. Find out who he was. Look at his face and see if he was the man he'd seen Lola with outside the cinema. But he didn't know what to say. He wasn't much of a conversationalist at the best of times, and this definitely wasn't the best of times. Small talk was completely beyond him. But he had to see the man's face; he had to know. He didn't much believe in coincidences. What were the chances of both of them showing up at this hospital, at virtually the same time, asking for Lola? No, that wasn't just chance, there was a reason. He nudged the young man ever so slightly in the knee as he shuffled around in his own seat. The young man raised his head. It was him; it was the same man who'd been laughing with Lola that night. The man she'd kissed outside the conference.

'Do you smoke?' asked Raphael.

The young man shook his head. 'You're not allowed to in here.'

Raphael nodded and put back the cigarette he had started to pull out of the box.

'Are you ill?'

'No, looking for someone,' he said solemnly. Clearly, he didn't want to talk.

'For Lola?'

The man looked at him with such a mixture of surprise and suspicion. 'Yes,' he said. Hanging his head again he barely audibly added, 'they say her body has been brought here.'

'Her body?'

'Yes, she's dead.'

Raphael gasped. Though he had been expecting it in a way, the words were still a shock. The world seemed to stop still for a second then jump back into focus. Raphael was confused. The woman at the desk had said nothing to him, why had she told this boy anything. Perhaps he had been mistaken; perhaps the young man was a relative of some kind.

'Are you family?' Raphael asked.

'No, I'm her lover,' said the young man, more forcibly than was required. 'And you?'

'Just a friend, we worked together sometimes. Raphael,' he added, holding out his hand.

The man took it reluctantly. 'Josue.'

Raphael was stuck for words again. There were so many things he wanted to ask, but his mind wouldn't frame the questions. They sat in silence, though it was not uncomfortable, both men united in their complete solitude and despair, their own thoughts about Lola. Josue still sat with his head in his hands, as though feeling faint. Raphael sat staring straight ahead, oblivious to his surroundings, fearing the worse. Now he couldn't think that Lola had been involved in some accident or had some serious illness, he felt sure she had been killed and he tried to think by whom, and more importantly why. But his mind jumped from thought to thought, image to image. Their last kiss, their argument, writing the note to her, looking into her apartment window on Saturday night. Why hadn't he gone in then? Why wait until today? It wouldn't have made much difference, she was already dead, and he wouldn't be here now sitting next to Josue, her other lover, of all the unbelievable things. Suddenly the words from *Casablanca* flashed into his head, "of all the gin joints in all the towns ..." He wanted to laugh at the absurdity of it, he knew it was just the shock; the mind played strange games at times like these.

Then Josue broke the silence, suddenly lifting his head and almost crying out. 'Why, why aren't they telling us anything? What can have happened to her?'

Raphael laid his hand across the other man's shoulder. Josue seemed naïve, innocent somehow. Raphael didn't think thoughts of murder were running through his head. 'When did you last see her?' he asked.

'Thursday night. It was beautiful.' Josue's voice trailed off as remembering he began to sob quietly and without tears.

Raphael squeezed his shoulder more firmly, feeling only compassion for the man, no rivalry, that would be pointless now. He knew suffering; he could tell that Josue didn't, he needed help navigating its dark alleys. How Raphael wanted a cigarette now, but he couldn't desert Josue to go outside.

A policeman came through the double doors behind reception and walked towards them and Raphael realised he hadn't asked Josue what had brought him here. If he hadn't seen Lola since Thursday what had made him come to this hospital, today, how did he know her body was here? He removed his arm from Josue's shoulder as the policeman arrived in front of them.

'Both of you are here for Dolores Rodriguez?'

Raphael answered. 'Yes.' Josue looked up and nodded almost imperceptibly.

'We need someone to identify the body.'

Josue looked shell-shocked. Raphael looked confused. The policeman seemed to be jumping ahead of the game here. He hadn't even been told that Lola had died, not officially. He didn't know that they couldn't start the post-mortem without an official identification and who performed that didn't matter much.

The policeman was surly and businesslike. He's got no time for sentimentality, thought Raphael. He just wants to get on with his job. Raphael continued to stare at the officer, dazed. The policeman didn't seriously expect Raphael to identify her, did he? Didn't they need a family member? He had only just stumbled in here on the off chance that ... On the off chance of exactly this situation occurring. Wasn't that what he'd been thinking when he'd walked in – that Lola was dead?

'Sir? We are sure it is Miss Rodriguez, there was identification in her bag, but we still need someone to officially identify the body. We'd rather not wait for the family if one of you could … So, we could get on.'

Josue looked at Raphael pleadingly and he knew he would have to do it. He raised himself slowly to his feet. The policeman nodded and Raphael followed him through the double doors. They entered a long corridor and the policeman paused and pulled out a note-book from his jacket. 'If I could just take your full name for the record. And your exact relationship with the,' he paused, 'deceased.' Raphael wasn't sure of his exact relationship with the deceased, but he said *novio*, the word meaning both boyfriend and fiancé. The officer looked surprised. 'The receptionist said the other man was her boyfriend.'

'So, it would seem,' replied Raphael.

'So …' the policeman decided to leave it, storing that information for later. 'If you'd follow me sir.' He turned and started walking.

'Her family has been informed then,' Raphael ventured.

'An officer has been dispatched to the family home,' said the policeman without turning round.

'When was she found?'

'This morning.'

Where? How? Why? These were the questions Raphael wanted answers to. 'What happened to her?'

The policeman didn't reply. He paused now outside another door. 'What …'

'I'm really not at liberty to say.'

'But is she … does she …? Er, does she look OK?'

'You will only see the face. I believe the face is undamaged,' said the officer matter-of-factly.

Raphael nodded. The officer pushed open the door and gestured him in. They entered a small, dark anti-room. Another policeman and a hospital worker in blue scrubs waited there. Light came in from a curtained window behind which Lola lay. 'Are you ready?'

With a nod Raphael showed that he was, although of course he wasn't. When was anyone ever ready to look at their lover on a mortuary slab? Lidia at least had died in his arms, in some semblance of peace after the terrible pain. Her lifeblood may have been flowing out of her, but at least she had the joy of having held her son, Raphael's hand stroking her forehead. Her death was unnecessary, preventable, but it had been natural.

The officer held the door open for him. The room was heavy with the smell of chloroform. The clinical smell of death hit Raphael full in the face and instinctively he took a step backwards wanting to leave again. Though he'd never been in a morgue he knew how he expected it to look. This was even more sterile than that, too unnatural, too metallic, before he'd even looked at Lola he wanted to pick her up and run out of there with her, sit under a tree with her in his arms. He felt more tender towards her than he had when she was alive, than he had felt recently. Now he looked towards the metal table in the middle of the room, the large white sheet covering a body shaped mound. He stepped closer. The man in scrubs pulled back the sheet to uncover her face. Raphael sucked in his breath. The room faded away and all he saw was that face. The closed eyes, the grey tinge to the cheeks, the blue lips. They had always been so full and wine red. These couldn't be her lips. He raised his hand to touch them and felt a hand on his shoulder. He turned. The officer's lips moved, but Raphael didn't hear him.

'Is it her?' The officer repeated.

'Yes,' Raphael said, but the word didn't seem to come out. 'Yes.'

He wanted to look at her again, kiss her, touch her face, but when he turned back the sheet was already being pulled over her. The policeman took his arm to lead Raphael out of the room. His legs didn't want to work; he felt paralysed and moved in a trance. He didn't know how he made it back into the corridor.

Outside the room he gulped in air greedily. It seemed so much fresher, less filled with the odour of death. Again, he wanted to run. He abhorred the cruel modernity that didn't even let people die in peace. He had seen more dead people than he cared to think about. All of them friends, loved, cared for, killed in horrific circumstances, with wounds too disgusting to look at. Yet none of them had smelt like that. They had been human, smelling of sweat, tears, blood. They had smelt of the earth. He had held them, touched them, breathed them in, felt the warmth ebb away from them, willing them to a more peaceful world. The magic words had been said in ancient tongues to send them on their journeys. '*Ri ralma' ri lok'laj, ri ralma' ri lok'laj'* the walls whispered to him. They were never left alone, between gunfire and dropping bombs they were carried to a safe place, the prayers were said, what flowers could be found were laid, or at least some sweet-smelling branches. The candles were lit and they were buried properly. Lola would be buried with Catholic mass and weeping relatives, but it wouldn't be right; it was too late. She had been violated and violated again. Dumped somewhere like garbage, left alone, then brought here to suffer the humiliation of a cold metal slab, a dark metal drawer in a wall, more people prodding and poking and cutting her. Raphael felt sick. He lent against the wall, hands behind his back feeling the cool plaster. '*Ri ralma' ri lok'laj, ri ralma' ri lok'laj.*' Raphael was vaguely aware of a voice.

'Are you all right?'

Slowly the officer came into focus and Raphael tried to drag himself out of his daze. The lights seemed very bright, unsympathetically so, had this place no respect for the living or the dead? He pushed himself away from the wall, ran a clammy hand across his forehead, pushing back his hair. 'Yes, sorry, bit of a shock.'

'I'm sure it must be sir.' The policeman laid a hand on his elbow to guide him down the corridor. Raphael's mind flashed to Josue's hand on Lola's elbow. He pulled his arm away and began to walk on his own, with every step the world came back to him, though he had the sensation of having been on a ship for many days as the ground swayed up and down beneath his feet.

Then they were back in the waiting area, the officer holding open the door. Josue looked up expectantly, clinging to some vain hope that there had been a terrible mistake and it wasn't Lola they had found. Raphael nodded with his eyes and Josue's head dropped towards the floor, his hands in continual nervous motion, as if he were trying to wring moisture out of them, then wiping them down his thighs. His trousers were wrinkled and slightly damp as though he'd been doing this since his arrival. Raphael sat down next to him and felt an overwhelming desire to take hold of his hands and calm them.

The policeman cleared his throat as though put off his stride by their emotion. Perhaps it crossed his mind that they were the lovers and the dead woman was some sort of cover for them.

'I'll need some contact information from both of you,' he said. 'In due course we'll be needing to ask you some questions.' Josue jumped, appearing shocked at the very thought that they would question him at such a time. 'Just routine,' the policeman added.

The officer began with Raphael, taking his home address, place of work and occupation. He did not ask again for his relationship to Lola for which Raphael was thankful. He didn't want to add to Josue's anguish. 'When will the body be released?' he asked.

'That will depend on our investigations. And it will be released to the family. I suggest you contact them.'

Charming, thought Raphael, they needed him to identify her, not wanting to wait for the family for that, but he wasn't good enough to claim her body. He felt a stab of anger strike him. 'I loved her enough,' he wanted to say. 'I'll take care of her.' But he hadn't loved her enough, and he hadn't taken care of her, that much was painfully clear.

When it was his turn, Josue answered calmly though in a feeble voice. He gave his full name, again stated his relationship as fiancé, gave his address and said he was a musician.

Raphael watched him. He looked soft, newborn, as though the world hadn't yet touched him, but with such emotion in his overly large eyes. He was well dressed, though not expensively so. His hands were elegantly manicured and clean as though he'd never so much as turned on a tap or lifted a pen. Raphael wondered what instrument he played, or if he sang. He couldn't picture him as a singer.

He was barely twenty if that, a good quarter century younger than Raphael, who suddenly felt old, weighed down and exhausted by death and at the same time full of compassion for the sensitive youth at his side, experiencing it for the first time. Probably his pain was greater, tied as it was with the lust of a love too young to have turned sour. Raphael found it easy to imagine how Josue might idolize Lola, how they hadn't yet had time for more than the lovers' tiffs of fresh romance that were lost within moments to the surges of passion. Perhaps she was even his first love, Raphael hoped not, if so it would take Josue even longer to recover.

The officer was taking his leave of them and retreating back through the double doors. Raphael glanced at Josue who, apart from his hands, was still sitting immobile. Clearly, he didn't know what to do next. Raphael expected that at any moment he might start rocking back and forth like a madman. 'Let's go and get a drink,' he said, resting his hand lightly on Josue's arm. Josue looked up speechless but appearing glad to have any decision taken for him.

Raphael was unfamiliar with the neighbourhood, but it seemed the kind that would have cafés so he walked in the direction away from where he had come. The relative fresh air outside snapped him back into reality, the reality of his own mind, which showed him image after image like a kaleidoscope, memories of Lola, memories of the jungle, imaginings of murders in city alleys. After about ten minutes he saw a restaurant on the other side of the street and crossed.

Inside there were few customers. They sat at a table furthest from the entrance. Raphael wanted alcohol to take the edge off things, but he was strong enough to know that wasn't a good idea. He caught the eye of the waitress and ordered coffee for them both.

'Have you eaten?' he asked Josue.

'No, but I ...'

'I know, but you need to.' He didn't feel like eating either. He had forgotten about food in his worry about Lola, but he could see he would have to be strong for this boy, for a little while longer at least. When the girl returned with the coffee he asked for a plate of tacos.

'What kind?'

'It doesn't matter. Whatever.'

The silence between the men continued. Josue added spoons of sugar to his coffee and stirred it in a daydream, eventually stopping as though a sudden realisation made the action seem out of place. He looked at Raphael and said, 'You're a good man.'

It seemed such a strange thing for him to say. 'You don't know that.'

'You're here with me; that's enough.'

Raphael shrugged. He didn't feel good, and would Josue think him so benevolent if he knew he was Lola's lover?

The food arrived. Raphael rolled a taco and bit into it tentatively. Josue followed, but after one bite he devoured them as though he hadn't eaten in days. They ordered another plate and more coffee.

'What happens now?' said Josue, his mouth still partly full.

Raphael wasn't sure what he meant. 'We go home and wait.'

'I mean, what will happen next? I don't know her family. We've only been together a few months.'

'I don't know. I don't know them either. I suppose the police will talk to us again some time. I have a number for her sister. I suppose I could call.' His voice trailed off. What on earth would he say to the sister he'd never met and who probably had no inkling of his existence.

'But,' Raphael paused, 'how did you know to go to the hospital?'

'Someone from the hospital called. I can't really remember now. It was such a shock. It seems when they brought her in they found a flyer for my concert in her bag. There was a hand-written note with my name and number.' He stopped, looking as if he might cry, looking as though he remembered writing the note and every emotion that had gone into it. 'I don't know why they didn't call her family, but I'm glad they didn't or I might never have …'

'Who knows why,' said Raphael, 'perhaps they were harder to find.' They sat in silence again, both stupefied with shock. Raphael found it hard to take in, even though he'd been expecting the worst. He was the first to break the silence. 'How long had you been there?'

'I don't know. It felt like a lifetime, a couple of hours?' Josue took a mouthful of coffee. 'And you? What brought you there?'

'I'd been away. Hadn't seen her for a few days and I couldn't find her, called, went to her apartment.'

'Her apartment?'

'Yes, er, I'd been there a few times, I knew where she lived, so I went to see. There was no sign of life.' Immediately Raphael regretted his choice of words, but Josue ignored that.

'You must be a very good friend. I've never been to her place.' He sounded petulant, betraying his age. 'How long have you known her?'

'A couple of years.'

Josue no longer seemed interested in why Raphael had been at the hospital, so he didn't continue. Raphael signalled for the bill and paid it. 'It's getting late, we'd better be going. Where do you live?'

Josue told him. How ironic that Lola should choose a lover from the same neighbourhood as him. The address hadn't registered when the policeman had been taking their details. 'Near me. We can go together.'

Dusk was falling. They walked, caught a bus, then walked again, two men together and alone with their sorrows. A few minutes from the bus stop Josue said, 'This is my street.'

Raphael said, 'I'll go to the door, it's not out of my way.'

Soon Josue stopped outside a door and pulled keys from his pocket. 'Come in for a minute?'

Raphael really didn't want to. He needed solitude like a drug, his own room, his books, his loneliness. Loneliness to think about Lola, to remember touching her, to hear her laughter again, but somehow he couldn't say no.

Josue closed the door and flipped a light switch; its dim glow barely illuminating the one room. A sink in one corner, a bed in another, books in piles, a small, badly made wardrobe, a guitar on a stand, the only luxury was a portable stereo, tapes scattered around it.

'Stay.' One word was all he said, with his mouth. With his eyes he said, please. Help me. I'm all alone.

'Don't you have anyone? Family, friends?'

'I'm an orphan,' Josue said matter-of-factly, 'but it's OK. I understand if you don't want to.'

'It's not that. I just thought … You don't know me, maybe a friend would be more comfort.'

'I don't need to know you. You didn't leave me. You knew Lola, cared for her in some way, you understand.'

Raphael shrugged in a way that showed he did.

Josue slumped on the floor leaning against the bed and nodded towards the only chair in the room, which Raphael sat in.

'You were more than friends, weren't you?'

Raphael raised an eyebrow.

Josue repeated, 'You and Lola, were you more than friends?'

Raphael hadn't wanted to tell him, but he couldn't lie. 'Yes.'

They looked at each other. 'Did you know about me?' said Josue. 'No. Well, I suspected. I saw you once, outside a cinema. Something about the way you looked at each other. I suspected. I used to tease her about her other lover. She always denied it.' Raphael didn't know why he was telling Josue all this.

'I thought she had someone else,' said Josue. 'But I thought it was just paranoia. I was crazy about her. Couldn't believe she wanted me.'

'Mmm, Lola could do that to you.'

They each held their own memories of her. Raphael continued. 'I accused her of having an affair. We argued. That was the last time I saw her.'

'I felt something had changed. She said we couldn't see each other again. I was devastated. She didn't really say why. Some crap about my age, too many differences. I couldn't believe that, I asked her if there was someone else. She said no, but it must have been you she'd chosen. But then she came back. That night, Thursday, she came back. Said she'd been wrong and that she couldn't live without me, and we made love like … sorry.' Josue looked down.

'It's OK.'

'In the morning she was gone before I woke, but she was going to come to my concert on Saturday. I made so many plans in my head, foolish plans. And then she didn't come and I thought she'd changed her mind again. I got drunk, very drunk. I went out with some friends after the concert and I talked badly about her, saying what a … I didn't know, I didn't know.' He began to cry.

Raphael went over and sat beside him and held him until the crying subsided. 'You weren't to know. How were any of us to know?'

'I didn't know what to do, didn't know whether to call or not. I didn't want to make a fool of myself.'

Raphael remembered it, that craziness of being young and in love, of not knowing what to do, how to impress, how not to screw it all up and lose the woman forever. He remembered it and kept silent. Josue fell asleep against him, exhausted from emotion.

Raphael lifted him onto the bed, removed his shoes and covered him with a blanket. He found a second blanket at the end of the bed and huddled under it in the chair, suddenly chilled to the core. It didn't occur to him to leave.

He slept badly. It wasn't the chair; he had slept in less comfortable places. It was his mind running amok, not letting him rest. He feared he would have a nightmare and wake Josue, but he was dead to the world, sleeping like a teenager, worn out by trauma.

At dawn a grey light filtered in from the one window and Raphael was wide-awake. He wanted to leave, but he couldn't, he couldn't leave Josue without a word, like a lover after a one night stand, lying in bed wanting desperately to get up and go, just run away and forget the night before, but not daring to move an inch for fear of waking the other. There was a door at the back of the room. Raphael eased himself out of the chair, went over to it and lifted the latch quietly. Beyond was a small courtyard with an outdoor shower and privy in one corner. He went and relieved himself, then crouched on the ground, Indian style, his back against the wall and smoked a cigarette. He was always surprised how quiet a city of this size was in the early morning. The poor people must be up and getting ready for work; women somewhere were already patting tortillas by hand over an open fire.

What had happened to Lola? Why had she been killed? He couldn't be sure that she had been, since the police had told him nothing, but a young healthy woman didn't just disappear and end up in a morgue naturally. The worse case scenario was also the most logical one. But why? True, she worked for an emerging opposition party, but she was a bit-player not one of the main actors. She did training and education; she was no threat to anyone. Was it to get at him? No, surely not, that was just his paranoia in overdrive. It had been some years since his subversive days and he had been just one of the million small hairs on the dandelion head, waiting to be blown away. If the authorities had wanted to catch up with him they could have done it any time. Maybe he hadn't been quite as low-key as he could have been in his writing, but it would be gross egotism and narcissism to think that his poetry and editorials might be the cause of anyone's death.

His thoughts turned to Josue. He seemed little more than a boy, but he was old enough to have loved and to have his love taken from him, to have lost his parents, no doubt in the violence, but maybe not. And what of siblings? He hadn't mentioned any; he appeared completely alone in the world, just like Raphael was alone. Had his family been wiped out? Had his whole village been wiped out? He didn't look particularly Indian, though he had an Indian surname, but there was something about his eyes. A child like that, drawn to the city, would try to hide where he'd come from. Raphael sighed; those were his own prejudices colouring his view. Josue could be anyone, he knew nothing about him; he could even be the son of a military man. For all he knew Josue could have something to do with Lola's death. It was certainly strange that he should have been at the hospital. Strange that of all the things they had found in Lola's bag the hospital staff had hit upon his concert flyer and tracked him down. Wouldn't it have been more sensible to look in her address book for family members?

But Josue was sensitive, Raphael could see it, feel it, they were alike in that way, alike and unique, there were not many people like that in this militaristic, macho society, not many men who dared to be different and risk being called *maricones*, poofs and worse. Was Raphael being sympathetic to Josue because he saw something of himself in him? Saw how he might have been? How he might have loved Lola? Raphael wondered how Josue had met Lola. At some concert? Through mutual friends? Lola had said she'd met him at a concert, hadn't she? When she was claiming he was just a friend. Was that why Raphael had been thinking about leaving her, because deep down he knew she was lying? Maybe Josue had bumped into her on the street? Or had Lola picked him up in a café, like she had Raphael? It didn't matter. Josue had been in love with her; probably loved her more than Raphael ever had or could. If Lola had told Raphael she loved another, he knew he would have given her up, let her go easily, too easily.

He stood up, his legs grown stiff; Raphael was too tall for such a position, not designed for it, and too old, though he had seen Quiche men twice his age maintain it for hours. Standing too quickly he saw shooting stars, like those he and Lidia had seen sometimes.

Josue stumbled out, eyes barely open, and went to the privy. Raphael went inside to wait for him. He folded the blanket from the chair, laid it on the bed, and sat down.

'Good morning.'

Josue nodded in reply, he looked like he wanted to collapse back into bed.

'Listen, I really need to go and do some things. Will you be all right?' said Raphael.

'Yeah. Thanks for staying. I didn't mean to put you out.' In daylight Josue seemed embarrassed by his dependence of the previous night.

'It's OK, no problem.' There was an awkward silence. 'Er do you want to get together later? See if there's any news?'

Josue looked relieved. 'Yeah that would be good. I'm working this afternoon; shall we say seven at Miguel's cantina?'

'OK.'

10

Raphael let himself out. The air felt good after Josue's claustrophobic room. He needed to walk, but there weren't many places to walk in the city that were free of traffic and people. At the corner he caught a bus north. He would go to the relief map, essentially a tourist attraction, few tourists ever found it, being rather out of the way and not near any other attractions of note. At this time of day there would be no tourists. The relief map was a large scale map of the whole country that one could walk around, surrounded by a small park, where in times past the richer citizens had sent their children to play with their Indian nannies.

He saw that the entrance to the map itself was still closed, but a gate to the park was open. The place was like a mirage in the desert and he had it all to himself. Raphael felt strangely calm and then he felt guilty for the feeling. Lola was dead and he didn't feel anything. Sometimes he thought he was immune to pain, he had already lost everything he cared about. He cried at the poignancy of poetry, music moved him, cinema reached out to him, but people left him untouched. Like a person afraid of dogs, he was tentative; he put out his hand only so far before pulling it back because he knew what would happen. The logical part of his brain told him the same boat couldn't sink twice, that he was beyond more suffering, but his reflex system drew him back to the known safety zone, the place where the ceasefire prevailed. He was shocked by Lola's death, he couldn't believe it, though it was tragically believable; it was as though someone was poking a needle in him, he could see them doing it, but he couldn't feel it.

Raphael didn't know how long he walked, but the sun rose high in the sky. After the days of fear and premonitions it was a sort of release to discover that something had actually happened to Lola. He had seen her body; he knew she had been killed; now he must do something about it. He decided to go to the office. He was in no rush to go back to his flat and be alone, for now he would be constantly alone, no relief from solitude in Lola's arms. A pang of pain and guilt stabbed him in the guts as he realised that was what he'd been thinking he'd wanted. He'd been thinking of finishing things with Lola and now that choice had been taken from him. Into the calmness sparked a flash of anger that she had been taken from him. That she had been stolen in the night before he got the chance to decide what he wanted, to say goodbye as friends, or to choose to spend the rest of their lives together. Everything in his life had been that way – the power taken from him. I want the power back, thought Raphael.

At the office, Raphael checked the previous day's news and the drafts of that day's edition for anything about Lola. There was nothing. Clearly the police hadn't yet released any details, but that was not unusual, and the morgue prowlers, reporters who hung around the hospitals hoping for leads to murder stories, hadn't picked up on it. Fortunately, *Siglo* was too high quality to attract that kind of reporter. He checked a couple of the sleazier papers, there was nothing there either; that was good.

He checked on a couple of small assignments and was about to leave when he saw a policeman at the far end of the room. One of his colleagues pointed to Raphael and the officer walked over. Raphael really wished the police hadn't come to his office, now there would be questions from his work colleagues. He could lie, but he wasn't very good at that. None of them had known about Lola, they wouldn't take his feelings into consideration. He'd have to be creative, invent a traffic violation or some misdemeanour, some ridiculous misunderstanding. Everyone knew the police were prone to be overzealous; he might get away with such a story.

By now the officer was at his desk. 'Raphael Sifuentes?'

'Yes.'

'Perhaps you could accompany me for some questions in connec …'

'Yes, I think I know what it's in connection with,' said Raphael quietly, not wanting him to spell it out in front of his colleagues. He gathered his things and followed the officer out.

One of the newer boys, a junior, gibed him, 'In trouble again Raf?' Raphael knew he meant it as a joke, but he wished he hadn't drawn attention to it. He wanted to complain to the policeman, ask him why he'd come to his work, but he knew better. The man was just doing his job, these things had to be cleared up and Raphael wanted Lola's killer brought to justice quickly, though his well-founded scepticism made him doubt they would find the right man. Someone would go to jail for it, but most probably not the real killer. It might even be him. He shouldn't think about that, he knew how the authorities worked, it could happen. The officer said no more until they were outside, where he gestured to a waiting police car. 'Be easier at the station, if you don't mind.'

Raphael got in the back of the car and nothing else was said on the short drive to the station. He hoped it was just a formality, he had identified the body after all, but he couldn't assume that would let him off the hook.

At the station he was led swiftly into a small cheerless room and told to sit down at the table in the centre. He was left alone for a moment before a different officer entered the room and introduced himself. Raphael noticed the shine on his black boots and his serious countenance. The policeman who had collected him entered and stood blocking the doorway. Raphael immediately felt nervous and locked in; there was only one small window high in the wall letting in light and no air. He wanted to smoke but didn't want to appear nervous; he was innocent and had nothing to hide.

However, the officer very deliberately opened a packet and lit a cigarette before offering one to Raphael. He took it.

With no preliminaries the officer launched in. 'Are you Rafael Sifuentes de Morales, of edificio 2a, avenida 13, la zona 3? Date of birth 8 January 1951?'

Raphael replied in the affirmative. The officer didn't look up from his notes and his face showed no expression. His uniform was immaculate and Raphael found himself focussing on the shiny buttons on his chest. Oiled hair was swept back from his forehead, a fraction too long for a policeman, giving him a shady, slimy look, which was accentuated by his military style moustache.

'You claim to be the boyfriend of Dolores Rodriguez.'

'Yes.'

'Josue Chan also claims to be her boyfriend.' He looked up to gauge Raphael's reaction.

'Yes, it would seem that we both were.'

'So, you were jealous?'

'No, I didn't know.'

'You didn't kill her in a jealous rage?'

'What?! I didn't even know she'd been killed.'

'But you identified the body.'

'I mean I didn't know how she'd died. How did she die, exactly?'

'I'll ask the questions, thank you.' The officer gave him a pointed look, which Raphael thought unnecessary. He also thought the line of questioning unnecessary, abrupt and jumping to conclusions, but that was what the police did best. Obviously, jealousy was a clear motive in their eyes for both him and Josue.

The officer adjusted his perfectly tied tie and changing tack went for the more straightforward questions. 'Where were you on Saturday night?'

'Chimaltenango.'

'What were you doing there?'

'Investigating a story.'

'Yes, you're a reporter, aren't you? For *Siglo Veintiuno*?' he almost spat the words out, showing the first sign of emotion. 'What was the story about?'

'Is that relevant?'

He gave Raphael that look again. 'It may be. I'll return to that later. How long have you known Miss Rodriguez?'

'About two years.'

'And did you live together?'

'No.'

'When did you last see her?'

'About ten days ago?'

'You can't remember?'

'Not exactly.'

'Why so long? You were lovers, weren't you?'

'Yes, but that's the way it was.'

'You parted on good terms, no falling out?'

'No. I mean no falling out.' Raphael definitely didn't want to mention their argument. 'I left on Thursday and didn't come back until Sunday, so I didn't see her then.'

The policeman paused in his questioning, perhaps wondering how best to continue, though it seemed to Raphael that he knew exactly what he was doing, had a plan worked out before he'd even come into the room. They were trained in interrogation techniques; they knew how to make people say things they didn't want to say. Say things they didn't mean and incriminate themselves. Raphael reached for the cigarettes from his coat pocket. The policeman started, catching the movement out of the corner of his eye. The officer at the door laid a hand on his gun, then removed it as he saw Raphael pull out a cigarette.

'And when you got back, did you call her?' he continued.

'Yes, I called her at home and went round to her flat. She wasn't there.'

'Do you have a key to her flat?'

'Yes.'

'So, did you go in?'

'No.'

'No? Why not?'

'I don't know, it didn't seem quite right. I didn't know anything was wrong.'

'But weren't you worried?'

'Yes.'

'So, you were worried, you had a key, you had an intimate relation-ship with her, but you didn't go into her house to see if she was all right? She might have been ill in there. Or was it because you already knew she was dead?'

'Of course not! Anyway, why would I go there at all if I knew she was dead?'

'Maybe to set up an alibi? Keep up appearances? So the neigh-bours could say they had seen you there looking concerned?'

'Have they?'

'Uh?'

'The neighbours, have they said I was there?'

'We haven't checked that yet, but we will.'

'Why would I lie?' Raphael wished he hadn't said that, but he was exasperated. He had thought, foolishly in retrospect, that this would be a simple interview establishing some facts to eliminate him from their enquiries, but it was turning into a nightmare of accusations and insinuations and being less qualified in that area than the officer he felt he was coming off badly.

'You tell me,' came the inevitable reply.

'No reason, no reason at all. I'm telling you the truth.' The problem was Raphael wasn't telling the whole truth. He was missing out bits that were convenient for him, that he felt would sound incriminating. Like their argument, like the fact that he had gone into her apartment and snooped around, and he suddenly realised, the fact that he had been back in the city on Saturday night when he'd said he returned on Sunday. But that had been a genuine mistake. He was flustered by the questioning. He couldn't change it now, it would sound even worse, and the main point was he hadn't killed her, whatever this officer said, so they wouldn't be able to find any evidence to convict him. But he wasn't naïve enough to think they needed physical evidence to convict him. Come to think of it he could have an 'accident' in a police cell and who would be any wiser? Who would care? He had no family. Lola might have wondered about it, but she couldn't now. El Pelon might make a fuss for a while, but realistically what could he do about it? Raphael felt sweat trickle down his back. His palms were sweaty, his face pale, his heart racing. He needed to calm down or his own fear would incriminate him. He lit another cigarette.

'OK. So, you went to her flat, but you didn't go in. Tell me your movements from then until last night. How did you turn up so conveniently at the hospital where her body was? Strange coincidence, isn't it?'

'It was just that, a coincidence. I called her office and was told she wasn't there, but it was Sunday, so I wasn't that worried. I had to work, after that I went back to her flat and went in. It looked like she hadn't been there for a few days.' He didn't want to mention that the place had felt altered, as though someone had cleaned it up. That was just an intuition, and if it wasn't then the 'authorities' were the mostly likely clean-up crew. 'I looked around for numbers for her family. I called her sister, but there was no answer. I decided I should probably try calling the hospitals to see if she'd been admitted, but I couldn't bring myself to, so I just started walking. After a while I found myself outside the Santa Maria Hospital and since I was standing right outside, I thought I might as well start there – go in and ask about her. I did and that's when I found out she was there. And that's where I met Josue.'

'Hmm it doesn't sound very plausible to me. However ... You went to her office the day you left on your trip, didn't you?'

'Er, yes.'

'Why was that?'

'I just wanted to see her, say goodbye.'

'But that wasn't because you'd had some kind of argument?'

What was it with this officer, did he know something? Did he already know they'd had an argument? Was he pinning his whole case on that? Or was he just fishing, trying to get Raphael to admit something they could later use against him.

'No, I've already told you that,' said Raphael wearily.

'And you left this for her?' The policeman pulled out a plastic bag from his file and slid it across the table towards Raphael. It was the note he'd written to Lola at her office.

'Yes. Where did you find this?'

'In her jacket pocket.'

So, Lola had gone back to the office on that Thursday after all. Then she must have read the note before she died. Had she known then that he loved her? Had it said enough, or only confused her and driven her to the arms of Josue? Or had she not gone back?

Never read it? In which case how did it get into her pocket? Presumably, the pocket of the jacket she was wearing when they found her if the police already had it.

'It's unsigned,' said Raphael.

'Yes, but a man fitting your description left it at her office. It sounds pretty final, like you were saying goodbye for the last time.' He stressed the word 'goodbye'. 'Why didn't you finish it?'

'I don't know,' said Raphael, thinking that this was becoming more and more like a clichéd detective film, but knowing it was deadly serious. 'I couldn't think of anything else to say.'

'A journalist lost for words!' The policeman said sarcastically. 'Why didn't you sign it? Was that deliberate? Because you knew how things would turn out? Because you knew we'd find it?' The policeman stabbed the letter aggressively.

'No. I didn't think about it. But I had no particular reason to sign it, she was familiar with my writing, she would know it was from me.'

'Yes, we found a number of letters from you at her flat.'

Raphael cringed at the thought that this man and his cronies had been in Lola's home, that they had touched and read and probably laughed at her private correspondence, his private correspondence. He wished he had taken the letters with him, but he hadn't been home yet either, no doubt in his absence his house had also been searched, either legally or illegally, and they would question why he had taken them. Would assume there was something incriminating in them and would read them even more closely looking for it.

'That's perfectly natural, we were lovers.'

'Yes, let's come back to that, shall we? You say you've known Miss Rodriguez about two years?'

'Yes.'

'And how did you meet?'

'Is that …' he was going to ask again about the relevancy of the question but saw the pointlessness of that in time. 'In a café.'

'A café? Just like that?'

'Yes, just like that.'

'I wouldn't have taken you for such a ladies' man!'

Raphael's temper was starting to rise. He gritted his teeth and lit another cigarette.

'And you saw each other regularly after that?'

'Yes, pretty much.'

'Did you know what she did?'

'What do you mean, what she did?'

'Where she worked?' the officer clarified.

'I knew she worked for *La Frente*, if that's what you mean.'

'And did you meet any of her family or friends?'

'No.'

'Strange, isn't it?'

'Not really, it's not as if we were going to get married or anything, it was a casual sort of thing.'

'Ah I see, casual. But not so casual that you didn't become jealous?'

'I've already told you. I didn't know about Josue and I wasn't jealous.'

'All right Mr Sifuentes. I think that will be all for now.' As abruptly as he'd started the officer stopped his interrogation, put away his pen and began pushing back his chair.

'That's it? I'm free to go?'

'Unless there is something else you'd like to tell us?'

'No, nothing else.'

'Then you can leave. We'll be in touch again if necessary. Don't leave the city.'

Raphael entered Miguel's, the local *cantina*, but there was no sign of Josue. A few regulars were sitting at the bar telling stories and laughing. He chose a side table and sat down. On an impulse he ordered a beer, he figured after the unusual and stressful day he'd had, one beer wouldn't hurt. From the police station he had gone home and had not been surprised to find that it had been searched. It was a professional job, most people probably wouldn't have noticed, but Raphael had been expecting it and had a good eye. Things had been moved ever so slightly, the dust had shifted, there was a sensation of someone unknown having been there. He couldn't tell exactly what they'd been through; he could only presume they had been through everything. What were they hoping to find? A bloodstained item of clothing? More letters? A murder weapon maybe? He still didn't know the circumstances of

Lola's death so he couldn't speculate on what that weapon might be.

The beer arrived and he took a sip, it was cold and though bitter tasted good, he liked the sensation on the back of his throat, the feeling of the cool damp bottle in his hand. Maybe he should lift his moratorium on alcohol. He had the self-control of a nun; he had proved it to himself over and over; there was no reason to think that if he had the occasional beer he wouldn't be able to stop. He took another sip.

Was that the usual nature of police interviews, he wondered? Raphael had heard more than one horror story of people beaten up in police custody, of people forced to confess, so in that respect he had got off lightly. They didn't seem to have made many enquiries yet, although they had managed to ascertain that he was the writer of the note in Lola's pocket, if the officer could be believed. Not much of a leap to imagine that a writer, who was known to be her lover, who was going out of town, would be the author of the note. But he still wondered about how the police had come by it. If Lola hadn't been back to the office, then she would never have received the note and it couldn't have been in her coat pocket. Maybe they were just trying to find a lead to follow up; it had been barely twenty-four hours since he had identified her body, there was a limit to how much they could have found out yet.

But did they seriously think he'd done it? Implying he was jealous, implying that he and Lola had fought. But they had argued at least, hadn't they? What if somehow the police had found out? Questioned people at the restaurant? The waiter would have had some idea that they'd been arguing, would probably remember them. Lola was a memorable woman. Had been. But how could the police know about that? They couldn't have already gone to the restaurant and talked to anyone there when there were much more obvious things to investigate. Now he was just being overly paranoid. But it wouldn't look good for him if they found out about the row now that he'd said they hadn't argued. What else could he have said though? If he had told the truth, they would've exaggerated it and twisted it, making out he was so angry that he'd killed her because of it, even though the fight was nearly two weeks prior to her death. They were perfectly capable of wrongly accusing him without any help from him.

The waiter asked him if he wanted another beer. He hadn't realised he'd finished the one in his hand. He did, but he ordered lemonade. Where was Josue? It was nearly an hour since the time they had arranged to meet. Perhaps he'd forgotten. Last night had been unique; it was only natural for them to cling together, holding onto the lifeboat that was their memories of Lola and the shock of finding her like that. Maybe now Josue had realised he didn't want or need Raphael's friendship. After all Raphael was the one who had 'won' her in Josue's mind, why would he want to associate with the lover of his woman? He was probably commiserating with other friends, letting them comfort him.

Raphael was starting to feel the beer, in a pleasant way, after so many years without a drink it was having quite a profound effect, though in no way would he describe himself as drunk. Music started playing in the background of the bar. It was a Mercedes Sosa song he vaguely knew. The words seemed to blow into his mind like a hurricane, like he was hearing them right inside his head.

… *tantas veces te mataron, tantas veces resusitará, tantas noches pasaras desesperando y a la hora del naufragio, de la oscuridad, alguien te rescapará para ir cantando …*

'How many times have they killed you? How many times have you come back? How many nights will you spend in desperation and at the hour of failure, of the darkness, someone will save you so that you can keep on singing.' How many times indeed? He had died inside when Lidia had died. He died again for Benigno. Was he to die again for Lola? And who would save him?

… *cantando al sol come la cigarra, despues de un año bajo la tierra, igual que el sobreviviente que vuelve de la guerra …*

'Singing to the sun like the cicada, after a year under the earth, just like the survivor who returns from the war.'

That was Raphael. He was the survivor. He had come back from the war, but he had been under the earth more than a year. It felt like a whole lifetime. A whole lifetime wasted mourning his losses, trying to keep the stitches in his wounds, scratching his scars, and it hadn't done him any good. Now the woman he could have loved was gone, and he had never truly loved her.

The tears were streaming down his face, Mercedes' strong voice creating wave after wave. Raphael laid money on the table and slipped from the bar. Josue obviously wasn't going to turn up, there was no point staying there and making a fool of himself. Out in the street, he felt unstable and rested his hand against the wall of the *cantina*. It was strangely clammy. His sensations were heightened. Everything was suddenly more alive and real. He ran his fingertips lightly over the wall feeling its rough surface as though it were the rim of a pitted volcano. The subtle breeze felt like a strong wind in his face. He smelt the smells of the *barrio*, the rubbish, the smell of beer wafting from the bar door, rotting fruit, old tortillas, he smelt his own slightly rank odour, the earthy sweatiness of his own skin. The rumble of the *periferico* in the distance sounded like the ocean, a rhythm to the syncopation of the local sounds; the bell of the ice cream seller, the giggle of a girl walking home with her mother, a dog's bark almost deafening. He walked home feeling like someone who had just had their cataracts removed. The spell was broken. Finally, after all the years since the death of Benigno he felt a pain other than that of losing his wife and child.

11

Raphael woke late with an uneasiness about Josue. The night they had met at the hospital he had seemed so alone, so desperate for any consolation that Raphael could give him, it seemed unlikely to Raphael now that he would have missed their meeting at Miguel's, that he would have found other friends to be with. He felt sure that Josue would have at least dropped into the *cantina* to explain that he had another engagement. Perhaps the beer had clouded his judgement last night, but hadn't he been even more aware than usual? Raphael remembered the feelings and sensations, the words of the song, how fully aware he had felt. He no longer felt like that, though he was more energized than he had been in several days. While he was so full of verve, he decided he should call Lola's sister, a task he'd been dreading, but it had to be done. Afterwards he would go round to see Josue.

As he made coffee Raphael consoled himself with thinking that even if it had crossed his mind last night that something had happened to Josue there really wasn't anything he could have done about it. He didn't know anything about Josue, who his friends were, where he worked, where he hung out. And he wasn't about to go to the police after yesterday's ordeal. Of course, the police! Perhaps Josue was being interviewed by the police last night and had no way to get a message to him. Since he had been at the station earlier in the day, it made sense that they would also have questioned Josue, unless he'd been at the station at the same time. But no, it was more likely that the same officer would question them both. Surely that was the explanation. He would go and see Josue and they could swap interview stories and see who was the more likely candidate as a suspect. But what if Josue actually was Lola's killer? Raphael couldn't begin to imagine that the young man could kill anyone, let alone the woman he loved. Raphael knew in his heart Josue couldn't have done it, his grief had been too genuine, his disbelief and shock too real.

Raphael finished his coffee and searched in his bag for the piece of card with the telephone numbers from Lola's flat. Panic set in as he couldn't find it. His first thought was that it had been taken when his house had been searched. Raphael pulled his jacket off the chair and rifled quickly through the pockets, pulling out scraps of paper. Some coins fell on the floor, jingling and rolling into corners. It wasn't there. He dumped out the contents of his bag on the bed. He spread out the papers and didn't see it, then back to the bag, agitated, he ran his fingers along the inside ridges as though the card had shrunk to a grain of sand. He felt the grit and fluff stuck in the seam. His fingers caught on something sharp. He pulled it out - a tiny silver hand, a *milagro*. He looked at it. Lola had given it to him not long after they had met. 'To protect your hands, so you can always write.' Raphael had said it wasn't his hands that needed protecting. She had taken his hand then and kissed the scars. 'Isn't it?' He remembered that look in her eyes of concern, of love? Of sadness, yes, she had been sad for him. He wiped his cheek with the back of his hand. Took the woven cross from his neck, untied the knot of the string and threaded the hand onto it. There it hung with the cross. Two women, two different loves, brought together by death.

More calmly he went back to the collection of papers and books on the bed. Had the police been through his bag? Had they taken the list of numbers? He picked up his spiral-bound notebook. The end was coming unravelled, caught in other things, it was untwisting. He tried to tuck the loose end back into the spiral, turning the book on its side, and the piece of card fell out.

Raphael sat on the bed trying to calm his breathing, staring at the card. He lit a cigarette and went to the phone. He waited with trepidation as it rang. After only three bleeps a woman's voice answered.

'Hello. Can I speak to Andrea please?' He wished he knew her surname, to be more formal, but he didn't.

'Yes, that's me.'

'Ah. I'm Raphael Sifuentes. There isn't really an easy way to explain this. I'm a …, was a, friend of …'

'Yes, I know who you are, Lola spoke about you a lot.'

'She did?' Raphael was taken aback. 'I'm sorry to be calling under these circumstances. I'd hoped we might meet sometime. But I was wondering if you've made any plans yet. I, erm …'

'The body hasn't been released to us yet. The police are still completing their examination.'

'Ah. Have the police been to see you?'

'They asked some brief questions when they came to deliver the news, that's all.'

'Would it be too much to ask you to call when you know something about the arrangements?'

'No, that would be fine, but maybe we should talk before that. Can you come to my house? It's not easy to get away, I have small children.'

'Certainly. Where do you live?'

She gave him the address. 'Do you know it?'

'Yes, I know where it is.' Lola had taken him past the house once, one time when they'd been out walking, and she was telling him some story about her youth.

'Can you come this afternoon? Shall we say around 2 p.m.?'

'Yes, that's fine. I'll see you then.'

Raphael was relieved that she had been so pleasant and understanding, and that she had known who he was, that made things easier. But he wondered why she wanted to see him. Perhaps it was nothing more than wanting to meet him and chat before the funeral. Maybe she would even ask him if he wanted to be involved. That was more than he could hope for, he had assumed that her family knew nothing about him and maybe wouldn't even want him to attend the service. He wasn't sure how he would feel about participating anyway, given the nature of their relationship and the nature of her death. And what about Josue? Had Andrea known about him too? Would he be invited? Surely it would be embarrassing to have two of her lovers present, and Lola not married to either. He would try and ascertain how much Andrea knew that afternoon. For now, he wouldn't mention the call to Josue, but he must go and see if he could find him. He pulled on a shirt and left the house.

It was still ironic to him that Josue lived so close, within minutes Raphael was in the street where he lived, and almost as soon as he turned the corner he saw something lying on the ground outside what he thought was Josue's door. It looked like an old coat, or maybe a bag of rubbish. It could even be a dead dog; the city was painfully slow in removing dead animals killed by traffic; it was not uncommon to see them stiff with rigor mortis by the roadside. As he drew closer, he realised it was a person and broke into a run. It was only a short distance, but Raphael was panting by the time he got there, adrenalin coursing through him. He knelt down and gently eased the body towards him. A groan emerged and Raphael saw his face. It was Josue, slumped against the wall, barely conscious. Josue lifted his head a little and looked at him. His right eye was swollen closed and purple. A cut above his lip was still moist with blood, and darkened, dry blood clustered around his nostrils. He winced as he tried to lift himself up on one arm.

'Where are your keys? Give me your keys,' said Raphael.

Josue started to put a hand in his pocket but didn't have strength to reach the keys and pull them out. Raphael extracted them and opened the door. He took Josue in his arms and half carried, half dragged him into the room and laid him on the bed.

'*Ai Dios*, Josue, what happened to you?'

'They kept me there all night,' he mumbled. It sounded like his mouth was full of blood. 'I thought they would never let me go.'

'Who?'

'The police.'

'The police did this to you?' asked Raphael. He knew it happened, but Josue was in such a state; it was hard to believe the police had left him like that.

'Yes.'

'OK, don't talk any more now, let me clean you up. You need to see a doctor.'

'No, no doctors. They'll only ask questions; it will make things worse.' Josue began to become agitated.

'OK. *Esta bien, calmate.*'

Raphael went into the kitchen and found a bowl. Then he went out to the back and filled it with water. It was cold of course, but he took it back inside and poured some into a pan to heat so the water would at least be warm. In the outside shower he had also found a washcloth, which he brought in with him. He looked around for some alcohol but couldn't find any, not wanting to bother Josue he made do with soap and took the bowl over to the bed. As gently as he could he washed Josue's face. The water soon turned red and he had to change it. Josue's eye really needed ice, but Raphael doubted there was any in the house or anything cold enough to be useful. Slowly he unbuttoned Josue's shirt and eased him out of it. His midriff was covered with deep purple bruises. He soaked these with the water too. Josue moaned.

'I think you may have a broken rib or two. Did they hurt you anywhere else? What about your legs?'

'No they're OK. Just my face and chest. They kicked me a lot. It's strange, I thought they would want to inflict injuries that wouldn't show. I'm sure they know how to.'

It was the first thing Josue had said that indicated maybe he wasn't such an innocent.

'Lie down. I'm going to go and see if I can get anything for your eye and some alcohol.'

Raphael left and went to the small store at the other end of the street. He was really looking for rubbing alcohol, but they didn't have anything like that. The only strong liquor they had was whisky, so he bought a small bottle. They had nothing cold either so he left with the whisky only, but as he went into the street he almost fell over a man selling *paletas* and ices.

'Hey, can I buy some ice from you?'

'I don't know. I need it.'

'I only need a piece. My friend's been in a fight, got a real shiner!' Raphael shrugged, putting on a face that said, 'these lads, eh, always getting into trouble.'

The man agreed, though he demanded a rather unreasonable sum for a piece of ice. Raphael hurried back before it melted and let himself in with the key he had slipped into his pocket. He quickly wrapped the ice in the washcloth and pressed it to Josue's eyebrow. 'Hold that.'

He went into the kitchen and put coffee on. While it was brewing. he moistened the edge of a cloth with the whisky and went and dabbed it on Josue's cuts.

'Ah Jesus, you're making it worse.'

'Hey if you survived this, you can survive a little sting.'

Josue sat up. 'What would I do without you, eh?'

Raphael didn't reply but went and poured coffee for them both with a drop of whisky in each mug. Raphael sat in the chair and sipped his coffee. 'Do you want to talk about it? I wondered last night when you didn't show up, but I didn't think until this morning that you might have been with the police.'

'They came round yesterday afternoon and asked me to go to the station. I thought it was just routine, though I wondered why they couldn't just question me here.' He took a sip of coffee, 'ah that's good,' and pushed himself up against the wall behind the bed. 'They started out with the usual things, name, address, age, how did I know Lola and so on. Then the *cabron* started implying that I'd been jealous of you and I'd got angry and done something to her. I told them I didn't know about you, that I'd never met you before the hospital.'

'I tried to tell them too,' said Raphael.

'What?'

'They interviewed me yesterday morning. Went and picked me up at work and took me to the station. He kept implying I was jealous of you and tried to intimate that we'd had a fight; me and Lola that is. They found a note from me in her pocket and he wanted to make a big deal out of it, saying it sounded like a final goodbye, and that later I hadn't gone into her flat because I knew she was already dead. He gave the impression that I was their main suspect, but then almost as suddenly he stopped and said I could go.'

'Lucky you!' Josue managed a weak smile, then winced as it re-opened the cut on his lip. He touched the back of his hand to it, wiped the spot of blood on his trousers and took a swallow of coffee. 'They just wouldn't take no for an answer, kept on about how I must have known about you and how I must be jealous. They asked me where I'd been on Saturday night and I told them about the concert and going drinking with my friends, but of course after that I was at home in bed and that's no alibi. They kept trying to get me to say that I'd got drunk and gone looking for Lola to sort her out. I did drink a bit too much, but I never went to look for her, I came home and went to sleep. I don't even know where she lives.'

'I know, I know.' Raphael nodded.

'Then they started being nasty about Lola, saying what a loose woman she was, they even called her a whore, saying it was an affront to my manhood, her having another man, probably more than one, trying to goad me, make me angry and say something I didn't want to. Then when I wouldn't say what they wanted he hit me in the face, that made my nose bleed. It bled a lot.'

Raphael looked at the shirt slung on the end of the bed and realised for the first time how bloody it was and noticed the blood splashes down Josue's trousers.

'The more I said I hadn't done anything, the more they hit me. I begged them to stop, I told them they were making things up, that they couldn't get away with it. That just made the main officer angry, he nodded to the more junior one and he took out his gun and pointed it at me. I thought that was it, I nearly shat myself, I swear, then he lifted it and hit the side of my head. I didn't feel the pain, but I must have fallen off the chair and passed out for a bit, because when I came to he was kicking me and the pain was excruciating. I don't know how long that went on. I couldn't hear what they were saying, but then they left me lying there.'

'What did he look like, the one giving orders?'

'Mean looking, one of those funny little moustaches and his hair greased back.'

'Yeah, that was the one who interrogated me too.'

Josue paused to finish his coffee and seemed to be reliving the ordeal, his eyes glazed over, and Raphael saw the mug shaking in his hand. He wanted to go over to him, but sensed that the touch might be too much, too painful.

'How did you end up back here?' Raphael asked.

'I lay there I don't know how many hours; I must have passed out again. Then I heard them coming back in, and the light was very bright above me, they threw some water in my face and picked me up. The older one got right in my face and said, 'we'll come back when you've decided to tell the truth, and if you tell anyone about this you know what will happen.' Then they led me out, down a corridor and out a back door to a car that was waiting. I don't think it was a police car, I can't remember. They brought me back here and threw me out onto the kerb. I don't remember any more, but it was already light, so I must have been at the station all night.'

'I don't understand why they'd beat you up to try and get a story out of you. Why don't they just investigate a bit and try to find who really did it?' As soon as he'd said it, Raphael realised how naïve that sounded.

'I don't know. The only reason they wouldn't investigate is if they are involved, or they know who is. They're going to frame one of us for this, and I suppose it's going to be me.'

'And why didn't they rough me up? I'm as likely a suspect as you, if that's the line they're taking?'

'Who knows Raphael, maybe they thought they could break me down easier, that I'd give in. Maybe your turn is coming. But I tell you this; I'm not going back there. I'll go away or something, go to another country, but they're not going to touch me again.'

Raphael went over and sat on the bed with him. 'You can't do that.'

'Why not? I've got nothing to stay here for.'

'Do you want to be on the run the rest of your life? They'll take that as proof that you're guilty. They'll find you. You know the death squads have followed people to Los Angeles and other places.'

'That was in the old days. Why would they care for the murder of one woman?'

'Somebody cares enough to have killed her, to try to frame you, to try to cover it up. Times haven't changed that much.'

'I'll take my chances.' Josue's eyes began to close, the whisky and telling his story taking their somnolent effect.

'You need to sleep. I'll come back later and bring some food. Listen I'll take the key, don't be scared when I come back in.'

Josue nodded weakly as he drifted off.

Raphael left, closing the door softly behind him checking in his pocket that he had Josue's key. It was time to go and see Lola's sister, Andrea. Her house was some distance away and he wasn't sure how easily he could find it again; Lola had only shown him the house once. Now he wished he didn't have to go. He needed time to think, to digest what had happened to Josue. He didn't think it was wise for him to leave the country, not at the moment, but he couldn't protect him. The police could come and get him any time they wanted, they could come now while Raphael was gone, though he hoped they would have a day or two of breathing space before the next onslaught. Could he hide Josue somewhere? Move him somewhere else in the city for a while? But where? And would it really do any good? If the police were set on framing one or other of them for Lola's murder then surely they were being watched constantly. He lit a cigarette and walked in the direction of the bus stop.

12

Raphael leaned his head against the back of the seat and tried to work out what to do next. At first he had a thought that he immediately felt ashamed of: why should he help Josue at all? He wasn't a friend, in fact he had been his rival; they were in the same boat, both possible suspects, the only viable suspects at the moment, and both it would seem were easy to frame. Neither of them had an alibi for the time the police were asking about, late Saturday night or early Sunday morning, and he had inadvertently lied about not being in the capital, which would look suspicious when they found out. If Josue were framed, he would be off the hook. Why didn't he just forget about Josue and look out for himself? But Raphael couldn't, for one thing, that just wasn't in his nature. He knew he was innocent, and he believed Josue was too. They were pawns in somebody's plan. This was bigger than just Lola; they had to stick together. They were both in the same situation, and nobody else knew about it, they could only rely on each other. For now, he was off the hook and Josue was in trouble, but that could change. It was up to him to come up with some sort of plan.

Raphael needed to find out more about what had happened to Lola. That could be tricky. He needed to keep a low profile and he didn't see how he could investigate her murder when he was suspected of it. He didn't even know how she'd died, when, or where she had been found, and if there were any distinguishing characteristics. Could her hands have been missing too, like the journalist Rosario? He didn't know, he had only seen her face. Her pale face and blue lips looking like a poor imitation of herself.

Raphael kept coming back to the death of Rosario, and the stories he had been working on. Were the deaths connected? And if so, was he somehow the link? He couldn't get rid of the old suspicion that Lola had sought him out for some reason, that their whole affair had never been about love, but had some other reason behind it. And that led him to the beginning of another upsetting thought.

What if Josue was somehow being used? It seemed strange that he had been beaten up so severely yet he, Raphael, hadn't been touched. Maybe the police had done it deliberately as a threat – 'see what will happen to you if you don't talk'. But if that were the case it meant the police knew he and Josue were friends, or at least that they knew each other. And in the short time since they had met at the hospital, how could the police have worked that out? Especially as most of that time they had both been in police custody separately. Would Raphael even consider Josue a friend? Wasn't he just doing what any decent human being would do? A comforting arm for someone grieving, a dab of alcohol on cuts and bruises. Hadn't he just minutes ago thought about letting Josue take the rap, so he could be spared? Raphael's head hurt from too much thinking. It was like a jigsaw puzzle he couldn't put together, too many pieces were missing and all remaining pieces were of the sky. He couldn't tell them apart.

Raphael got off the bus and walked along the main road; looking for the side street he remembered Lola taking him down. He realised he should have looked at a map. The next street looked like the right one, with that stubbly tree on the corner, and he turned into it. About halfway down was a smaller road on the left; he checked the address in his pocket; this was it. The houses were big and the neighbourhood clean and airy, whoever Lola's sister had married, she had done well for herself. He hoped she wouldn't be a right-wing conservative like his brother, but he doubted that from the way Lola had talked about her. He reached the house and paused a moment to take it in. It was not a house of the super-rich, but definitely middle-class, well-kept and recently whitewashed; no doubt there was a maid who cleaned and maybe cooked. Raphael tried not to feel intimidated, he had grown up in similar circumstances, though not quite so grand, but after so many years of living hand to mouth, this kind of luxury disgusted him, even more so as he knew that not two miles away people were living on a trash heap, scavenging like rodents. He sighed, went up the path and rang the bell.

Almost immediately the door opened, as though the person behind had been standing just there or watching him from a window. The gap widened and a woman ushered him in. It was dark inside and after the glare of the sun, Raphael couldn't see properly. Once in the hallway his eyes adjusted, but the woman was already half-turned away from him saying, 'Come in.' She led him into a large sitting room with a tiled floor, and modern but simple wooden furniture of the kind that could be bought cheaply in any of the numerous furniture shops on the Avenida Bolivar. Raphael was surprised by the ordinary, pine furniture; he would have expected something more extravagant. Now the woman turned to him and extended a hand. Until then he hadn't been sure if she was a maid or the woman of the house. He bit his lip, trying not to gasp out loud. It was the woman in the photo on Rosario's desk. He was sure that Lola's sister was Rosario's fiancée. Stunned, he took her hand with its remarkably firm shake.

'Raphael, pleased to meet you.' He felt like he was about to fall over and hoped she would soon invite him to sit down.

'I'm Andrea Hernandez. Please have a seat. I made some coffee; I'll just get it.'

Raphael sank gratefully into the sofa and watched her leave the room. She was shorter than Lola but moved with the grace of a dancer. She was a couple of years older and in the flesh looked older than the picture Rosario had of her, though of course that could have been an old photo. Perhaps they had been lovers in the past and Rosario just kept telling people she was his fiancée. Maybe he was mistaken, but no, Raphael was sure it was her. She came back in with a tray and set it on the table. He watched her pour the coffee. She even did that with style. The fine china cup didn't shake at all in her hand as she passed it to him. It seemed as though nothing could perturb her, the complete opposite to Lola's fidgety nature. Andrea was attractive, though her hands belied her maturity, and flecks of grey speckled the short hair above her ears. She was definitely the woman from the photo. He accepted the cup from her. So far, she didn't give the appearance of a bereaved woman, but people reacted differently to death, perhaps she was still in shock, unbelieving as he was.

They sat silently for a moment, Andrea demurely sipping coffee and glancing at him. Unsure of what to say he came out with, 'Where are your children?'

'They're at nursery. They go two days a week just to get used to it. Pedro will be starting school soon and Mimi always cries when he's gone, so she goes too; she's four. Would you like to see photos?'

'Er yes, yes please.' What else could he say? In fact, he was interested to see her family, but it seemed incongruous in the circumstances. Andrea went over to a bookshelf and came back with a framed snapshot of herself, the two children and a man considerably older than her.

'And that's my husband,' she said pointing to him. He had an upright sort of sternness about him, with his grey hair and glasses.

'Ah, right, and what does he do?' asked Raphael, keeping the small talk going.

'He works in banking, all rather boring. I think people always wonder why I married him.' She gave a nervous laugh. 'They assume it was for the money.'

Since she'd given him the opportunity Raphael said, 'And was it?' Thinking almost immediately that was too crass.

'Perhaps at first, but I came to love him; apart from his work we have similar interests. He is very gentle and surprisingly good with the children. He looks a bit stern, doesn't he,' she said looking back at the photograph.

Raphael turned his head on one side, not quite nodding, not disagreeing.

'Not a very good photo,' she said, putting it back on the shelf. She sat down and turned back to Raphael. 'He's a good man, and he doesn't bother too much about what I get up to.'

Raphael looked at her more closely. There was more to this woman than the obvious appearance of wealth and security. From Lola's sister he really shouldn't be shocked. Perhaps picking up men ran in the family. No, that was unkind, he didn't know her circumstances. But he had to ask, he had to know about Rosario.

'So,' he ventured tentatively, but buoyed up by her previous confidence, 'Forgive the impropriety since I've just met you, but did you ... have a ... a friend, a boyfriend called Rosario; a journalist?'

She looked at the hands in her lap so Raphael couldn't see her expression. She played with her fingers and it was some time before she answered. 'Yes, so sad what happened to him. And now Lola. I can't believe it, I can't, not either of them. I thought things were getting better.' Her dark eyes looked sad, but there was anger in her voice.

'Yes, I'd hoped that too, but it seems things are just as they always were.'

'I'm glad to have finally met you,' she said changing the subject. 'Lola spoke about you a lot.'

'Really? She kept saying we should visit you, but we never seemed to get around to it.'

'She cared a lot about you, you know.'

'I wondered sometimes.' Raphael looked around the room again, finding nothing remarkable in it, but really he was thinking about Lola. Andrea looked puzzled, and Raphael felt he needed to explain, 'I always wondered what she saw in me, why she chose me. She did choose me, you know, picked me up in a café.'

'Just like Lola!' Andrea laughed. 'Don't put yourself down, from what she told me, you're a good man. She was waiting for you to propose.'

'What? But she never gave any indication,' said Raphael.

'In some things she was traditional, that was your move to make.'

Silence followed for a few minutes as they both sipped their coffee. Propose? Raphael had had no idea. He felt emotion welling up, but he didn't want Andrea to see it. He looked down at the rug, noticing it was a roughly woven blanket from Momostenango. Just like Lola's flat, the room was sparse, but had touches of femininity and indigenous culture, rare in *ladino* homes. Perhaps he had misjudged Lola, in many ways. He looked back at the sister, just as she raised her eyes from her lap.

They both began to speak at once. 'After you,' said Raphael.

'I was just going to say, we don't really know what's happening yet, the body hasn't …,' she let the sentence drift off, as though it was too hard to finish. 'But I suppose there will be a mass at the church she attended and then a private burial with just the family. The priest has already been to see me.' Absently, she poured herself, more coffee, then as if remembering her upbringing, offered some to Raphael. He declined by raising his palm.

'So, things are in hand?'

She nodded.

'And, how are your parents coping?'

'Father is no longer with us.'

Of course he knew that, what a tactless thing to say.

'Lola was always his favourite; this would have destroyed him.'

'I didn't know. She didn't talk about him much,' Raphael said.

'No, I think his death hit her hard. It's been a few years, but …' again she let the sentence hang. 'Mother, I don't know, she seems to have retreated into herself; she doesn't believe it. I don't think I will either until I see her …' She broke off, ran her hand through her hair, reminding Raphael of Lola. 'When the police came round, they said Lola had already been identified, you don't know who did that, do you?'

'I did,' Raphael mumbled.

'You? How did you come to …?' Her face showed surprise, but of course that would be a shock to her. He noticed her fiddling unconsciously with her wedding ring.

'It's a long story,' he said, reluctant to have to tell her the details.

'I've got time.'

Raphael swallowed the last dreg of coffee and set the cup back on the table.

'I'd been worried about Lola for days, had a strange feeling something bad had happened. She often didn't call for a few days, it's not like we saw each other every day, that's just not the way things were, you know.'

Andrea nodded as though Lola had spoken to her about it.

Raphael told her how he'd gone to look for Lola and ended up at the hospital. 'And she was there. Right there at the first place I tried.'

'How bizarre.'

'Yes, and it gets stranger. But I have to ask you something first.' Raphael leant forward and lifted his cup. Realising there was nothing in it; he set it down again.

'Shall I get some more?' asked Andrea, starting to rise.

'No, it's all right.' He paused briefly. 'Did Lola talk to you about anyone else she was seeing?'

'What do you mean?' asked Andrea.

'You know, another man, another lover?'

'No, she never talked about anyone but you and her work colleagues.'

'You're sure? She never mentioned anyone called, Josue?'

'No.'

'Hmm, and she'd tell you, you think?'

'You never know, but we were always pretty close since we were girls, I think she used to confide in me about most things.'

'And you with her? Did she know about Rosario?'

'I did tell her about him. He was a bit special; we were together a long time. I didn't tell her about the others.'

120

'How many were there?' Raphael heard himself sounding scandalized. 'I'm sorry, you don't need to answer that, it's none of my business, but you look so, so …'

'So what? Middle-aged and proper?'

Raphael smiled. That hadn't been quite what he meant, or had it? She didn't look like a woman who'd had a string of toy boys.

He thought he detected a sigh as she said, 'I'm happily married, I love my children and I would never leave my family, but I have needs my husband can no longer fulfil. There've been a few, but I don't go around just picking men up, it's always someone I meet naturally, as it were.'

'So how did you meet Rosario?'

'At a photography exhibition. Poor boy, I think he always expected more, thought I'd run off and marry him. I told him from the start how it would be, I never deceived him.' She smoothed her skirt over her thigh, not because it needed it, but to avoid Raphael's eyes.

He felt almost embarrassed watching her. He coughed, nervously. 'You know he had a photo of you on his desk, told his colleagues you were his fiancée.'

'No! How do you know that? You didn't work with him, did you? I thought you were at different papers.'

'We were, but I was asked to write something after … after what happened, so I went over and looked at some of his files and stuff. He had one of my books of poetry.'

'I gave him that.'

'Really?'

'Yes. I love your work.'

'Well thank you.' He smiled. He liked this woman, and not because she was now flattering him, but because of her openness and honesty, her willingness to trust him. 'I wish we had met sooner; I think we would have been good friends.'

'Why? Because I like your work?'

He wasn't sure if she was flirting with him, or not. 'No. I admire your honesty; it's rare these days.'

'I am who I am; I make no apologies for it.'

'Why do you trust me?'

'My sister respected you, that's good enough for me. She told me about your wife, I'm sorry. Is that why you couldn't commit to Lola?'

'I suppose so. I never felt like I could truly love anyone again after Lidia. But I always thought Lola was happy with things the way they were, that she liked the freedom and didn't want more. Now it's too late, I think I did love her. Not like Lidia, nothing could ever be like that.' He rubbed an invisible fleck from his trousers. 'But I loved her.'

'It's never too late for love.'

They were silent again. Raphael cleared his throat, uncomfortable with the shift in the conversation to his feelings. He needed to get things back to Andrea. 'Love, ha, love only brings pain,' he said reverting to his usual cynicism.

'Oh Raphael.'

He looked up at her, though he didn't want to see the pity he heard in her voice. 'You've lost a lover and a sister, how can you still think it's good to love?' he asked.

'I don't know … Rosario was not mine to keep, and Lola … Lola I keep expecting to walk through the door and start talking her head off before she's even given me a hug. It hasn't hit me yet, I suppose.'

Raphael looked at his watch. He knew it was an obvious thing to do, but the conversation was getting into the uncomfortable area of feelings and loss. He wasn't ready to go there. 'I should be going,' he said.

'There's no rush. I'll make some more coffee.'

Andrea seemed genuinely keen for him to stay, but Raphael had things to deal with. He had to go back and see Josue, worry about what they were going to do, try to find out more about Lola's death. Suddenly all his obligations and preoccupations crashed back down on him.

'No, I'd better go. I have things to do. I wish I could stay; being here is as though none of this has happened.' Raphael hesitated. Should he tell her about the police? That he was possibly a suspect? Well, she'd been honest with him. 'I think the police may suspect me, ' he confessed, eyes down, almost as if he thought they had a reason to.

'Oh Raphael. But surely, they can't really think …? It's just routine, isn't it?'

'Probably, but you know they don't need any evidence. If they wanted to …' It dawned on him with more conviction that the police could set him up easily if they wanted to. 'And there's circumstantial stuff I'm sure they could exaggerate,' he continued. 'They have a note I wrote to Lola, which they're blowing out of all proportion. But they suspect Josue too.'

'Who?'

'You know, the guy I met at the hospital. Says he's her boyfriend.'

Andrea looked confused, her brows almost meeting as she frowned.

'Sorry, I never finished telling you, did I? When I went to the Santa Maria Hospital, Josue was there, said he was her boyfriend and that someone from the hospital had called him. He was completely broken down, I had to take him home and stay the night with him.'

'But why did you believe him?'

Raphael shrugged. 'Why else would he be there? And I'd seen him before, with Lola. At the time I thought they were lovers, there was something about the way they looked at each other. We had an argument about it actually and she denied it. That was the last time I saw her.'

'I'm sorry.' She smiled at him. 'But I'm sure Lola wasn't seeing anyone else. Maybe she wouldn't tell me if she was, but I really don't think she would do that to you.'

Raphael shrugged. 'Lola was a true enigma; I never understood her. Anyway, Josue and I were supposed to meet last night, he never showed up. I went to check on him this morning and found him all beaten up. He said the police had done it to him.'

'I thought they were more subtle than that now. They don't have quite the impunity they used to.' Raphael realised from the comment that Andrea kept up with things, had her finger on the political situation, just like Lola.

'I don't know, but I feel like I should help him; he doesn't seem to have anyone else.'

'But you don't really know anything about him,' said Andrea, with reservation in her voice.

Raphael was surprised that Andrea might be suspicious of Josue's intentions, but he didn't stress the point. Changing the subject, he asked if he could help her with any of the funeral arrangements.

'No, I think you're busy enough. I can manage. The priest seems very good. I'll let you know when we have a day and time.'

'Good, here let me give you my number.' He pulled out his wallet and removed one of the business cards he never used. On the back he wrote his home number and address. 'I don't think I'll be at the office too much, so here are my home details.' He handed her the card. 'Josue is going to want to go to the funeral, you know.'

'I suppose so, but I've really never heard of him. Are you sure he's a friend of Lola's?'

Raphael shrugged. 'I don't see why he'd lie about it.'

He stood up and she followed him. She gave him a light hug. 'You can call me any time.'

13

Outside Andrea's house, the sun beat down, but the world seemed a colder place. Raphael was having a hard time digesting the conversation they had just had, not to mention who Andrea had been going out with. She had told him the most intimate things, but perhaps she felt like she knew him already since Lola had told her so much about him. That had surprised him too, not that Lola had talked to her sister about him, but the things she seemed to have said. He had always thought he was a bit of fun for Lola, nothing serious, certainly not that she loved him as much as Andrea had claimed and that she was hoping he would marry her. And that combined with the fact that Andrea didn't know anything about Josue made Raphael suspicious of him. He didn't think Lola would lie to her sister, but maybe she wouldn't tell her everything. Maybe Lola didn't feel she could tell Andrea she was seeing someone else after she'd told her how much she loved Raphael. But surely, she knew about Andrea's affairs, knew that she wouldn't criticize her for such an indiscretion, that given her experience Andrea would be the perfect person to give advice to someone in love with two men?

Raphael had passed the bus stop deep in thought. He paused and looked around him. He wasn't really sure where he was. A split second of panic passed through him, but he was on the main street the bus had come down, so he couldn't go too far wrong. He kept walking in the direction he thought he'd come from earlier, on the journey to Andrea's house that now felt so long ago.

It was true he didn't know anything about Josue. He seemed to be a man without a past, and without much of a present in a way, an unknown quantity. Perhaps he should try to find out a bit more about him. Raphael was a journalist; he knew how to investigate things, not like the police, but for his own satisfaction. What harm would it do to try to find out a bit more about Josue? If the police were really set on taking Josue down, then nothing Raphael said or did would change that. Perhaps it wasn't wise to take Josue too much into his confidence, or to be seen to hang around with him too much.

But if Josue wasn't who he said he was, how had he ended up at the hospital that night? And why had he been so grief-stricken and distraught? Surely, he couldn't be that convincing an actor? He thought about Andrea's calmness – was that a more natural response to grief? Had Josue's distress been too extreme, not realistic because it was overdone? But if he was in love with Lola ...?

Raphael thought about his own reactions; he was shocked and sad, but not so much, and he had been with Lola for two years, even though all that time he had tried to convince himself he didn't love her. Wasn't Josue's reaction a bit over the top? Now he was letting Andrea's doubts cloud his mind; he couldn't think clearly, just because he had seen Josue with Lola a couple of times, he had immediately believed he was her lover, but maybe there was another explanation. The hospital receptionist had said so too, but only because Josue would have told her that. If Josue had been following Raphael, he could have slipped into the hospital while he'd been smoking outside, told the receptionist his story, maybe even paid her to go along with him and then sat down to wait for Raphael to make his appearance.

But why? What did any of it have to do with Josue if he wasn't Lola's lover? These were conspiracy theories too large to consider. They rested on the idea that everything had somehow happened to get at Raphael and he couldn't believe that. The security forces may have had a reason to kill him years ago; being a guerrilla was enough to warrant that, but now? He was a second-rate journalist and an obscure poet. If they wanted to get him, they could have killed him any time, there was no need for elaborate plots.

Raphael looked around him. He thought he recognised the furniture shop across the street from the bus trip. He seemed to be going vaguely in the right direction. A bus passed him, but he wasn't ready yet to stop walking. It helped him work through things. Things that were too bizarre to contemplate, that Lola had picked him up and stayed with him for two years to entrap him, and then why had she been killed? That Rosario's death was part of a bigger plot, that Rosario had been the lover of Lola's sister, but maybe that was just a coincidence? He should have asked Andrea more about Rosario – if he was working on any big story he'd told her about. But that would have been too much all at once, and he wasn't even sure they had still been together. It may have been a while since she'd seen him. Raphael needed time to think, but he didn't believe thinking would help; it just raised more questions and threw up more inexplicable possibilities.

Raphael sighed. He stopped to light a cigarette, looking up to see a billboard advertising the tourist attraction of Tikal. If only he could get away; escape to the ancient pyramids or the beach; anywhere but here; anywhere where none of this had happened. He felt trapped in a nightmare, and yet, in the past couple of days he had felt more alive than he had since he'd been with Lidia. He had connected with people for the first time in years. Josue had needed him and he had helped him and for one night at least they had been true friends, friends like he used to have. Now he had met Andrea and felt as though he had known her for years, felt a strange peace in her presence. What was the message? That hiding from pain wasn't the answer, you had to face it head on and deal with it? He dropped the stub and ground it with his heel. It was all too philosophical, too much to take.

He couldn't work things out, so he decided to just shut his brain down for a while, concentrate on practical things. Things he could do. He could smell roast chicken and saw a rotisserie up the street. He'd promised to take Josue some food and he would. Maybe Josue wasn't who he said he was, but for now he was hurt and needed help. Raphael stopped at the restaurant and bought some chicken soup and tortillas; then he went back to Josue's house and let himself in.

Josue was asleep on the bed, much as Raphael had left him. He looked at him sleeping. Despite all his bruises he still appeared innocent, childlike. Raphael couldn't believe he was other than who he said he was – a young man who'd fallen in love with Lola. Maybe it was never reciprocated. Maybe that was why Lola had never told Andrea; perhaps in her mind they had just been friends? That wouldn't have stopped him being in love with her, that wouldn't stop him mourning her loss as only a lover could.

Raphael set about finding bowls for the soup, noisily so that Josue might wake up. He did. Slowly at first, dazed as though he was drugged, and wincing as he sat up; then for a moment he seemed scared as though he didn't know where he was and the police were back again, ready to beat him. Raphael looked at him and saw the fear. He knew what fear felt like. Only now he wasn't afraid. Not even of being framed for murder. If he was jailed, how much worse could it be than all he'd been through?

'Oh, it's you,' said Josue. 'What time is it?'

'It's about six. Here I brought you some soup.' Raphael handed him a bowl and a tortilla and sat in the chair. The tortillas were already cooled but he wasn't going to the bother of heating them; the soup was hot enough and tasted heavenly. He bit into a sweet, juicy hunk of corn, burning his tongue. Raphael realised he hadn't eaten all day. He wiped the soup off his chin with the back of his hand. Josue sipped the hot liquid gingerly trying to avoid touching the cut on his lip. They ate in silence for a while; Raphael refilling his bowl while Josue still struggled with the first one.

Raphael didn't know what to say; he was unsure of Josue now, and couldn't quite trust his motives, though he didn't want to betray that, so he simply asked how he was feeling.

'Sore.'

'Have you been asleep all this time?'

'I suppose so.'

'So, you haven't had chance to think any more about what you're going to do?'

'No, but I don't think I can do anything much until I'm a bit stronger, so I'll just have to hope they don't come back for a while. What are you going to do?'

'Lie low I suppose. Not much I can do either, I'm not going to leave, so if the police want to pick me up, they can do it any time.'

'Have you heard anything from Lola's family?'

'No.' Raphael didn't want to tell Josue about Andrea and he still didn't know anything about funeral plans. He was starting to feel uncomfortable though he wasn't sure why. 'Listen, I'd better get going; you need your rest.'

'OK. Thanks for the soup. I'm so lucky I bumped into you at the hospital; otherwise who'd take care of me? And to think at any other time I probably would have wanted to beat you up if I'd known who you were!'

'Yeah, weird how life turns out,' said Raphael standing up. He put his bowl in the sink and went towards the door. 'Oh, here's your key.' He laid it on the low table. 'I'll pop in tomorrow sometime and see how you are.'

Raphael stepped into the street and closed the door behind him. He thought about what Josue had said about it being lucky they had met. Was it luck? Could Josue really be so alone? It was possible that he had no close family, but surely he had friends? Maybe he couldn't talk to them about what had happened. Raphael at least knew the situation he was in and had known Lola. Or was he just being taken for a ride?

Revived by the food, Raphael walked briskly home. When he opened his door, he felt a weight descending. Back at home, his body felt worn out, but his mind was too confused to sleep and it was still early. He had a shower and opened the door to his tiny balcony to let in the evening air, with it came the gentle background noise of the city, the buzz that was constant until the curfew fell. He stood there a few minutes just listening to the sounds of evening. Then sitting at his desk, he opened a drawer and pulled out some plain paper. It felt so long since he had sat down and written a poem, written anything. Now he began making lists of all the facts he knew that related to Lola's death, all the theories and possible related events.

First was a page for Lola:

Killed Saturday night/early Sunday morning.

Found – where exactly?

Killed by whom; why; how?

He drew lines to himself and Josue as Lola's lovers. A line to Rosario the journalist connected through her sister Andrea. Was it possible that Lola had known Rosario other than through her sister? He circled the question and wondered how he might go about finding out.

Then he had a page for Rosario:

Killed 24 April, four days before Lola.

Found in an alley near where he worked.

How? Method unknown, but hands cut off – indicative of paramilitaries – assumed *Mano Blanco*.

Why? Was he getting too close to Colonel Lopez? Had he found out something in connection with the murder of Manuel Chavez in Chimaltenango? Why had Rosario written so many stories about Lopez? Did he have any hard evidence or only suspicions? Raphael drew a red circle around the fact that Rosario had been going out with Andrea; that was a definite link to Lola. It could be a coincidence, but Raphael didn't believe in coincidences.

Next, he started a page for Josue. Other than his name, it was conspicuously empty. He knew nothing about him. He tried to think if there was anything he knew about him that Josue himself hadn't told him and there wasn't, except for having seen him outside the cinema with Lola. Could he even be sure about that? It had been raining hard and the light hadn't been good. But then he'd seen them outside the conference too. Lola had kissed him, and later on when pressed she had told him his name was Josue, so Lola definitely knew him, even if they hadn't been lovers. He had to try and find out more about Josue.

Raphael began to make a list of things he could look into, hopefully without drawing any attention to himself. He could see if Josue really was a musician; if he gave concerts there should be a review written somewhere. He could ask Ricardo, the cultural events reporter; see if he'd heard of him. He could try and find a record of him being an orphan. It wouldn't help him know who Josue was, but he could see if he'd been telling the truth. It would mean going into the office, which he didn't really want to do, but maybe it was best; if he didn't go into work his colleagues would wonder what was going on with the police, and if he was being watched the best way to look innocent would be to carry on with his normal life, to go to work as though nothing had happened, as though nothing had changed.

He took another sheet of paper and made a list of inconsistencies: the way Lola's apartment had been so clean and orderly as though someone had been there to tidy up. The fact that Josue had just happened to be at the hospital when he had arrived there; all the strange things Josue had said to him. Raphael pondered the various comments Josue had made to him that had struck him as odd: 'You're a good man. You're here with me; that's enough.' But Josue barely knew him, how could he say he was a good man? 'Help me, I'm all alone.' 'I'm so lucky I bumped into you.' Why was that lucky? And was it luck? Raphael didn't believe in luck, any more than he believed in coincidences. 'Any other time I probably would have beaten you up.' Why couldn't Raphael believe in his own goodness? He had been good to Josue, more than was necessary. Why was he so uncomfortable with Josue's gratitude? It was natural that he'd be grateful for Raphael's support, wasn't it?

He thought about how Josue had announced, 'I'm an orphan' just like that with no further explanation, but maybe there was no other way to say it and he didn't want to tell the story that went with that statement; Raphael could understand that.

He thought about how Josue believed it was Raphael Lola had chosen to be with, and how much Andrea had claimed Lola had loved him. Had he really been blind to Lola's love? Did his own pain and refusal to love pull a curtain over his eyes, blocking out her feelings for him? He had always thought she wasn't that bothered about their relationship, that she could take it or leave it, that it was sex she enjoyed more than anything else. Maybe he had been wrong; maybe he had just convinced himself of those things? She had picked him up in the first place after all; she had chosen to sit at his table not anyone else's and perhaps she had no other motive than attraction to him.

The words of the policeman in the interrogation came back to him, "strange coincidence" both he and Josue showing up at the hospital at the same time. It was. Had Josue been following him? No, how could he have been, how could he even have recognised him? Had the police been following him? But why? Nothing made any sense.

Raphael paused to go and check the phone book for the name Josue had given the police at the hospital – Josue Chan. There were not so many entries for the surname Chan. It was a typical enough Indian name, but perhaps not so common in the capital and many people with that name probably wouldn't have telephones. The fact that Josue had an Indian name at least made it plausible that he had lived in one of the villages that had been wiped out, and he was young enough that if he had made it to an orphanage in the city he could have lost contact with any remaining family and people he knew. It would also make him wary about making close friends with people, so it was not completely beyond belief that he really didn't have anyone he could trust in his current situation.

There were two listings for J. Chan, one of which corresponded to Josue's address. So, he had a legitimate address and telephone number at least. Having paused from his work, Raphael rolled a cigarette and went out to the balcony to smoke it. He couldn't feel the tears taking shape, but he felt their cold trajectory down his cheeks. He brushed away the drip forming at his chin. He'd spent so long convincing himself he didn't love Lola, only to find out too late that he did.

The city gave the appearance of serenity. It no longer held the fear of previous years, except during the early hours of the morning when the streets were completely deserted, though Raphael had more reasons than most to know the dangers and evils that ran below the surface. He couldn't believe Lola had been killed, that he might be a suspect, that apparently there could be much more to it all than even his fevered paranoia could dream up, that in a few short days the earth below him had shifted as though struck by a strong *temblor* and nothing would be the same again. What had happened to Lidia had at least been believable, but now the war was over, and Lola's body had turned up in an alley, like some hideous nightmare.

14

Raphael got up to close the balcony door that was tapping in the breeze. He stood looking at the dust motes in the beam of sunlight across his bed and turned to watch the miniature twister swirling on the balcony. It felt like the windy season of November; the season when children bought flimsy kites of brightly coloured tissue paper without even realising that the tradition behind the plaything was to fly away the spirits of the dead, but it was the wrong time of year. He remembered trying to fly a kite with his brother in the small patio of their house. 'Fly it, fly it, there it goes.' Raphael had jumped up and down in excitement until the red and yellow kite crashed into the floor tiles yet again. 'Let me have a go,' he'd begged.

Benjamin shoved it at him. 'Knock yourself out shorty.' Raphael jumped, throwing the flimsy wood and paper kite into the air, but he was too short, he couldn't get it to catch the wind at all. Benjamin laughed at him. 'Why don't you try the roof? That's the only way you'll get that stupid thing to fly.'

'OK, I will,' Raphael had said defiantly. His brother didn't believe he would climb onto the roof. He was always egging him on to do dangerous things, or things he knew Raphael would get into trouble for. Benjamin had a malicious streak, but Raphael couldn't resist proving him wrong. '*Mira, mirame, ya veras!*' That would show him. The kite had soared away as Raphael let out the string, dancing it backwards and forwards, letting it swing, and then a sudden gust had caught it and hurled it to the ground.

'You bastard, I'll get you for this,' Benjamin had cried as he picked up the tangled mess on which he'd spent his meagre pocket money.

Raphael wanted to fly a kite now, go to a hill on the outskirts of the city and fly it until all the spirits of the dead were blown away, but he couldn't. Lidia and Benigno were always with him, he always felt the comfort of their presence. Lola wasn't present, he couldn't feel her with him, but his guilt sat on his shoulder watching him like Lola's ghost and he didn't think it would go away until he discovered who had killed her. Why didn't she help him, send him a clue? He didn't believe much in religion, but he believed in the power of the ancestors and the rituals designed to keep the world spinning, maybe he'd be better off going to a shaman than digging up Josue's past and trying to discover the story behind Lola's death, if there was one. Maybe it was just one of those random, meaningless murders that happened often enough. He sighed. It must be late and daydreaming of kites wouldn't help him.

'Hey, the jailbird returns!'

Raphael had expected such quips from his colleagues. With the threat of death never too far away it helped to have a sense of humour. 'Just helping the police with their enquiries, you know how it is, wrong place, wrong time, all cleared up now.'

'Yeah likely story.'

He checked his desk for messages. There was a note saying his editor wanted to see him, but he glanced over to the glass fronted office and was glad to see that El Pelon wasn't there. He went over to one of the computers used for reference and checked all the papers again for a story about Lola. A short paragraph appeared in a couple of them including his own paper. It was on the third page, not big news but not completely buried.

'Dolores Rodriguez was found dead in the early hours of Sunday morning. The police have released no further details. Ms. Rodriguez, aged thirty-eight was a resident of Guatemala City and worked in an educative capacity for the new political alliance *La Frente*. Police ask anyone with information about the incident to come forward.'

Raphael grimaced, as if anyone was going to come forward with information! He picked up the phone and called the reporter who had written it, or rather who had picked up the press release from the police. 'Hi, it's Raphael, you know from editorials. I wanted to know what else you've got about the Dolores Rodriguez thing?'

'Why's that? You're not going to write a piece on that, are you?'

'No, I knew her slightly, friend of a friend, I just wondered what the scoop was.'

'No scoop, that's all the police gave out and the chief said it wasn't worth chasing up.'

Fortunately, it sounded like he hadn't heard about Raphael being picked up by the police; he didn't make any jokes or leap to conclusions as to why Raphael might want to know about Lola. 'Hmm that's interesting, since she worked for *La Frente* there must be some angle. It's got to be a bit fishy when a political type gets killed.'

'Yeah, you'd think, but the boss said not to bother for now, that's she's small fry, no story.'

'OK, well thanks anyway. Let me know if you hear anything.'

'Sure, but don't hold your breath on that one.'

Raphael replaced the phone slowly. That was strange, El Pelon not wanting to follow up a story like that. There wasn't much to go on, but that was often the case with the stories they got, it was up to the reporters to delve. Lola hadn't been much of a political player, but in the current climate being even vaguely associated with a political party was enough to annoy certain quarters. Not to mention that coming so soon after the blatant murder of Rosario, even if the deaths weren't linked, he could play up the general impunity factor and the moral decline since the signing of the peace. It didn't make sense to make so little of the story, unless the editor had been got at, or unless he knew Raphael had been involved with Lola, which he doubted. The other paper had the same information almost word for word, so he didn't bother calling them.

Since he didn't have a particular work assignment, he decided to go through his list of things to find out and see what he could discover about Josue and his links to Lola. He started with the easiest thing and called Ricardo the arts reporter.

'Hey man, how's it going?'

'Raphael, if you need bail, you're calling the wrong man; I'm just a poor cultural reporter.'

'Very funny, no I don't need your money, just a bit of information to tie in with something I'm working on.'

'OK shoot. Not literally of course!' Ricardo laughed heartily.

'Don't give up the day job just yet; your stand-up routine needs a little work. You ever heard of a guy named Josue Chan, plays the guitar, I believe?'

'Yeah, he's not bad, heard him a couple of times. Why? Thinking of taking your honey out on the town?'

'Something like that. I heard he teaches too.'

'I expect he does. Who can afford to go to concerts these days? But I wouldn't know about that. Probably does it privately anyway, hit those rich kids' parents for some serious money. Check out my by-line for the last few months, there's probably a review of one of his gigs.'

'OK, thanks.'

'And stay out of trouble, right!'

'I'll try, but you know how it is.' Raphael laughed.

Josue had checked out again, at least his story about being a musician and giving concerts held out to a certain degree. Raphael quickly checked the computer database and did find a small piece about him. His style of playing was described as exquisite, but you couldn't trust those cultural writers, they loved to use flamboyant words. The piece didn't give Raphael any more information except the name of one of the places where he'd played. He made a note of it so he could drop in later and see what they knew.

Raphael felt in his leather bag for his address book and pulled it out. From stories in the past about street kids and orphans he had contacts at two orphanages in the city. He'd decided it was worth a phone call to see if anyone knew anything about a boy named Josue Chan. He called the first place and asked for Maria.

'*Soy yo.* It's me.'

Raphael briefly reminded her of who he was. She didn't seem annoyed or surprised to hear from him, so he asked about Josue.

'I don't think we ever had a boy by that name, but I'm better with faces than names, I'll go and check.' Raphael doodled on a scrap of paper while he waited. 'We did have a Josue Chan.'

Raphael's heart leapt, perhaps he would finally find out a little about who Josue really was.

'Let me have a look here.'

Raphael drummed his fingers on the desktop as he waited for Maria to scan the file.

'No, he'd be too old for the man you described. Sorry, but I'm pretty sure this isn't who you're looking for.'

Raphael thanked her. It had been too much to expect he'd find something on the first call. He thought he probably wouldn't have much luck with his next call either. He was right; they had never had a child by that name. There was one more thing to try before he began cold-calling orphanages, which probably wouldn't give out any information anyway. A year or two previously there had been a big scandal about an orphanage just outside the capital that had been found selling children to be adopted by foreigners, and there was a rumour that some were never adopted but were sold to have organs removed for transplants. He thought it highly unlikely he'd find anything there, for one thing Josue was too old to have still been there and also no real names of children were given, but since he had the tools at hand to find the story quickly he glanced through it. There was nothing of interest, except the name of the disgraced orphanage owner, Ephraim Lopez. Any relation to Colonel Lopez? A million to one chance with such a common name, but Raphael stored it at the back of his mind as a piece of trivia that might one day come in handy; so many things and so many people seemed connected in some way to Rosario's death, and possibly Lola's, that it didn't make sense to discount anything just because it was a ridiculous long shot.

He continued to doodle, Rosario, Lopez, Andrea, Josue, Raphael, and Lola in the middle, like spokes of a wheel all the connecting lines went out from Lola and then some intertwined like tangled string – Andrea to Rosario, Rosario to Lopez, Rosario to Chavez to Lopez, himself to Rosario though that was tenuous, just about anyone could have been asked to write about him, and other people had, himself to Josue, that was tenuous too, not to mention recent and unstable. He had reached a full stop again, without really getting much further forward. Josue had a real address, a real name, and did the job he'd said he did, but did that mean he was who he said he was? Had he been Lola's lover? And either way could he be trusted? Raphael logged out of the computer and was standing up to leave when El Pelon walked in.

'Ah Raphael, come into my office, I want a word.'

Raphael groaned inwardly, the last thing he wanted at the moment was to talk to his editor. Rather than inviting him to sit, El Pelon inclined his head towards a chair. Raphael closed the door and sat down.

'So, Raphael, a bit of trouble with the police?'

'No, not really, just helping with their inquiries, all sorted out now.'

'What inquiries?'

'Er, they thought I'd witnessed an accident, but I didn't really see much.'

'And they came all the way over here to pick you up for that? In a police car?'

Damn he must have been looking out of his window when Raphael had been driven away; he didn't even think he'd been there. 'Easiest way to find me I suppose. It was a pretty big accident, they took my name at the scene, I must have told them where I worked.'

'Careless Raphael, careless. Sloppy. Never tell a cop you're a newspaper man, you know that, might as well sign your own death certificate.'

'Yes, you're right,' sighed Raphael. He was used to the editor's wealth of expertise in all things related to journalism. The man just loved to share his knowledge.

'I hope you're being up front with me here. I can't protect you if I don't know what you're up to.'

What does that mean, thought Raphael. Does he know something I don't? How could he protect me anyway?

'So, what's your next big project?' asked the editor.

'You tell me sir, what have you got for me?'

'Not much, things are a bit quiet just now.'

'What about the death of that woman from *La Frente*, isn't anyone covering that?' Raphael knew he was taking a risk asking about it because it wouldn't be a good idea for him to follow it up and he didn't want to show too much interest, but since he knew the editor had dumped it, he thought it was a safe question.

'Not much of a story there. Could be political infighting. Anyway, not sure it's even murder; the police haven't released much on that one.'

'Exactly, doesn't that ...'

'What's your interest, eh? Don't know the woman, do you?'

'Only vaguely, friend of a friend, I recognised the name that's all.'

'Hmm.'

'Well, if you haven't got much for me, perhaps I'll take those days off we talked about?'

'Excellent idea,' said the editor cutting him off. 'I'm sure you're due it. Go and have a few days' rest, go and get hammered or whatever you young men do these days.'

'Er, yes sir.'

'Right. Let me know when you're back. A week or so, do you?'

'Yes, a week will be fine, thank you.'

Raphael escaped from the office and the building as quickly as he could without making a scene. Yet more unusual things for him to wonder about. His boss not having something for him to work on was completely unheard of; he always had an idea of some sort even if there was no story to it. His dismissal of the death of Lola seemed completely out of character too, and his keenness for Raphael to take some time off was unbelievable, even though Raphael had mentioned it before. Did El Pelon know something? Did he have a source in the police department? That was certainly possible, a lot of hinted at material came their way, which could only have come from a police source. Raphael hated the thought of his editor knowing he was involved with Lola, and the possibility of him thinking that he could have killed her, or be a suspect, made him break out in a sweat. And yet, he had to admire the man for his discretion and his attempt to shield him by burying the story. He would never have expected anywhere near such loyalty and concern from that distant and soulless man.

Raphael went to the café across the street and ordered a coffee. Being off work wasn't necessarily a good thing. He wouldn't be able to use the computers there, if he needed more computer access, he would have to go to another newspaper office and try and cajole computer rights. Of course, he could always go to the University, as a member of staff, albeit part-time, he had access to their library and computing facilities. At least it would free him up to do some investigating out on the street and gave him a valid excuse to be out of the office in case he was picked up by the police again. He just hoped the police wouldn't show up at work while he wasn't there. No telling what people might say in all innocence, not to mention that it would set the office gossips going again.

This was the café where he'd first met Lola. He looked fondly at the table where they'd sat, picturing her in his mind with all her packages around her. He stirred his cup in a daze.

Raphael swallowed his coffee. Brick walls, that was what he kept running into, dead-ends and brick walls. He thought about going over and talking to some of Rosario's colleagues, maybe they knew something more about his death, or at least something more about his life that might give Raphael some clues.

He paid the bill and walked the short distance to the office of *La Prensa* and remembered the last time he had taken that walk, the talk with Rosario's editor, his subsequent, seemingly pointless trip to Chimal, the Chavez story, and how much his life had changed since then.

Josue clearly trusted Raphael: that was a comfort to him. Why couldn't he trust Josue? Why did his story have to be a lie? It didn't. Why did their meeting have to be a plot of some kind? It didn't. It could have been a pure coincidence, much stranger things than that happened in life. And just because Lola hadn't told her older sister about Josue, that didn't mean they hadn't been lovers. Andrea believed Lola told her everything, but maybe she didn't; she certainly hadn't told Lola about all of her lovers. But she had told her about Rosario Recinos. His name kept popping up in Raphael's mind. Rosario, the chain, the link, but was he? He needed to talk to Andrea about Rosario and his work.

At the offices of *Prensa Libre*, it was clear security had been stepped up since Rosario's murder.

'Can I help you sir?' asked the mature woman at reception as though she were training to join the civil patrols.

'Yes, I'm from *Siglo Veintiuno*. I wanted to talk to a couple of your reporters.'

'Let me see your identification.' Raphael showed her his press card. 'Which reporters?'

He tried to think of a name, or someone he knew, or whose by-line he had at least read, someone who had covered the murder, but he couldn't think of any names. 'Just someone in the news-room.'

She gave him a look, the sort of look that meant he was on the list to be transported to the next model village, sighed and picked up the phone. 'What was your name again?'

'Raphael Sifuentes.'

She mumbled something into the phone, hung it up and said to him, 'One of the boys will come down, please wait.'

He moved as far away as possible from the uncomfortable penetration of her gaze, sat on one of the low, vinyl-covered benches and picked up a pristine copy of *Prensa Libre*, of which several were artistically placed on a coffee table.

The headline stunned him, especially as he had scanned today's papers that morning, but then he remembered he had only done a search for Lola's name.

'Arrest made in murder of journalist Rosario Recinos.' Raphael read on. 'Police confirmed today that they have arrested a twenty-three-year-old man in connection with the killing of the journalist, believed to be the work of the paramilitary group *Mano Blanco*. Inspector Pedro A. Lopez who is leading the inquiry, said that it was still unclear what connections, if any, could be made to the paramilitary organisation, which until recently was believed to be defunct. He said police were pursuing various avenues of investigation. The name of the detainee was not released.'

Raphael inhaled deeply, feeling faint, and leaned back against the wall. Pedro A Lopez. Colonel Almendrez Lopez again, or was he being paranoid? It was no surprise that the name of the arrested man hadn't been released. Raphael wondered if he even existed, or if he'd just been picked up for being drunk, or if Lopez was more clever than that and was tidying up several loose ends by clearing Rosario's murder and framing someone he wanted to get rid of. How convenient that Lopez now worked for the police after his military retirement, so easy to cover up murder if you were the investigating officer. What was it Rosario had found on Lopez? And could any of it be connected to Lola? The thought of that made him feel ill; in fact he thought he might be sick and was about to run out of the front door and incur the disdain of the receptionist, when a man appeared from a door behind reception and walked over to him.

He held out his hand, 'Lucio Martinez, from the newsroom, you wanted to er, you look a bit rough, are you all right?'

'Ugh yes, yes thanks,' Raphael swallowed and tried to compose himself. 'Bit hung over, sorry.'

'Ah right, bit of a night was it?' He nudged Raphael conspiratorially. 'And I bet our Maria did nothing to make you feel better.' He nodded his head towards the receptionist. Raphael smiled weakly. 'Thought not. Come on up, I'll see if I can find some coffee.'

Raphael followed him through the door, ignoring the glare from Maria that he felt on the side of his neck as they passed, and down a long corridor with several doors off it. Outwardly at least the offices of *Prensa Libre* were more ostentatious, but *Siglo Veintiuno* had the more liberal reputation, perhaps that's why their offices were shabbier. At the end, the young man pushed a door and they were in a large room full of cubicles, most of them filled by busy looking newspapermen typing or talking on the phone. He didn't immediately notice any women. Papers were still a man's business and maybe just as well given the possible dangers.

Lucio showed him to an empty cubicle. 'Have a seat, I'll grab some coffee.'

Raphael sat down. He was still clutching the copy of the paper and he glanced at the front page again. He was still reading through the rest of the article when Lucio returned and held out a small Styrofoam cup of black coffee.

'Feeling any better?'

'A bit, thanks.' Raphael sipped the coffee carefully, wanting the caffeine but not sure how his stomach would react. 'So, they think they've got his murderer then,' he said inclining his head towards the headline.

'That's the theory.'

'What do you think?'

'I suppose I'm glad they've got anyone, but I don't know, something doesn't seem quite right. It's like the lone gunman theory. They're saying he's connected to *Mano Blanco*, but they don't say how. If it was them, there had to be more than one person involved and if it was one man making the decision it certainly wasn't a twenty-three-year-old. He may have been the knife man, but I'm not convinced he was the brains behind it.'

'And the police just sent this over in a press release or what?'

'Yeah, didn't you guys get it? Maybe we got it first because he was one of ours, but they usually send stuff round to everyone at once.'

'I'm sure we got it. I don't work news. I do editorials. I was working on something else this morning; I hadn't seen the new stuff.'

'Right. So, what was it you wanted anyway?'

'Well actually I was coming over to find out a bit more about Rosario. I wrote our editorial on him, you might have seen it, and I wanted to try to find out a bit more about him, thought it might tie in with something else I'm working on. Did you work with him?'

'Yeah, I knew him pretty well; he was a nice guy, hard working but didn't take it too seriously. I don't know why he got bumped off, there are plenty more around here who made more of a career out of it, you'd think they would be higher on the list.'

'Maybe he had something on somebody, someone in the military maybe?' suggested Raphael.

'An exposé? Not his style, he was more of a plodder than a big story man, he did his job, he did a good job, in ten years maybe he might even have made editor, but Rosario wasn't stylish, not a go-getter.'

'Did you socialise with him much? Ever see his beautiful fiancée?'

'Ah you saw the picture, huh? That was a bit of a joke among the guys, he talked about her all the time, had that picture above his desk, but none of us ever saw her and he never talked about getting married. I worked with him two years and he was engaged the whole time.' So, it had been a long-term thing with Andrea, either Rosario was fantastic in bed or there was something else about him she liked, but not enough to make her leave her husband. 'Not that we went out much,' Lucio continued, 'it was more like drinks after the print run. But Rosario went drinking with us most of the time. If I had a woman like that waiting somewhere for me, I wouldn't be hanging around with this bunch.' Lucio glanced out at the sea of cubicles.

'Did you ever go to his house?'

'No. We were work mates, we got on well, but we weren't really friends, you know?'

'Yeah I know. So, could anyone come up with a reason why he got it and not someone else, or was he just unlucky?' asked Raphael.

'You want my opinion – he was unlucky. I really don't see that he could have annoyed anyone that much. And I don't think he was the type to make a big investigative discovery unless he literally tripped over it. *Que descanse en paz.* I'm not saying he wasn't intelligent, but he didn't quite have that edge you need to be a good journalist. He was too nice. You know what I mean, the really good reporters, they aren't always nice people. Rosario was nice, not much of a compliment I know, but he was, he would have made a good husband and father with a boring desk job somewhere.'

'OK, well I guess I won't keep you anymore.' Raphael got up.

'OK. Good talking to you, and for what it's worth I read your piece on Rosario and I liked it, but if I were you, I'd leave it alone. We both know what happened to him, we don't need another good man with no hands.'

'Thanks. Yeah you're right.'

'Hey just make something up, it's not worth the risk.' Lucio smiled and shrugged his shoulders.

Raphael wasn't sure if he was joking or not, but the remark made Raphael lose any respect he might have had for the man. Now he wasn't sure whether to believe him about anything he had said, except that it all rang true. Rosario, as far as he could tell, did seem like a nice man and he must have had something going for him to have stayed so long with Andrea. And what Lucio surmised about the arrest seemed logical too. If it really had been the work of a group like *Mano Blanco*, then it wouldn't have been down to one man and certainly not one so young.

Out on the street Raphael lit a cigarette and wondered who he knew who had inside information on the police. There must be someone. He wanted to know about the arrest. He needed to know if this Lopez was in fact the same Colonel Lopez from Chimaltenango. There was nothing at all to say that he was except Raphael's gut feeling and the fact that a senior police job would be a cushy number for a recently retired military man with some loose ends to tie up. Who could he call? Who did he know? He racked his brains. One of the *Siglo* reporters? No one sprang to mind, and anyway now he was on holiday. El Pelon? He surely had police contacts, but none Raphael could tap into. He didn't have the pull to get favours from the chief and he'd only wonder why Raphael needed to know. He decided to call Andrea, see what she knew about Rosario. Probably nothing. If Rosario really loved her, he wouldn't tell her anything about his work, especially something that could be dangerous.

There was a *Pollo Campero* round the corner. He went in and ordered coffee. The smell of fried food was repugnant, yet there were people eating greasy chicken at an hour Raphael considered far too early for it. He asked the girl serving him if they had a phone.

'There's a phone over there,' she replied with disinterest.

Raphael took a sip of his coffee. It wasn't good. He set it on a table, went over to the phone and dialled Andrea's number.

'Hello.'

'Andrea, it's me, Raphael.'

'Hi. Are you all right?'

'Yes, but I need to talk to you.'

'OK.' There was a pause as though she expected him to talk.

'Not on the phone.'

'Right, right, of course, um …'

Raphael was wary about arranging a meeting, but a pay phone should be safe enough. 'I'm near the offices of *La Prensa*, could you meet me there?'

'Yes.'

'You know where it is?'

'I think so. Downtown on Avenida 2?'

'Yes, just wait outside the foyer.'

'It'll take me at least half an hour.'

'That's fine. I'll wait.'

Raphael sat back down to wait, though he didn't want more of the foul coffee and the smell of chicken was making him nauseous, while he had time to kill, he might as well make some more phone calls. If he could find the address for the bar where Josue had played, he could go and check it out later. He looked around for a phone book. Of course, there wasn't one. He called the office and asked for Ricardo.

'*Diga.*'

'Hey, it's Raphael.'

'Twice in one day? People will start talking! What can I do for you?'

'I checked out your review on the concert. Very nice.'

'Yeah, yeah, cut to the chase.'

'It was at a bar, *La Luminaria*, what's the address?'

'Hang on a minute. OK it's 8 Calle 22-24, zona 10.'

'Where's that?'

'Off the Avenida Reforma. The rich part of town.'

'That's why I don't know it! OK thanks.'

'You're really keen to see this guitar player, eh? He's not *that* good, you know!'

'Oh, you know us editorial types, have days to kill putting a story together.'

Raphael played with the unravelling spiral wire of his notebook. He couldn't think who else to call. He went outside for a smoke. From there he could see the entrance to *Prensa Libre* and see Andrea arrive.

'Hello Raphael,' Andrea took his arm, 'I was worried; you sounded concerned on the phone. Is something wrong?'

'No, not really, but I need to know more about Rosario. Things aren't adding up about his murder, and maybe it's even tied to Lola, I don't know, maybe not, but … You heard they arrested someone for his murder?'

'No, I hadn't, I …' She looked shocked, more stunned than Raphael had yet seen her.

He handed her the crumpled newspaper. 'Let's walk. I think there's a park just down here, then you can read it.'

Entering the park, they might have been mistaken for a couple meeting for lunch. They sat on an empty bench and Andrea read the first paragraph of the story. She looked up at Raphael. 'You don't believe they've got the right man, do you?'

'I don't know. He may have been the one who actually killed him, but I'm sure someone else masterminded it. I'm puzzled by this story Rosario was working on – the murder of Manuel Chavez in Chimaltenango …'

'Oh yes, he mentioned that,' she interrupted.

'Did he? What did he say?'

'Oh, nothing of consequence. I knew he'd been to Chimaltenango and then I read his story. I read all his work.'

'Well, a Colonel Lopez was implicated in that murder and Rosario seems to have written an awful lot of other stories about him. I wonder it he had some hard evidence to link Lopez to Manuel's murder and that's why he was killed. And now Lopez is investigating Rosario's murder.'

'What? How can that be?'

'He retired from the military. I think he works for the police now. Lopez is a common name, but his maternal surname is Almendrez – not so common. And look, "Pedro A. Lopez, investigating officer."'

'But Raphael that could be anyone.'

'OK, say he's not the police officer. He still had the connections to get Rosario killed if he'd found out something. Did Rosario ever tell you anything about Lopez? Any big story he was working on?'

'No, no he never talked about his work except in passing; I just read the stories in the paper like everyone else.'

'And he never gave you anything for safekeeping? Any papers or files?'

'No.' Andrea looked pensive. 'But wait, around that time he did give me a framed photo of Lake Atitlan. I thought it was a bit strange, because he usually didn't give me things. He tried to give me flowers, but I told him not to. I didn't want my husband asking questions. But this picture, he said I had to keep it, even if I hid it.'

'And you've still got it?'

'Yes, it's at home. I put it in my sewing room.'

'Can we go and look at it?'

'Of course. But why? It's just a photo of the lake.'

'It's not the photo I'm interested in.'

Finally, Raphael was thinking like a journalist, like a researcher. Maybe Rosario wasn't as uninspired as his colleagues believed. Maybe he'd given Andrea something to hold onto until he had more evidence, or until he worked out how to expose Lopez, only Lopez got to him first.

Andrea drove, and back at her house led Raphael straight to her sewing room in the back. 'That's it,' she said pointing to a medium sized artistic photo in a cheap frame. Raphael took it down, pushed back the metal clips and eased out the cardboard that backed it. There was a black and white photo taped to the underside. One of the men in the photo Raphael recognised as Manuel Chavez, the other he strongly suspected was Lopez. The photo wasn't clear, probably taken at night, but it was fairly obvious that Manuel was being taken against his will.

Andrea looked over his shoulder. 'Manuel Chavez,' said Raphael resting his thumb on the man on the right.

'And …'

'Colonel Lopez is my guess.'

'*Hijole*! What are we going to do with it?'

'I don't know, but I think Rosario was killed because Lopez either knew or suspected that he had some evidence like this.'

'But what does this really prove? Even if it is Lopez, it only shows him leading Manuel away somewhere; surely he could talk his way out of that easily enough?'

'Hmm. Maybe Rosario had something else that combined with this made more of a case, and he didn't want to keep things together in case they were found. Or he was hoping to gather more evidence. Presumably Lopez doesn't know this exists, or at least not where it is, and as you say, it's not too much use on its own, but since Lopez is the type who kills with little provocation …' Raphael left the sentence hanging.

Andrea and Raphael looked at each other. 'Let's put it back where it was for now,' he said.

Raphael was in a quandary about what to do with the photo, but he knew it was a no-win situation, they couldn't reveal they had it, and they couldn't just hide it indefinitely. So, for now he carried on with his plans – to look into Josue's background and that afternoon he headed to *La Luminaria*. It was indeed in the more exclusive part of town, where the foreign diplomats and high up civil servants lived. It was not far from a cinema Raphael had been to once that showed foreign films with subtitles rather than dubbing. Fortunately, the bar was open; it looked like the kind of place that only opened in the evening, and only to men wearing ties and ladies in posh dresses. He was surprised that Josue had played in such a place, knowing where and how he lived.

As he went through the door the man wiping down the bar looked up at him dubiously. 'Can I help you?'

'Are you serving?'

'Yes.' He was refined with freshly washed hair and clean hands, and looked at Raphael as if to say, 'isn't that obvious.'

'Then I'll have a lemonade please, *con soda*.' Raphael sat on a stool in front of the barman. 'A friend of mine said you have music here in the evenings, that right?' Raphael was trying to be chatty. He didn't want to play the journalist card unless he had to.

'That's right.' He set the drink before Raphael on a paper drinks mat.

'What kind of music?' He took a sip from the lemonade. It was sharp but good.

'Sophisticated music.' The barman was a monosyllabic type. Raphael wondered if ritzier customers got the same treatment.

'Ah huh. Any guitar players ever? I like guitar music. You know, the sophisticated kind.'

'Yeah we have someone plays here once a month.' The barman managed to string a sentence together.

'Any good?'

'I suppose. Not my thing. But I'd have to say yes. We get a good crowd when he comes.'

'When's he playing next?'

'Next week, I think. There are some posters and things on the board by the door. There's marimba tomorrow.'

'Marimba? Isn't that a bit ...'

'Ethnic? Yeah I know, but we get a lot of foreigners in.'

Ethnic had not been the word Raphael was thinking of. 'You ever get a pretty woman in here, long hair, green eyes.'

'What's with the third degree? We get a lot of pretty women in here. If your woman's two timing you, it's none of my business.'

'Hey, I was just asking.'

The barman shrugged.

Raphael downed the rest of the lemonade, the sharpness making his mouth water.

'*Cinco quetzals*,' said the barman, eager to get rid of him.

Five quetzals! Raphael could get a whole dinner for that in his own neighbourhood, but he refrained from making any comment. He handed over a five note and couldn't resist saying, 'keep the change.' At the door he paused to inspect the board. There was a flyer with Josue's photo and several dates he had played there. He was due to play again a week from Saturday. Raphael wondered how much Josue earned for playing in a place that charged five quetzals for a lemonade. He wondered how many of the children in the surrounding area Josue taught and if they paid him in dollars. In theory he could be, probably was, making a lot of money. Well good luck to him if he does, thought Raphael and then wondered what he spent it on. It clearly wasn't his house, and his clothes while good quality were not expensive. Still what Josue did or did not spend his money on was not the issue. So far Raphael had only been able to prove that he was who he said he was and did what he said he did. It didn't bring him any closer to knowing what his relationship with Lola had been, or why he had been called to the hospital when she was found, or if he had anything to do with her death.

15

Late that evening, back at home, Raphael went into the closet in his bedroom to look for his old files. He was still pondering what, if anything, to do about Andrea's photo of Lopez abducting Manuel Chavez. He had to think of a way to expose Lopez, whilst keeping Andrea safe, and find out what had happened to Lola, and why. He had to find out if Josue was involved. He knew if he didn't keep busy, he would just sit comatose in a corner not knowing what to do, or what to feel. He was already feeling overwhelmed, exhausted, on the edge of sanity. He had to keep his mind and body occupied to keep himself from going crazy. So, he let his rational side take over, the side that wrote cutting newspaper copy.

The side that tracked down leads. The side that had joined the guerrillas with barely a second thought.

The walk-in cupboard was filled with cardboard file boxes. On the left side a metal rail with the few items of clothing he owned vied with the pile of boxes underneath. He opened the door wide to let in light from the dim bulb hanging naked from the ceiling. His filing system was a struggle between what would remind him of the content of the boxes and the desire to make it hard for anyone else looking for something. It was a symptom of his paranoia. Consequently, the outside of the boxes only gave the relevant year. Inside, the files had names, but in a sort of code, something that would jog his memory, but had no obvious meaning. So, his file on Rigoberta Menchu, for example, was not called Menchu, or *indigena*, but Pablo Neruda because he was a Nobel Prize winner too.

Raphael was looking for the notes he'd made on the orphanage story. The way Josue had calmly announced that he was an orphan was still bothering Raphael. He was pretty sure of the year of the story, but what would he have called the file? He flipped through the folders: 'smoked fish' – a story on abductions round Lake Atitlan; 'sheep fur', 'dolls house'. What on earth was dolls house? He looked out of curiosity. It was a story he'd forgotten, though he shouldn't have. It was a particularly poignant piece on street children, with a photo of a girl holding a doll made of rags.

Then Raphael found what he was looking for, 'church plays' – 'organ'. The thrust of the story had been that children were being sold for their organs, rather than being adopted by rich families in the US. He pulled out the file and had just opened it when the phone rang. He set the file on top of the box and scrambled up toppling the boxes behind him.

He grabbed the phone. 'Hello.'

'Hello. It's Andrea. Is this a bad time?'

'No, no, it's fine. I was just looking through some old files. I'm surrounded by boxes. How are you?' Raphael was a little surprised to hear from her again so soon. He hoped she wasn't worrying too much about the photo still hidden in her house.

'Oh, all right, I suppose, plodding along.' She was quiet for a minute. 'Lola's body has been released.'

'Right.' Incredibly he had almost forgotten that he'd first contacted Andrea to find out about funeral arrangements. That seemed like days ago. There was a pause, neither of them knowing what to say.

'The funeral will be Friday, with a wake at mother's house tomorrow night. You're welcome to attend both.'

'Thanks,' said Raphael. She sounded so officious. She'd been busy he thought. While he'd been embroiled in his investigations, she had the tasteless task of arranging Lola's funeral. As the only sibling with an aging mother, it would fall mostly on her. 'Are you … Is there anything I can do? It must be hard.'

Andrea cut him off as if not wanting him to slip into sympathy. 'The priest has been very good, and her friends … Here, I'll give you the details.' She told him the address of her mother's house and the time the house would be open. Wakes typically went on all night, with close family there constantly and friends and more distant relatives dropping in. 'The Mass will be at San Bartolome, at noon.' Burial would follow at the central cemetery. 'I would have liked you to say something, but it was rather taken out of my hands.' She paused, and Raphael thought he heard a sniff. 'Her work colleagues …'

'Yes. I understand. It's probably better.'

'Right, well I'd better be going.' She sounded so disheartened, so flat and empty as though reality had finally sunk in. There was none of the excitement of that morning.

'Yes. It's just …' she said.

'Yes?'

'What are you going to do, Raphael?'

'I don't know.' He was fairly confident that his phone was bugged, if not before Lola's death then certainly since it. 'Actually, we probably shouldn't talk about this on the phone.'

'Right.'

'So, I'll try and come tomorrow.'

'Yes. Have you …' her voice trailed off.

'Have I what?'

'Nothing. See you tomorrow Raphael.'

He hung up the phone. He felt a deep sadness, a weight on his chest, and he wasn't sure if it was for himself, or for Andrea. He wished he could see her again, comfort her. Her tone was so different from the upbeat, almost bubbly person he'd experienced before. But then that attitude hadn't seemed quite right either.

Raphael sat thinking and an awful thought emerged – what if Lola had been killed by mistake? What if they'd got the wrong sister? Maybe the police suspected that Rosario had given something to his girlfriend and they'd mistakenly thought that was Lola. Her place had been searched. Maybe she interrupted them and that's why they had to kill her? Was Andrea in danger too? Wouldn't the safest thing be to keep the photo hidden where it was for now? Presumably Lopez didn't know where the photo was. Maybe he didn't know it existed at all. Raphael's heart beat faster and he wanted a cigarette, but he had to stay calm, to keep working.

He went back to his boxes. He started tidying the box that had toppled over. A couple of files had slid out and partly emptied their contents on the floor. He scooped up the file and a photo of Lola fell out. He picked it up and held it to the light. She was looking particularly alluring, hooking her hair behind her ear, her faced turned slightly in profile as though she were talking to someone out of shot. It wasn't a photo Raphael recognised. In fact, he didn't think he'd ever seen it before. He opened the file. There were photocopies of notes in Lola's handwriting, but they weren't to him. They looked like diary entries. He began to read. '31 de mayo, 1995. Met R for coffee. He's working on a new story, but he wouldn't tell me about it. Back to mine. The usual. He complains of nightmares. I know he's thinking about her. I hate it.' Raphael shuffled the pages, looking at others. They were not in chronological order; they seemed to be random pages and random dates. Another, from only a month ago said, 'I can't do this anymore. Don't make me. I have to stop. It's tearing me apart.' What was tearing her apart?

The more he read, the more he began to think that they weren't private diary entries but reports about him to a third party. But to whom? And why? And why on earth were there copies of them in his private filing system? Who had put them there? Had Lola been informing on him to the police? Surely not. Unless, they had some hold over her, something in her past, a mistake, some misdemeanour on record. The military? Raphael couldn't believe that; not after what she knew of his life, not after the intimacies they'd shared. Even if it hadn't been love, she couldn't be that cruel. Who then? Something political? Something to do with *La Frente*? Was she hatching a plot to get him involved in politics? To get him revolutionised again? No. She would know that blackmail wouldn't work. She ought to have known that nothing would work. He was done with all of that.

He looked through the pages again. The last one was dated June 1994. Wasn't that around the time they'd first met? 'I met him. He was where you said. As you said. Intriguing. You didn't say he was attractive! Are you sure you want this?' Want what? Who was she talking to? Who could have told her to meet him, and described him, and why? Raphael rocked back on his heals. The file slid from his hand and fell to the floor. Then he saw the name on the file tab *la pesadilla*, the nightmare. It was. The police must have planted the file when they searched his place. How else could it have got there? Lola never came to his apartment; he always went to hers; so it couldn't have been her. Maybe it was fake, just to get him wondering, just so it could be found later and displayed as a reason for him killing her. She'd been informing on him, had been all along, she had never loved him. He'd found out and that had been it. But the police had mentioned nothing when they'd interviewed him; they had only focussed on his jealousy of Josue. What kind of cat and mouse game were they playing? Or was someone else playing? Raphael felt bombed, shell-shocked; it was all too much to take in. Every time he thought he was getting a little closer to working things out, something else slapped him sideways.

He flopped down onto his backside, stretching out his legs and wiping a hand down his trousers. He looked again at the notes. It *did* look like her writing. Raphael scrambled up and went to his desk. Opening the drawer, he rifled through it, looking for a letter from her. She never wrote him letters. A note, anything. He pulled out papers, put them on top of the desk in a pile, running his hands over them rapidly trying to locate something in her hand. They fell on the floor like leaves, floating down, poems and receipts, unpaid bills, but nothing from Lola. He felt in the drawer for more and it fell on the floor with a clatter. He just pushed it away with his foot. There, something that said 'Raphael.' He pulled it out. 'Can't meet tonight after all. I'll call you tomorrow.' He compared it with the photocopies, definitely the same writing. He wiped his forehead. He was sweating. Sweat ran down his arm in a cool trickle. He sat back in the chair and took a cigarette from the box on the desk. The paper stuck to his dry lips and pulled off a piece of skin. He tasted blood, the blood of betrayal. He had doubted Lola. Doubted her love, but never her loyalty; never for a minute thought she could do this. She might betray him with another man; that didn't matter to Raphael, but to inform on him? Why? For what gain?

His head was swimming. He needed to walk, but it was too late to go out. He got up and shoved the desk. The feet screeched on the floor and more papers fell off. He kicked the box of files. He kicked it again, then the chair. In a frenzy he pushed all the papers off the table. Then he dragged the chair over to the balcony and sat in the doorway, his anger spent almost as quickly as it had come over him. He lit another cigarette, taking a fleck of tobacco from his lip and flicking it to the floor. How could she have done that to him? And now she was gone, the bitch, now he'd never know the truth. He kicked the metal balcony, sending a shiver of pain up his leg. So, their first meeting had been a set up, just as he'd thought. And had she just been stringing him along since then? Had she ever loved him? Andrea thought that she had, but maybe she only told Andrea that to make her cover more convincing. Well, he couldn't ask Andrea about it. He'd have to wait until after the funeral to broach the subject and maybe not even then. If Andrea was in the dark about what Lola had been up to, how could he break it to her now? Slander the name of the dead? He couldn't. And if Andrea had known then he couldn't trust her.

16

Several hours later, Raphael was still sitting in the chair mulling things over, surrounded by cigarette butts. The sky was attempting to lighten in preparation for dawn. Moths fluttered around and bumped into the light bulb. He was exhausted, but not tired in a way he could sleep. He went inside and began tidying things. He picked up the papers around the desk and without looking at them, shoved them back in the drawer. He pushed the chair carefully under the table. Then he began tidying the boxes. The papers from the *pesadilla* file were spread around it and Raphael got sidetracked reading the pages again. He read them all this time, still incredulous. Then he put them back in the file. He looked once more at the photo of Lola, the unnecessary photo, as though signposting her betrayal, saying 'look at me, look what I did.' He put the box back in the closet as though he'd never found it. The other box with the orphanage file was still sitting in the middle of the floor, but Raphael had no interest in pursuing that now. What was the point? What was the point of anything? Did it matter any more who had killed Rosario? Who had killed Lola? Whoever it was had done him a favour.

He stood up and wiped his hands down his trousers, leaving dusty trails. In the bathroom he surveyed himself in the small mirror. What a state. His shirt was unbuttoned and looked like he'd been wearing it for several days. There were rings of dry and damp sweat under his arms. His hair looked like he'd been running his hands through it all night. He rubbed a thumb over his dark beard, then splashed cold water on his face and looked more closely at his bloodshot eyes. He needed a shower, but he didn't have the energy. Coffee first.

Dawn had broken and Raphael turned off the light and lit the gas to make coffee. While it heated, he looked around for something to eat. Not that he was really hungry. There was nothing. To compensate he put three spoons of sugar in his coffee, blew on it and sipped. The phone rang. He hesitated to answer it. Who could be calling so early? He thought maybe it was Andrea, not able to sleep, wanting to talk or needing help with some last-minute arrangements.

'*Diga.*'

'Oh thank goodness. Raphael, it's me, Josue.'

'Josue? What's the matter? Where …'

'I've been arrested. They finally let me use the phone. I didn't know who else to call. I …'

'*Esta bien.*'

'Please come Raphael.'

'Which police station are you at?'

'The one where we were taken before. Raph ...'

Raphael heard someone else say '*basta*' and the phone went dead. Going to the police station was the last thing he wanted to do, and he wondered again why he should help Josue. But if he didn't go he would only stay there feeling sorry for himself, breeding hatred for Lola and wondering how he could ever have been stupid enough to have trusted her. Just when he was thinking perhaps he'd made a mistake in not committing to her, by not freeing up his feelings, keeping everything locked inside. But that was no answer either. He could help this boy, but what would it cost him?

Swallowing the dregs of coffee, he splashed more water on his face, changed shirts and left. Raphael knew some lawyers, but none he thought he could afford. The state would have to provide Josue with a lawyer, but Raphael knew how bad they could be. Why hadn't the police arrested him instead? He had an even more convincing motive for killing Lola now. Anger rose in him again as he went over her notes in his mind. 'You didn't say he was attractive.' 'He was just where you said he'd be.' He had less to lose than young Josue with his whole life ahead of him. But the police didn't care about that. They just wanted someone to take the rap and remove any shred of a link to Lopez. Raphael was surprised he hadn't been questioned again. Did they have some hard evidence against Josue? Or were they just playing them off against each other, seeing who would break first?

The city was starting to wake up. It was cool, and Raphael huddled inside his jacket on the bus seat. A woman across the aisle sipped steaming *atole* from a plastic mug. Its sickly smell made Raphael feel both hungry and faint. This was the bus route he usually took to work, but never so early. He looked out of the window and let the gentle rocking lull his brain to numbness. He didn't want to think. He didn't want to think about anything ever again. Whatever he did or didn't do, life just happened to him. The one good thing there had been – Lidia, had been taken away.

Everything seemed different at this hour. The city was calmer as if shrouded in mountain mist. The lottery ticket stand on the corner was shut up and padlocked. The shoeshine boys were not yet out in the park. The shutters on all but the bakeries were pulled down. Raphael got off the bus a stop before his usual one and could see the police station as soon as he was on the street. He walked over and entered.

'I'm here for Josue Chan,' he said to the officer at the desk, barely more than a boy with fluff above his lip and a smooth chin.

'*Que?*'

'You have a Josue Chan in custody. He called me.'

'When was he brought in?'

'I don't know. Probably during the night.'

'What's he charged with?'

Raphael thought to himself, who's the policeman here, I know more than he does. 'I don't know. He didn't say.' The sleepless night and other preoccupations were niggling Raphael's patience.

'Take a seat. I'll have to go and see. I just came on duty. I've got no reports here.'

The officer went through a door behind the desk and left Raphael. There was no one else around. Raphael paced back and forth. He was conscious of the aching muscles in his legs, but he was too tense to sit down. He remembered the feeling from when he'd been a guerrilla; never having enough sleep, body aching from languor brought on by over exertion, from the endless tramping through the jungle, from lying in damp, cold clothes.

He tapped his fingers on the countertop, looked at the hard wooden benches against the wall, the green and white marble floor. Raphael wondered if the cell floors were also made of marble; what it would be like to fall on one. He shivered. What was taking so long? It crossed his mind to go to the door for a cigarette, but if he did the officer would surely choose that moment to come back. He looked at the cork notice board, with notices of recent crimes, people wanted by the police, even a reward for the return of some stolen jewellery in an old lady's spindly handwriting. Raphael looked at his watch. He'd been there half an hour. He went to the counter to see if there was a bell to ring. There wasn't.

It couldn't be right to leave the desk unattended for so long. Then the door opened and the young officer came back out.

'Can I see him now?' asked Raphael.

'I'm sorry sir, you can't see him.'

'But he asked for me. This can't be right.' Raphael raised his voice.

'The chief said you can't see him. Only a lawyer.'

'Has he got a lawyer?'

'No.'

'Isn't there a duty lawyer or something?' said Raphael, exasperated.

'He hasn't been called. I think it was assumed you'd bring a lawyer, sir.' The boy said everything in a deadpan tone, as though he had no emotions, or opinions. He would make a great policeman.

'What has he been charged with?'

'Murder.'

'Actually charged, not just questioning?'

'Yes, he's been charged.'

'But ...' Raphael's mind went blank.

'Sir?'

'Eh?'

'Will you be providing a lawyer?'

'I'll have to look into it. Does Josue know I'm here?'

'He's been told.'

'But I can't speak to him?'

'No, and he's refusing to answer any more questions without a lawyer.'

'Right, well, I'll have to see.' Raphael looked at his watch. It wasn't yet 8 a.m. Lawyers wouldn't be in their offices until 9 a.m. at the earliest, probably later. 'Who's the investigating officer? Who should I call if I sort something out?'

'Inspector Lopez.' The boy handed him a card, just a little too quickly as though he'd been waiting for Raphael to ask that question.

Raphael looked at it. 'P.A. Lopez. Detective Inspector.' The police crest was in the top right-hand corner, a telephone number and a pager number below his name. The world blurred for a minute. Raphael saw himself standing staring at the card, but he couldn't move. He felt a shiver move down his spine as though he'd touched evil.

'Are you all right sir?'

158

Raphael blinked and looked up. 'Hmm.'

'I said, are you all right?'

'Yes, yes. I'll get back to you. It could be a while. Offices won't be …' Raphael's voice trailed off and he left.

Opposite the police station he saw a low wall. He crossed over and sat on it. The stone was cold through his thin trousers. He still had the business card in his hand. He flicked it back and forth across his thumbnail. Bloody Lopez was everywhere. It must be the same man, he thought, everything revolved around Colonel Almendrez Lopez. Raphael couldn't know for sure that the Colonel Lopez implicated in Manuel Chavez's murder was the same man now working for the police, the same man in charge of Rosario's case. But he knew it was. He just knew, and it made his blood run cold. The thought came back to him that maybe Josue wasn't innocent. Would the police have arrested him if they didn't have at least some evidence? What if he *had* killed Lola? If Raphael could be fooled and betrayed by his lover of two years, he could easily be fooled by this young man he barely knew, that he'd only met as a result of Lola's death. Nothing was certain anymore. The only thing he knew for sure about Josue was that he'd known Lola. He'd seen him with her on two occasions, in close proximity, in what might be called intimate poses. Whether they were lovers he didn't know. Friends – *quien sabe?* Had it all been a show for his benefit? – Could be. He couldn't trust anything now, not even his instincts – all the unbelievable things had happened. Lola had been killed. Lola had betrayed him. Josue had appeared as if by magic, right on cue. Andrea had been having an affair with Rosario. Rosario had been killed. Rosario had written about Manuel Chavez. Manuel had been killed by Lopez, and Rosario had the proof of it. Rosario had been murdered by Lopez. Now Lopez was 'investigating' Lola's murder. Full circle back to Lopez. Raphael had thought all the unbelievable things in his life had already happened.

But to get back to the matter in hand – did he believe Josue was innocent, and was he going to do anything to help him? Raphael had thought all along that Josue wasn't killer material. Not everything added up neatly with him, but was he a killer? Raphael had to say that no, he was not. Was he going to help him? That really wasn't up for discussion because Raphael was not the kind of man who could not help him. I had more reason to kill her than Josue, he thought, if they are going to pin it on anyone it should be me. He had to track down a lawyer he could afford. Or at least get some legal advice and try to keep tabs on what the state appointed lawyer did. Raphael put Lopez's card in his pocket and pulled out his cigarettes. The nicotine felt good. He inhaled slowly and deeply and felt himself grow calmer. At the taco stand near his office he bought a couple of *gorditas*. They were doughy and stuck to the roof of his mouth. He gagged on the first bite, but then the taste of the pork scratchings in them won him over.

He needed a phone and a phone book and while he hated to have to go into work, the newspaper office was the closest place with both those facilities.

'Hey Rafa, they said you were on holiday; funny looking holiday!'

'Hey man, you look like *mierda*! Must have been some party?'

Raphael took the jibes and continued thumbing through the phone book. He just hoped El Pelon didn't show up, because he didn't want to have to make up some explanation for his presence. He had two names of lawyers in mind; one he could remember and one he couldn't. He ran his finger down the list in the book and found the address for Daniel Hernandez. He wrote it down and kept looking. 'Arturo, Raul Arturo, but what was his surname?' Ortiz, that was it.

Some time later Raphael was across town in zone 9, sitting in the waiting room of R.A. Ortiz and Associates. The receptionist had said Mr Ortiz wouldn't be free all morning. Raphael had said he'd wait anyway. He wished he had a book to read or some paper to write on. Uncharacteristically he'd come out without his satchel. He felt bereft without it and he worried about the notes it contained. The notes he'd already made about the case – the links between the various players, questions to ask about Josue. They didn't really give much away, but he wouldn't want the police reading them, and clearly they, or someone, had access to his home. He was probably being watched. They would have seen him leave without his bag. His hands were clammy.

He tried to think logically about things, but his mind was a black hole, swallowing all the information and releasing nothing useful.

160

He had so many things to think about that he couldn't concentrate on anything. He didn't even know how long he'd been sitting there. The comfortable chair was starting to make him sleepy and a disturbing thought was coming to the fore of the confusion in his mind. What if he were to confess to Lola's murder? Get Josue off the hook. He had nothing to lose. He'd already lost everything, Lidia, Benigno, Lola, trust. How could he ever trust anyone again after what Lola had done? Could he trust Josue? How did he know he wasn't setting him up somehow? Getting him to pay for a lawyer, when he probably earned more than Raphael did, playing at that fancy bar. Raphael couldn't think like that. He couldn't live his life looking over his shoulder anymore; he'd done it for too many years. Always waiting for the knock at the door in the night, the hand on the shoulder dragging him down an alley, the story discrediting him and losing him his job, the security forces had many ways to destroy a man, not simply by killing him. He'd always expected something to happen sooner or later, he just hadn't expected the betrayal to be so close. But hadn't he always wondered what Lola saw in him? Why she'd picked him up in the first place? Had he been so desperate for love of some sort that he'd over-looked the rules of self-preservation?

No, he'd blatantly disregarded them. For so long he had wanted to just die, wanted nothing more than to join his wife and child, he'd given Lola an open invitation. His whole being proclaimed 'I don't care anymore' as though it were printed on one of those cheap T-shirts sold for tourists in the central market. He was exhausted, worn out with running and hiding, hiding mainly from himself and his feelings. If he were in jail there'd be nowhere left to run. There would be no need to look over his shoulder, they couldn't catch him twice. And there would be no need to hide.

A door opened and Arturo poked his head out. The receptionist inclined her head towards Raphael and said something that Raphael couldn't hear. Arturo looked over at him with no recognition on his face, but then it had been many years since they'd been at college together and they'd pretty much lost touch after that. He came round the desk and crossed the room.

'Raphael?'

'Yes.' He stood up and the lawyer extended his hand to shake, laying the other one across his back.

'Come in. I've got a few minutes to spare.' Arturo closed the door. 'I didn't recognise you.'

'Must be the beard.'

'Listen, I'd love to chat, fill in the missing years, but I really haven't got long. I take it this isn't a social call?'

'No.'

'Are you in trouble?' Arturo sounded concerned, in that practiced manner of lawyers.

'Yes, but not in the way you think. I need to know if you can represent a friend of mine and how much it would cost?'

'I'd need to know a bit more about the case. What's he been charged with? Has he been charged?'

'Murder.'

'*A la gran*! Nice crowd of people you mix with these days.'

'It's not like …'

'I'm sorry. I shouldn't joke about these things, but you've got to have a sense of humour, eh?'

'Why you never had one before?' said Raphael, staring at him.

Arturo looked suitably chastised and in a serious tone said, 'Tell me more.'

'In brief, my girlfriend was murdered.'

'Oh Raphael I'm …'

Raphael held up his hand to stop him. He needed his expertise not his sympathy. 'And well, this is going to sound ridiculous. It is ridiculous, but just bear with me. This man, Josue, I think they were having an affair. I'd seen them together a couple of times, but … Anyway, he claims to be her lover. And we met at the hospital when they'd found her body. And to cut a long story short, we were both interviewed by the police and both treated as suspects – the "killed her in a fit of jealousy" scenario. Josue was beaten up by the police and now he's been arrested. He called me early this morning and I went down to the station. They wouldn't let me see him, but they said he'd been charged and he needed a lawyer.'

'So, let me get this straight. You're here to try to obtain my services for a man you barely know, but who was probably having an affair with your girlfriend and who may well have killed her.'

162

'But I'm sure he didn't.'

'How can you be sure? Were you with him at the time of the murder? Do you even know anything about the man?'

'Well no, not much, but …'

'You always did have a soft spot for lost causes, didn't you Raphael? And you're going to pay for his defence too?'

'That depends.'

'On how much it costs? You can't afford it.' There was a waggish bite to Arturo's voice that didn't suit his profession.

Raphael sighed. Arturo had always been hard work. 'There's more to this Arturo. It's complicated.'

'Spare me your conspiracy theories.'

'I can see I came to the wrong man,' said Raphael jumping up and heading for the door.

Arturo stood up too. 'Wait. Just sit down for a minute. Look, we did each other lots of favours back in university, but I think I still owe you.'

'I don't need your charity, Arturo.'

'I wasn't about to offer charity. For you I might,' he stressed the word *might*, 'do this pro-bono, but not for someone I don't know, for someone you can't even vouch for and who probably did it, despite your intuition.'

Raphael tried to interrupt, but Arturo continued. 'Why don't I go down there, see what's what. Maybe this Josue character can afford me, if not I'll see if I can pull him one of the better state appointees.'

Raphael shrugged his consent.

'Your gratitude overwhelms me.'

'I didn't mean. It's just …'

'Hey, I'm looking out for your interests here. I don't care about this Josue character. What is his surname, anyway?'

'Chan.'

'OK. And I'll waive my usual fee for the service.'

'You don't need to do that.'

'I know I don't need to. Are you trying to piss me off? It's obvious you've been through the cane thresher with this. It's bad enough losing your girlfriend, and you may not be out of trouble yourself. You've been interviewed once; they could come back to you. I hope you realise it's not in your best interest to help this guy.'

Raphael nodded.

'Right.' Arturo thumbed through his desk diary, but without really looking at it, like he knew his schedule off by heart. 'I've got a small window of opportunity at 3 p.m. this afternoon.'

'That's great. Shall I meet you there?'

'No. I think it's best if you stay out of it for now. I'll meet you afterwards.'

'All right,' said Raphael.

'That El Salvadorean place?'

'No,' he said a bit too emphatically. That was where he and Lola had had their argument. He didn't want to go there again. 'How about the Pan American Hotel?'

The lawyer chuckled. 'You think I'm picking up the tab as well?' Raphael smiled. 'All right, I'll meet you there at 4.30 p.m.'

'Should I call the police station and let them know?' asked Raphael.

'No, I'll do that. I'll do it now. Who's the investigating officer?'

'Lopez.'

'Never heard of him. Have you got a number?'

Raphael handed over the card and Arturo made the call. When he hung up he said to Raphael, 'All set,' and looked at his watch as though he'd already used up too much of his valuable time.

Raphael stood up and extended his hand. 'Thank you, Arturo.'

'Don't mention it. See you later.'

17

Raphael stood outside the offices of Ortiz and Associates. He felt faint. He leant against the cool wall and felt the breeze coming up the stairwell. He just stood there, his mind blank, now there was nothing to do for a while. It was hours before he was to meet Arturo again and find out what the situation was with Josue. He should probably go home and rest, but just thinking about getting the two buses and the walk involved and then coming back downtown again, exhausted him. He slumped to the ground, his back against the wall. His head throbbed lightly. His whole body ached.

Eventually he stood up. The blood rushed to his head and he nearly toppled over, closing his eyes until the flash of stars and colours cleared. He must have been there some time; his joints were stiff, and no feeling was left in his buttocks. There was no longer a breeze blowing up the stairs, but the rising heat of midday. Reluctantly Raphael went down the stairs and out into the glare; he didn't want to still be outside the office when Arturo left. He shaded his eyes and looked around him. He had no recollection of how he'd got to the office. Nothing around him looked familiar, but then it was not a part of the city he knew well. Since he didn't know which way to go, he turned left; force of habit, they had always done that in the guerrillas when they didn't know which way to take, because what self respecting guerrilla could ever turn right – *siempre a la izquierda.*

After a while he saw a small park, an open space with trees and benches. At the entrance was a man selling drinks. Raphael bought a bottle of a very orange fizzy drink and some banana chips and sat on the first bench he came to. The tree provided a little shade, but it was still hot. He took a gulp of the drink. It was cool and sweet, just what he needed. The fried *platanos* were already making the paper bag greasy. Raphael didn't really want to eat, but he forced one down. It oozed oil inside his mouth as he chewed it. He continued to eat them for the satisfying crunch of each first bite.

Arturo's words came back to him. 'I hope you realise it's not in your best interest to help this guy.' Wasn't it? Perhaps it was the best thing he could do. The only thing he could do. Not help Josue get off, but set him free, take the rap, offer himself up as the sacrificial lamb. If he didn't, what would his life be? He'd always be paranoid. Why not take the power out of their hands and give himself up willingly? He'd wanted control of his life, now he could take it. If he chose of his own volition to say he'd murdered Lola, while knowing he hadn't, wouldn't he have won? Wouldn't he have won against the enemy that had caused the death of Lidia, that blew up his only son, that killed his lover? Wouldn't it royally stick two fingers up at all of them and finally take the bitterness out of the bile that had churned inside him for all these years? It would.

Raphael believed it would. And with those thoughts swirling in his mind and bringing a crazy calmness to him, he lay back on the bench and fell asleep.

Raphael woke up confused. He sat up slowly, blinking his eyes. His back hurt from lying rigid on the bench. His right leg had taken the weight of the other leg and pins and needles ran through it as he got up. He rubbed his face; it felt scorched and sweaty. He looked at his watch. 'Shit.' It was past four. He'd never make it to the Pan American by 4.30. He stumbled up, feeling drunk, dizzy from dehydration, hunger and disorientation. He made his way back to the entrance of the park. The drinks seller was still there. Raphael bought another soda and asked him how to get to the centre. He hurried in the direction indicated and got a bus.

Arturo sat sipping iced tea and looking at his watch.

Raphael rushed in. 'I'm sorry.'

'It's all right. What happened to you? You're all red in the face.'

Raphael sat down. 'I …' no, he didn't want to tell Arturo he'd fallen asleep in a park. He knew what he'd think of that. 'I got caught up in some stuff, lost track of time. So how did it go? What's going on?'

Arturo took a sip of his drink, caught the eye of the waiter and beckoned him over. The waiters at the Pan American Hotel wore traditional Indian dress, which Raphael didn't approve of. He thought it belittled them for the tourists and affluent, especially as most of them weren't Indian. But the hotel served good food, and it was central and the first place he'd thought of. Lola used to eat there a lot when they had foreign visitors. In fact, it dawned on him that they had eaten there after the conference when he'd been trying to apologise for making a scene about Josue, but he didn't want to remember Lola just now. The waiter stood by their table expectantly.

'Lemonade with soda,' Raphael ordered.

'Do you want something to eat?' asked Arturo.

'Yes actually.' Without looking at the menu Raphael ordered a typical plate with strips of beef, mashed black beans and fried bananas. Arturo ordered nothing.

'So,' said Raphael, leaning forward.

'Well he's in a state, very nervous. No, scared out of his mind actually. For what it's worth, I don't think he did it. He kept saying what a good man you were, and such a friend and how good you were to be helping him.' Arturo took another sip. 'I offered to represent him for a reduced fee, but he doesn't have the money. But he was quite adamant that he didn't want you to help him out financially, that he didn't want you paying for a lawyer.'

'Are you just saying that?'

'No. Come on Raphael, what do you take me for. You know me better than that, even after all these years.'

Yes, thought Raphael, I know you. Arturo had always been a slightly smarmy character. Raphael didn't know how they'd ever become friends, but somehow, they'd hooked up despite studying different subjects. Arturo had always had his eye to the main chance, being interested in money and position more than anything else. Raphael was his complete opposite, an idealist wanting to save the world. It was clear who'd come off better, but was he happy, Raphael wondered. His drink arrived and he sipped it demurely, though he could have gladly gulped it down and ordered another. 'So what did you arrange? How did you leave things? What's going to happen?'

'Take it easy. I said I'd organise a state appointed lawyer. I already called the public defenders' office and got someone I know vaguely. He's not bad; he'll do his best for him. Should be there already while Josue makes a statement.'

'And what have they got on him? How's his case looking?'

'Not so good. They weren't supposed to tell me anything as I'm not going to represent him, but I managed to ascertain ...' he gestured with his hand going under the table, 'they say he has no alibi for the time of death, but that's circumstantial. More worryingly, they claim to have found his fingerprints on the murder weapon.'

'What?'

Arturo raised his eyebrows, as if to say keep your voice down.

'They've found a murder weapon?'

'A knife apparently.'

'But surely, his fingerprints?'

'You and me both know there are any number of ways they could have got on there without Josue ever having touched it. Hey, it's enough that they say his prints are on it.'

The waiter brought Raphael's food. After the first tentative bite he realised he was ravenous. Apart from snacks, he hadn't eaten all day, and he felt like he'd been awake for a week. Between bites he asked, 'Will I be able to see him?'

'Not until after the case is heard and he's remanded for trial.'

'When will that be?'

'They'll hear it on Monday. Bad luck being arrested so close to the weekend. He gets to languish in a police cell a couple of extra days.'

'I doubt luck had anything to do with it,' said Raphael.

'Well, much as I'd like to sit here and watch you eat, I do have things to do. Call me if you need any help yourself.'

Raphael nodded. He knew what Arturo meant.

'And if I were you, I'd stay well out of it. Be glad they arrested someone other than you, but then you've never taken my advice.'

Raphael smiled. No, he hadn't and he probably never would. They moved in different circles, had different views of the world. Their paths hadn't crossed in over twenty-five years, and Raphael suspected they would never cross again, whatever happened.

Arturo tossed a twenty-quetzal note on the table. 'That should pretty much cover it.'

Raphael made to get up.

'No, don't get up.' Arturo gripped his shoulder. 'Take care Raphael. Stay out of trouble.'

18

Raphael wanted to go home. He was so tired and he'd done all he could do for now. He'd arranged a lawyer for Josue and since he wasn't allowed to see him nothing else could be done until after the weekend. He thought about just going down to the police station and confessing, getting it over with, but he knew the police would keep him up all night questioning him and he didn't have the strength. And he would have to have his wits about him. If he wanted his confession to be convincing, he'd have to be alert and keep his story straight, even though he imagined the police would be more than happy to accept his confession. But there was another reason to wait, Lola's funeral. Raphael felt that he had to go to it, even though it would be painful. Since he'd found out she'd betrayed him he wasn't sure what he felt about her, but he had to go. He had to put her to rest. And Andrea would expect it. The thought of Andrea reminded him that he also had to go to the wake.

Wearily Raphael followed Andrea's directions to her mother's house. Twilight was falling and street lamps began to flicker on. The day was in that hazy zone between wakefulness and sleep, as was Raphael. In the not too far distance he could hear traffic, but the neighbourhood felt secluded and cut off. He should have gone home to change, he must look terrible, not to mention what he smelled like after sweating in the sun all afternoon. He had taken advantage of the plush bathrooms at the Pan American to wash a little and run water through his hair, but even so he wasn't going to make much of an impression. He tucked in his shirt more firmly and put on the crumpled jacket he'd been carrying round all day. He felt like he'd been travelling all week, tramping round the dusty city, from one bus to another. The ground beneath him moved up and down as though he'd just got off a boat. Exhaustion was starting to set in again after the brief respite of dinner at the hotel. He should have brought some food with him too, as a gift for the family, but it couldn't be helped.

He saw the big black bow on the house before he noticed anything else. He registered that he was in a clean, affluent area, not unlike where Andrea lived, but he was too worn out to focus on much other than finding the right house. When Andrea had called to tell him the arrangements, he had planned in his head to arrive later at the wake, at the time when most visitors might be expected, so that he could pass through and pay his respects with the minimum of fuss and conversation. He realised with a glance at his watch, though he already knew it, that he was too early. They might not even be ready to receive guests. That would be embarrassing. But as he went up the path, he saw that the door was open.

Raphael stepped through the open doorway into the darkened hall. He immediately smelt copal, which surprised him as the incense was more commonly used by Indians than *ladinos*. A wave of olfactory memory swept over him. Yellow flowers, trees, the dense smoke of copal, Benigno's tiny coffin lowered into the ground. An older man just to the right of the door welcomed him and ushered him down the hallway towards a back room. As he shook his hand, Raphael recognised him as Andrea's husband from the photo she had shown him. What a long time ago that seemed, that pleasant afternoon before events had completely overtaken them. He went down the hall to the back room. It was full of flowers, white and yellow, the colour typically used for death. The smell of incense was overpowering. The curtains of the room were drawn, blocking out the last remnants of daylight. Candles dotted around added to the atmosphere though little to the illumination. Raphael immediately felt hot in the claustrophobic room. The candles were throwing off a lot of heat. Combined with the pungent incense it was a heady mix. It took Raphael back to Indian churches in the highlands with their myriad candles on the floor. Indian women kneeling on hard earth floors, rocking back and forth in prayer, mumbling beneath their breath. He heard again the incantations, like a chant that lulled him, '*ri ralma' ri lok'laj Benigno. Beniigno.*'

Andrea sat just inside the door. She stood up as he entered, taking his outstretched hand in both of hers and then kissing him on both cheeks. As Raphael had feared, he was the only person there who was not close family. Andrea took his hand and led him over to the older, distinguished looking woman sitting at the other end. Close up he could tell she'd been crying. She kept her eyes on the thin cotton handkerchief that she was unfolding and screwing up in the hands in her lap. Andrea leant forward and whispered in her ear and she looked up at Raphael.

'I'm so sorry,' he said, offering his hand. She took it limply. Raphael was glad of the dim light so she wouldn't see his dishevelled appearance and bloodshot eyes, but she was too consumed by grief even to notice who he was. There seemed to be nothing else to say. He half turned to face the coffin. He'd expected an open coffin but was greeted by the smoothness of dark wood with a simple bouquet of flowers on top. Naïve of him, even in the cool storage of the morgue, after all these days Lola wouldn't be a pleasant vista for most people. And yet, Raphael realised he had wanted to hold her one more time, hold her hand, kiss her forehead.

Andrea had returned to her seat. He went and sat next to her and took her hand. They sat that way in silence for some time. Raphael tried to think good thoughts about Lola. He pictured her in the café the first time they'd met, in full flow at a workshop, naked in bed after they'd made love, making him coffee, but the main thought that kept intruding on all the others was, how could she have betrayed him and why? Why? He was no risk to anyone – a destroyed man, a grieving ex-guerrilla who'd given up the fight. What had forced her to inform on him? Who had coerced her? He couldn't believe she had done it of her own volition, or just for money. But then when they'd met, she hadn't known him, had she? She'd had no feelings or emotions to interfere with business. How long had it taken her to fall in love with him? If in fact she had. How long had she struggled, fought that dichotomy of loving the man she was obliged to watch and report on? She'd pulled it off so well, so seamlessly. Had she died because of him, because she'd refused to carry on informing any longer? Because she'd told them she couldn't do it anymore? Had he then chosen that moment to accuse her of infidelity? The precise moment when she'd chosen love over obligation? Chosen him over whatever her assignment was? Had he spurned her just when she had made the sacrifice for him, and so led to her ultimate sacrifice? Had he somehow caused this? Had he caused the death of another woman?

He'd always thought it was somehow his fault that Lidia had died, wished it had been him in her place, felt the guilt of the survivor, and then had it made manifest ten times over when Benigno died – he should have watched him better, if only he hadn't taken his eyes off him, if only he could have watched him every second of every day he could have stopped that bomb from falling. But he could fix it now. One simple act could wipe the slate clean.

Andrea squeezed his arm. He looked at her and realised his eyes were blurred with tears. He wiped his face and stood up. He heard

171

voices in the passageway, and he moved towards the door. Andrea stood too and followed him out into the kitchen.

'How are you Raphael?'

'All right, and you?'

She shrugged.

'Your mother seems …'

'Yes. I'm not sure she'll get over this. It's not the death, it's the nature of it. She never expected to outlive her children.'

'No one does,' said Raphael.

She squeezed his arm again as though realising how well he knew that fact. 'I have to get back,' she said. 'Mother shouldn't be alone.'

Raphael nodded.

'Have you made a decision?' she asked.

Yes, he'd made a decision, but not with regards to what Andrea was thinking about. She meant the photo still hidden in her house. He shook his head.

'But you're OK? You'll be at the funeral tomorrow?'

'Yes,' he said, 'we'll talk then. He recognised that she was indirectly asking if he'd had more problems with the police. 'They've arrested Josue,' he whispered.

'Good.'

'Good?'

'Maybe he did it Raphael. I want whoever did it locked away forever. He should never see the light of day and even that would be too good for him.'

Her vehemence shocked him, but now was not the time to argue with her. 'I'll see you tomorrow Andrea.'

19

Raphael breathed in the night air, enjoyed the slightly damp coolness of it. He walked slowly up to the main street, avoiding the nearest bus stop. He needed space. What were they going to do about the photo? On its own it didn't really prove anything, but

Raphael had to consider Andrea's safety. Presumably no one knew she had it, but was it only a matter of time before Lopez realised that it was still out there somewhere? Before he realised he'd searched the wrong house, the wrong sister? Raphael couldn't allow that to happen. There had been too much death already.

If he exposed Lopez in a newspaper article he would surely be killed. But if Raphael didn't expose him, would he go on killing? Would he go on looking for people who might be able to link him to crimes? And could Raphael live with himself if he let Lola's murderer get away with it? He could be wrong about that though, that could just be his overactive mind making links that weren't there. But he was sure now that Lopez had been involved in the death of Manuel Chavez and consequently of Rosario Recinos. There had to be a way to bring that into the open.

If he sent it anonymously to the legal authorities, it would no doubt be covered up or simply overlooked in the swamp of murder cases. What if he sent it to the United Nations task force? But they had more than enough work investigating war crimes and extra judicial killings. They had years of work ahead of them, and so far, it looked like military personnel would be exempt from prosecution, or at least the higher ranks. Was Lopez superior enough, protected enough to escape justice? Would his new job in the police enable him to get away with his crimes indefinitely? I don't even know for sure it's the same man, thought Raphael.

The story needed to come out with no hint of who'd supplied the information. Easier said than done. If Lopez had killed Rosario because he knew he had information on him, then any new information must have come via Rosario, mustn't it? Wouldn't that tighten the net to him and Andrea? Or maybe Rosario's colleagues would come under suspicion. But clearly Lopez was not a man who would allow himself to be caught. But that is not my problem, thought Raphael. If I confess to Lola's murder I'll atone for my mistakes, my lack of vigilance. Fate can take care of Lopez.

Raphael slumped on a bus seat and curled up, his head against the window. The bus was fairly empty though a few people were still heading home from work. He must have dozed off. He woke with a dry mouth and a crick in his neck from leaning against the window. He stretched his neck to the right by tilting his head and heard the bones pop.

He arrived home before he was able to come up with any solution to the dilemma of the photo. He wished they'd never found it. Maybe, just maybe, it gave a reason for Rosario's death, but did it help when he couldn't do anything about it? Raphael wanted to just lie down on the bed in his clothes and go to sleep, but he forced himself to get undressed and have a shower. The water was warm at first and soothing but within minutes it turned cold. Raphael quickly took the soap off his body and got out. He shivered though the night and his house were warm. The house was stuffy from having been closed all day, but he didn't have the energy to open the door to the balcony. Half dry, he dropped the towel on the floor and eased under the sheet.

Hours later he woke from a nightmare. Lola bound and gagged, blindfolded in a dark cellar. A man had a gun to her head. 'Will you change your mind?' he asked her.

'No.'

He shoved the gun in her ribs. 'Will you?'

'No.'

He put the gun to her head and released the safety. 'Now?'

'No.'

He removed the gag, forced open her mouth and put the gun into it. Slowly he pulled back the cock and asked her again. 'Are you going to keep working for us?'

Lola shook her head. The man pulled the trigger just as Raphael came running in saying, 'Tell them Lola, tell them anything they want to know about me, I don't care.' He saw the back of her head hit the wall.

Raphael sat up. The sheet clung to him. He was soaked in sweat. His tongue was parched and his hands were shaking. He reached for the cigarettes by the bedside and with difficulty lit one. He watched its tip glow red in the dark and thought of the twin gods in the dungeons of hell, how they tricked the Lords of Xilbalba by putting fireflies at the end of their cigars rather than lighting them, and that way they burned all night but never got any shorter. The thought made Raphael smile, relax a little. He watched the red glow get brighter as he inhaled.

He was even more convinced that he had to confess to Lola's murder – nothing to do with Josue. It had to do with him and only him. He'd survived when he shouldn't have, and now Lola may have died because of him. He had to pay for it. He couldn't think logically that if Lola had been informing on him it was her choice, her decision, if she'd died as a result it wasn't his fault. He couldn't think that maybe the file of memos from Lola was a fake, planted by the police or Lopez's cronies just to make him do something reckless. He couldn't think that maybe her death had nothing to do with him, that maybe it was just one of those things that happened. People got killed for senseless reasons, for no reason. Lola was one of them, as simple as that. He couldn't think that maybe, just maybe Josue *had* killed her, out of jealousy, or insanity, or because the time and place was right or maybe even because someone had paid him. He could only think that everything revolved around Colonel Almendrez Lopez and Rosario, that Lola's death must be connected. That she'd been killed because she'd refused to pass on information about him anymore and so it was his fault she'd died. Raphael could only think that he had been the cause of her death and so he had to pay for it.

The more he thought about it, the more he realised it was the only solution. It was an idea both unsettling and invigorating. An idea that could change his whole life and Josue's. An idea too scary to put into words. The police were just looking for someone to blame, anyone, so they could close the case. For now, they had picked on Josue, but if he confessed, they would leave Josue alone. They weren't interested in the truth. Raphael was sure they could find evidence against him, or plant evidence. He'd inadvertently lied about not being back in the city on the Saturday night. All he had to do was wait for the police to discover that then admit that he'd lied about where he was. Come to think of it, if they'd done any investigating at all they would have found out that lie by now. Why hadn't they been back to interview him again?

Raphael lit another cigarette and sat up straighter in bed. He was wide-awake working things out. There was the note to Lola the police had already found and believed implicated him in her death. Yes, there was enough circumstantial evidence for them not to dismiss his confession. But wouldn't that be playing right into their hands – confessing to a crime he hadn't committed? Raphael didn't care any more. It didn't matter. He was worn out, tired of trying to make a life when his life had gone. Whatever the truth, whatever the real story, connected or unconnected, Raphael had the opportunity to do something good. He could save a young man's life, give him another chance, and at the same time pay the penance he owed, make his libation. He had nothing to lose, he'd lost Lidia, he'd lost Benigno, and he'd lost Lola, all through his own carelessness. The worst he could get would be twenty years or so for manslaughter. Wasn't his life already like being in prison? He could write in jail, and if he died before his time, well so what, it would hurry him on the journey he was eager to take to Lidia and Benigno. Yes, it was a thought that made his insides curdle and his heart race and yet it calmed him like an absolution. Raphael would submit to his penance. So, relieved of his burden through contrition, he fell asleep again.

It was late when he woke, very late. He looked for his watch and found it on the floor with his clothes. He only had an hour to get to the funeral.

As Raphael looked through his wardrobe for something suitable to wear, he thought how fed up he was of rushing around. His life had been a disaster since Lola had died. It would be a relief to be in jail, comforting to have a set routine, no buses to catch or phone calls to make, no waking up at strange hours not knowing where he was. He would wake up at the same time every day, eat the same breakfast, probably do the same monotonous task, have his light turned out for him at the same time every night. No decisions, no questions, no responsibilities. He wouldn't even have to worry about what to wear. It would be a salve on his wounds, a salvation of sorts.

He pulled out a navy suit he hadn't worn in years and laid it on the bed. Now was the time to shave off his beard. It was a new beginning, a new era in his life; it called for a certain rite, a symbolic removal of his past, a fresh face to the world. As the dark hair fell against the white porcelain, he felt his worries fall with it. He'd found a way out.

Raphael tied his black tie. He hated wearing ties, always had, couldn't bear the suffocating tightness of it around his throat, but now the constriction felt good – a restriction chosen, just like the cell bars would be. The suit was loose on him, but he couldn't see the full effect, as he had no full-length mirror. He combed his hair in front of the small piece of glass in the bathroom. Clean-shaven he didn't look too bad, almost handsome. The hours of sleep had improved his appearance from the day before to almost human. But it wasn't the sleep so much, as the decision. He straightened his back and felt more of a man than he had in years.

20

San Bartolome was already full when Raphael arrived. He sat near the back and looked around him. It was a small church, fairly traditional, candles dotted around in front of the various saints. Lights sparkled over the head of the Virgin like Christmas decorations. The air was cool and humid. Light came in from windows behind the chancel, but the church was still penumbral. Raphael looked around to see if he recognised anyone. He was not well placed as he could only see the backs of people, not their faces. Soon he gave up. He only knew a handful of Lola's friends and colleagues anyway. Now he knew why, he thought bitterly. She couldn't let him into her life because her life was passing on information about him, from the beginning that had been the basis of their relationship, she had been asked, told, forced, or paid, to betray him, befriend him, sleep with him – had that been part of her assignment too? Or an optional extra? And let a third party know … know what? If he engaged in criminal acts? If he missed his wife and son? What his innermost thoughts were? If his poetry or teaching might incite rebellion? If he was somehow a threat to the state?

She couldn't let him meet her family and friends, her colleagues, couldn't let her guard down, what if someone said something they shouldn't, what if she did? Had Andrea been the only one Lola had confided her feelings in, or had she been duped too?

The service had started while Raphael had been thinking these thoughts, but it passed in a haze. It was as if he wasn't really there, like someone had given him a drug so he could hear and see everything, but not experience it, an anaesthetic, he was conscious, but not feeling. He heard people talking about Lola, her good qualities, her beauty, her passion for life. Her colleagues talked about her valuable work for *La Frente*, what a loss she would be, how vivacious she'd been. Raphael felt only anger. Now he'd never know why she'd done it. He'd never be able to confront her. And if she had denied it would he have believed her? Of course, she would say the notes had been planted. How could he possibly believe that of her? She loved him.

The bell rang. Mass was said. Raphael went through the motions of sitting and kneeling, kneeling and standing, crossing himself. Unconsciously he mumbled the words he'd known all his life, and then he was mumbling words in Quiche, the words they'd said when they had laid Lidia to rest, the words he hadn't been able to say then, '*ri alma' ri lok'laj Lidia, xe' jawjechi' xpewi.*' He didn't perceive the man standing next to him who looked at him strangely. No one else noticed that Raphael was saying something different. And then they were carrying out the coffin.

Outside the sun blinded Raphael. It somehow wasn't seemly that the day should be so gloriously bright and sunny, so full of life; that the world went on without pausing to acknowledge Lola's passing. The sun gods didn't care and the rain spirits were oblivious, she wasn't worthy of their tears. The coffin had already been loaded into the hearse and Lola's family were gathering in cars behind for the drive to the cemetery. Raphael walked around the church to a side street and lit a cigarette. He was reluctant to go to the cemetery but felt obliged. He also thought it would do him good to see her actually lowered into the ground, gone forever, nothing but a memory. He walked further along the street to where it intersected a main road and there, he hailed a taxi.

It was pleasant walking down the avenue into the cemetery. Raphael's feelings and the beauty of the day combined to make things even more surreal. A very slight breeze blew against his bare face and he ran his fingers over his smooth chin. He felt a strange mixture of sadness, anger, and release, but he had to let the anger go. Being angry with Lola now would achieve nothing. He was doing the right thing; he had to concentrate on that. Cut off from the noise of the city, he could have been far away in the Mayan ruins of the *selva*; birds sang in the trees, the aroma of flowers starting to dry and wither hung in the air, a lizard ran across the path in front of him. The heat radiated up from the gravel, and the glare reflected off the white headstones, producing ethereal haloes. It dawned on him that this might be the last such walk he would have, out in the open air. It made him want to find a place to sit, away from the main path, and write poetry.

Raphael was roused somewhat from these peaceful thoughts by the entrance of Lola's cortege. It crawled past him and he made note of where it stopped, increasing his pace slightly to arrive at the same time as Lola's coffin was laid on the ground next to the newly dug grave.

Andrea looked up and smiled at him. Not a smile of joy, but of recognition, of relief that he was there. He moved closer, though he didn't want to impinge on the familial positions closest to the grave. The priest arrived as if from nowhere and re-aligned his stole and found and re-found the place in his prayer book over and over, while more people gathered. He looked young, and nervous, as though this were his first funeral and he was unsure of the words, but when he spoke his voice was strong and confident with no hesitation.

Raphael felt the sweat around his hairline and the stiffness of his collar. He hoped no one would faint, done up as they were in their ensembles of black. On the other side of the group, in the background, he thought he saw Josue, but it couldn't be. Josue was in jail and he was sure they wouldn't have let him out for the funeral. It was just his mind playing tricks on him.

'We therefore commit her body to the ground; earth to earth, ashes to ashes ...'

The mention of ashes sent Raphael back to the burning of Benigno's belongings, the smell of burning and ash.

The smell of burning fills the air. It is tinged with chrysanthemums. I don't know where they found the flowers. I see yellow everywhere. I'm covered in black; soot smudges my clothes and face. I hold Benigno's corn doll. It's just a

179

dried out husk of corn. I rub the withered ears with my thumb and it crumbles. I throw it into the fire where it sparks and crackles.

Raphael's nostrils were filled with the smell of smoke. His nose hair tingled with the memory of the singeing. He felt the pain again, that heart-rending agony of the loss of his son. For that he shed tears, not for Lola. Had he shed any genuine tears for her, or only for the other sadnesses of his life? It didn't matter. He would make his confession and pay his penance for all of them.

The priest said the *Nunc Dimittis* in Latin as the coffin was lowered and invited them to throw in the earth. Lola's mother went first, stooping slowly and stiffly, looking even older than she had the night before. Andrea and the rest of the family followed. There was a pause. Andrea looked at Raphael. He bent and picked up a handful of soil. It was moist and cooler than he would have expected in this heat. He pressed his fingers into its earthy dampness. At last he could bury them properly. It was no longer Lola he was saying farewell to, but Lidia. He saw her grave by the tree, the wild flowers on top, limp from him holding them too tightly, and it was Lidia he said goodbye to. *'Que descanse en paz querida.'*

Raphael looked around at the small crowd that was dispersing. He noticed the fat man from *La Frente* he'd met in Chimaltenango. The man nodded in recognition. Raphael remembered the strange conversation they'd had in the restaurant. What had he been trying to warn him about? Had he known that Lola was betraying him? Had he subtly been trying to warn him away from Lola? No, that was paranoid nonsense. Probably he hadn't been trying to warn him of anything. He just didn't want him snooping around his Presbytery, his work, making trouble for them by his presence. The man smiled in a genuine way as he turned and walked away.

Raphael wanted to speak with Andrea, but he could see people going up to her, giving expressions of condolence, pressing palms and rubbing backs. He leaned against a tree and waited. His gaze wandered over the graves. It was a restful scene. Even the movement of mourners leaving didn't disturb it. They talked in muted tones and walked away discreetly. Soon there was no one left but Andrea as the gravediggers moved in to start filling the hole. She watched them. Raphael left her to her moment of solitude. She looked up then and saw him. She walked over.

'Are you coming back to the house?'

'No, I don't think so.'

Andrea nodded as though she understood his reluctance to be in a house full of people he didn't know, reminiscing about the woman he loved.

'I like it here,' he said.

She nodded again. 'Will I see you soon?'

'I don't know. I'm going away.'

'That's good. I think that's good for you. Where?'

'I don't know yet.' He wanted to tell her what he was going to do. During the committal he had made his mind up finally. He was going to confess. He wanted to tell her, but he thought she would try and talk him out of it. And he remembered her words when he'd told her Josue had been arrested, her vehemence, her desire for vengeance on the man she seemed convinced had killed her sister. He didn't want her thinking, even for a second, that his confession somehow implied guilt. It did, but not of the crime of killing Lola. He wanted Andrea's respect. He didn't want their newfound friendship spoilt so soon by doubts.

'Will you call me when you get back?' she asked quietly.

'Yes.'

'I'm sorry, Raphael.'

'What do you have to be sorry about?'

'That you lost someone else.'

He shrugged. 'It's not your fault. And so did you.'

She smiled. 'I'd better go. People will be wondering where the hostess is.' She turned to walk away, then turned back. 'What about the photo?' she whispered.

'Just hold onto it for now. Can you do that? I think it will be safe if you don't talk to anyone about it.'

'All right, Raphael, but we have to do something, don't we?'

'We will. We will.' He took her arm. 'Just let me think. We have to find the best way.'

Andrea nodded.

Raphael stayed a long time in the cemetery. He watched the gravediggers finish their job, smoothing the freshly dug earth. He watched other mourners come and go, taking flowers to gravesides. And he watched the dusk fall, the sky moving through its kaleidoscope of blues until it reached the dark cobalt he loved.

21

Today was the day Raphael was going to confession, but first he would get his things in order. He was thinking rationally and practically again. He couldn't see any hint of madness in his actions, only the obvious conclusion to a terrible time, and horrific events.

Having drunk coffee with a couple of cigarettes out on his balcony, enjoying the sights, sounds and smells of the *barrio* waking up, he set about cleaning his apartment. First, he went through his belongings and selected the few things he would want with him in prison. It didn't amount to much – a few books including the *Pop Vuh* and his beloved copy of Otto Rene Castillo's poems. His own poems and writings, collected in notebooks and a thick handful of papers held together with an elastic band. He thought about the letters and poems of his that he'd found at Lola's apartment. Where were they now – still at her place? With the police? Or had they been returned to the family? Should he go back and look for them? He still had a key to her apartment. No, he was finished with Lola; he didn't want any memories of her. He didn't want any reminders of his life before this day, nothing to remind him of Lidia or Benigno. Nothing from his life as a guerrilla or as a journalist. Today was the first day of a new life, without memories. He was expunging them by his act of contrition. He felt the cloth cross around his neck with the silver *milagro* from Lola. He was about to remove it, but he hesitated. Best to keep one thing as a reminder of the transitory nature of love. Nothing is forever.

He put a few more things in the box, his favourite pen, the watch from his father and all the blank writing paper and notebooks he could find. Then he sealed the box and set it on the table, labelling it 'Raphael Sifuentes – to be picked up.' He pulled all the file boxes out of the closet and without looking in any of them stacked them by the front door. He was going to need more empty boxes. He went out the corner shop to plead with them for all the boxes they had. As soon as he was out on the street, he smelt fresh tortillas from the stand on the corner, but he had no thoughts of food. He picked up the boxes and went home.

It did not take long for him to pack up the rest of the things he didn't want. He stacked them by the door with the file boxes. Then he packed the rest of his books and stacked those boxes against the wall with a sign on top labelled "library". His clothes also went in a box with a sign saying "charity" though he considered most of them too shabby for even the homeless to want. He swiftly cleaned the apartment and had a shower. Then he went out to hire a car.

Raphael had to go some way on the bus before he got to a car rental place as no one in his neighbourhood could afford to rent cars even if they'd wanted to. Most places were near the airport or on the *periferico* near the business and tourist districts. It was a beautiful day, clear blue sky and sun. The weather perfectly matched Raphael's mood and resolve. Everything was going to be fine. Having secured a car, he drove back to his apartment, loaded up the boxes and drove to the city dump.

The dump was a desolate place even in sunlight and despite the growth of communities around it building hope out of nothing and lives out of the *basura*. He drove as far as he could, to where the trucks came and opened their backs and let the detritus fall out down the ravine. The smell was terrible. He took off his shirt and tied it over his nose and mouth. Raphael unloaded the boxes and laboriously dragged or carried them to the edge. Some he kicked over, watching the little cloud of dust that rose up as they tumbled down the hillside, bouncing off the collection of other people's rubbish. But somehow that didn't seem enough. He took the lid off a box of files and flung it out over the precipice like a Frisbee. He watched it glide, rising and falling in a spiral with the heat vents from the smouldering rubbish, which lifted shafts of hot air like the thermals that the vultures rode. There were several *zopilotes* circling overhead in a menacing way, hoping perhaps that Raphael would jump to his death, or produce an animal carcass from his boxes.

He threw lid after lid, like a child with a new toy watching them spiral. He was tempted to throw out the papers in the same way, to watch them flutter and spin to their final resting place below, but he wanted something more terminal for them. He took out a handful and carefully lit the corner with his lighter. He delighted in the flames, feeling the heat near his face and growing closer to his fingers. He dropped the last piece just in time and peered over to watch it tumble away sending out little sparks as it rolled. He lit handful after handful, throwing them over the edge and watching the paper curl and blacken, the large pieces of soot soaring and swirling. The smuts soon covered him. His arms were dusted with ash; dark soot speckled the hair on his arms, his white vest looked like a soldier's daubed in camouflage paint.

The fire was cleansing. Raphael felt like he was ridding himself of everything that had gone before. The sour smell of burning was like honeysuckle, the crackle of the burning cardboard like the chuckling clatter of cicadas. He was covered in ash, just like he had been after Benigno's death, but this time he was healed by it. This time it purged like it never had before. He watched the final box go over in a cascade of sparks and flames, watched it roll down the hill setting light to other rubbish, leaving specks of orange in its wake. Raphael wished it were night-time, so the fire's glow might be highlighted against the blue of the night sky.

Raphael untied the shirt and wiped his face. He was soaked with sweat from the flames and the heat of the sun. As he opened the car door he caught a glimpse of his face in the side mirror and gasped. He was thrown back to another time. Not his own face, he'd never seen his own face in camouflage. They had no mirrors in the mountain camps. But the faces of his comrades, smeared with shoe polish and ashes, charcoal taken from the fires and rubbed over faces providing a flimsy disguise. He spat on his hand and rubbed his face, but it only made things worse. Raphael realised he couldn't return the car looking like that. He returned to his apartment, showered again and put on clean clothes from the charity box, putting the sooty clothes in the one remaining rubbish bag by the door, which he threw in the dumpster on his way out.

Raphael returned the car. There was only one thing left to do before he went to the police station. He walked to his favourite restaurant near the newspaper office and ordered chicken soup. They made the soup there just how he liked it, watery but full of taste, chunks of chicken floating beside the pieces of corn cob, coriander, carrots and potatoes, specks of bright red chilli. And with it came as many tortillas as a man could eat. Raphael inhaled the scent, warm coriander, a hint of chilli condensed on his nose and he wiped it away. He ate slowly, tasting every flavour that combined to make the whole. He wondered what the food would be like in prison, if they ever got chicken soup. More likely it would be tortillas and beans most of the time. But Raphael was used to that. His guerrilla training would become useful again.

Raphael stood calmly outside the café, rolled a cigarette and lit it with unshaking hands, then he walked over to the police station and asked to see Inspector Lopez. This time he was not made to wait but shown almost immediately into an interview room. The Inspector came in. He was shorter than Raphael had expected given what he knew of the nature of the man, but he had dark eyes, deeply set and slightly too close together. He certainly resembled the man in the photo hidden at Andrea's. So this was the infamous Pedro Almendrez Lopez, killer of highland pastors, kidnapper and conspirator. He seemed a rather pathetic man.

'How can we help you Mr Sifuentes?' His voice was high pitched and monotone. He made no effort to add inflection to the question.

'I think it's more how I can help you.'

'Really? Do you have more information concerning the Dolores Rodriguez case?'

'You could say that. I wish to make a confession.'

'To her murder?' Lopez seemed incredulous while keeping his icy composure.

'Yes.'

'We already have someone in custody. He's been charged.'

'You have the wrong man.'

'Are you implying my investigation was flawed?' Lopez said with annoyance, slightly raising one eyebrow.

Raphael had thought Lopez would welcome his confession. 'We both know the police sometimes make mistakes.'

'But you claimed in your original statement that you were in Chimaltenango at the time of Miss Rodriguez's death.'

'I was mistaken. I lied. If you'd checked my statement at all you'd know I was back in the capital on the Saturday night.' Raphael was goading him now, pointing out his mistakes, telling him he knew he hadn't investigated properly, and he was enjoying it.

'And how did you go about killing her Mr Sifuentes?'

Raphael took a gamble. He still didn't know exactly how Lola had been killed, and obviously her murderer would know those details, but he took a chance on knowing that they'd said Josue's finger-prints were on a knife. Even the police couldn't bend the truth too much. 'I stabbed her.'

'How many times?'

'I don't remember. I was very angry. Maybe thirty-three?' Raphael looked Lopez right in the eye as he said that, remembering in a moment of brilliant lucidity that Manuel Chavez had been stabbed thirty-three times.

'No. She was not stabbed that many times.' Lopez said briskly.

'Like I said, I don't remember.'

'And why did you kill her?'

'Jealousy. Pure and simple, just like the other policeman thought when he interviewed me. I found out about her and Josue and I flew into a rage about it.'

Lopez seemed to think for a moment or was it just that he couldn't believe his luck and he was revelling in it. The frame of Josue Chan was pretty solid but a signed confession from her known lover that would be even better. 'Let me go and get your previous statement. We need to go over it, we can't just accept your word that you killed her.'

Raphael smiled inside at that. Since when did the police care about the truth, or a proper investigation, or checking the facts? 'Perhaps you could leave me a piece of paper to write my confession?'

'You just wait here. I'll be right back.' Lopez snapped.

Raphael lit a cigarette. He was enjoying this. Enjoying making Lopez squirm, letting him know he knew about his crimes, even if he was playing right into his hands by confessing. It hadn't crossed his mind that he would enjoy it. Raphael couldn't remember when he'd last had so much fun. He hadn't had any fun for a long time.

Lopez came back in with a file and sat down opposite Raphael. 'So, let's go through this again, shall we?' He scanned the papers in front of him. 'My colleague was of the opinion that you killed Miss Rodriguez in a fit of jealousy.'

'That's right.'

'What were you jealous about?'

'You know perfectly well,' said Raphael looking him right in the eye. 'I found out about her and Josue.'

'But you'd fought about that previously, hadn't you?'

So, the police had found out about his argument with Lola. Why hadn't they come back to question him more? Did they know he would come in to confess? But how could they have known that when Raphael hadn't known it himself? 'Yes, before I went away.'

'So you were still angry when you got back? Angry enough to kill her?'

'Yes, we fought again. She kept denying it, but I knew. I just knew, the whore.' Raphael threw that in for dramatic effect. Well, she had betrayed him, he had a right to be angry, but he shouldn't overdo it, he might even end up believing he had killed her.

'And then what happened, did you hit her?'

'Yes. We were struggling and I lost it, I hit her and knocked her out.'

'Where was this?'

'At her place.'

'But Miss Rodriguez was found in an alley, some distance from her home.'

'I took her there.'

Lopez looked at him in disbelief.

'I may not look it, but I'm a strong man you know. I used to be a fighter.'

'A fighter?'

'A freedom fighter.' That should be a good strong nail in his coffin, admitting that, though of course Lopez already knew all about his past.

'Hmm. How exactly? Was she already dead? How did you get her through the streets without arousing suspicion?'

'I don't know exactly what happened, I must have lost control. Then I realised I'd stabbed her. We were covered in blood. I wrapped her in a blanket and then I half carried her out, like she was leaning on me. It was the middle of the night by then, you know what it's like, the streets were deserted. There was no one around. It was easy, easier than I thought. The adrenalin, you know, gives you extra strength. I'm sure you know, being an ex-military man.'

Lopez did not rise to that. 'And is that why you went to her apartment the next day? To clear up the mess?'

'That's right.'

'Yes, you were seen by one of the neighbours, but she didn't find anything strange about it. Said she'd seen you many times before at her apartment.'

Raphael smiled; it was all tying in neatly, his innocent visit to check on Lola. Although if he were hearing this story from the police, if they were trying to pin this version of events on him, he'd be decrying its implausibility, proclaiming his innocence.

'So, if you were jealous of Josue as you claim, Mr Sifuentes, why did you arrange legal representation for him? It was perfect for you, him being accused of your crime.'

Raphael hadn't thought of that. He had to come up with an answer quickly; he couldn't be seen to be thinking too much. 'I don't know what you mean. I never arranged any representation for Josue.' He stared Lopez right in the eyes, trying to appear confident.

'So, the lawyer who showed up here, wasn't a friend of yours?'

'What lawyer? I don't know what you're talking about. I don't know about any lawyer.' Raphael's hands were sweating now. He tried to wipe them inconspicuously on his trousers. He went to light a cigarette.

'I don't believe you,' said Lopez.

'What?' Raphael laid the cigarette back on the table.

'You didn't *lose it*. You planned it. You had it all planned out from your previous argument. Your trip to Chimaltenango to provide an alibi, telling us you didn't get back here until Sunday, conveniently turning up at the hospital and being the one to identify her, pretending you were shocked. And this letter.' He waved Raphael's note at him. 'Telling her goodbye. Saying you're sorry. It was a threat, wasn't it? You were letting her know you were going to deal with her when you got back? Don't think you'll get away with manslaughter Mr Sifuentes. This was premeditated. This was murder. You'll get life for this.'

Lopez paused for dramatic effect. 'Chan would have gone down for it.' He smirked. 'So why the confession, Raphael. Guilt too much for you. Playing games with your mind, is it?'

Raphael stared at him. It took him a few seconds to compose himself, to come up with a response. 'What are you talking about? If you were so sure it was murder, why didn't you arrest me? Why have you got Josue in custody? You don't know what you're doing.'

'Oh, I think I do. My officers were going to pick you up later today.'

'Bullshit. You've got Josue's fingerprints on the murder weapon!'

'Do I? And how would you know that, Mr Sifuentes? You shouldn't believe everything your lawyer tells you. They can be fed information. Everyone's open to a bribe.'

Now Raphael didn't know what to say. Was Lopez telling the truth? Had they really been on the point of arresting him? It wasn't hard to believe that Arturo could be persuaded by money. He always had been. Why had he gone to him? Of all the lawyers he could have picked, why him, the least trustworthy person? Someone he didn't know at all would have been better.

'Well. What have you got to say to that?' asked Lopez. 'Perhaps you should think about it in a cell for a while. Then you can write your confession. Make sure you get all the facts right.' Lopez pushed back his chair with a loud screech against the floor.

Raphael sat on the hard cot in the cell looking at the wall. Suddenly, winning was feeling very much like losing. He'd played right into Lopez's hands, done exactly what he'd wanted him to, and if he hadn't he would have been arrested anyway. Or would he? Raphael didn't know what to believe. Surely Lopez was lying? He hadn't been going to arrest him. They had Josue all stitched up for it. The police twisted everything. Raphael's own mind twisted everything. He could easily see how after a few hours of interrogation by

189

Lopez he'd believe he really had done it, and not just in a fit of jealousy, but a carefully plotted plan as Lopez had said. Just the way Lopez planned everything, with precision. He wondered if Josue had admitted guilt, if he'd been ground down by the incessant questions and manipulation of the facts. But what were the facts?

Fact – Lola was dead.

Fact – what else? He couldn't say for sure who'd committed her murder, or why.

Fact – Raphael hadn't killed her. But how long would it take for that fact to become fuzzy.

Fact – Lopez had killed Manuel Chavez – but that wasn't proven, was it? It was only a supposition. A theory put forward by Rosario. And all Raphael had as corroboration was a shadowy picture of Lopez leading off Manuel.

Fact – Rosario was dead. Killed by Lopez? Inconclusive evidence your honour.

Fact – Raphael was screwed. Whatever he said or did now, Lopez had him; there was no turning back. Best to go along with everything Lopez said. Keep the questioning to a minimum so he could at least keep his sanity.

He wondered if Josue was still in the same police station. Maybe he was in the cell next to him, separated by just a few feet of stone, wondering what would become of him, what would happen at his hearing, if he was going to spend the rest of his days in jail. Or was he in on it? Had Josue been told Raphael had been arrested? Was he rejoicing, knowing that he'd only have to spend one more night in this hole and tomorrow the case against him would be dropped? That he'd be a free man again? Raphael looked round the cell. It didn't take long – the thick iron door, the bare, narrow cot, the bucket in the corner. He could almost reach out and touch the opposite wall. Surely proper jails were better appointed than this? He'd have a desk maybe where he could write. But would he have any time to himself? That was the point of prison, no free time. They took away your right to a moment's peace. Maybe he'd have to share with a crazy man, a murderer, a rapist. What might they do to him? He hadn't thought this through and now it was too late.

But his mind would still be free, they couldn't imprison his mind. That was better, wasn't it, to have his body imprisoned and his mind free? No more guilt, he was more than paying for everything. Yes, it would be all right. He would find a way to cope. He always had. He had lived through Lidia's death, through Benigno's, through Lola's betrayal. He was strong, stronger than he thought, stronger than anyone believed him to be. Lopez couldn't beat him. He had won. Raphael's conviction in the validity of his actions was unshaken.

The door opened and he was taken back to the interview room.

'So, are you ready to make your confession Mr Sifuentes?'

'Yes. Give me a piece of paper, I'll write it all out.'

Lopez's face showed no emotion. 'I have some more questions.'

'No need. I did it. I'm going to write it all out and sign it. You don't have to worry about it holding up in court.'

'Very well.'

22

Three weeks later. Pavoncito jail, outside Guatemala City.

'What are you doing here?' whispered Andrea urgently.

'I confessed.'

'What? I don't understand. What do you mean?'

'I confessed to Lola's murder.' Andrea turned her head away, looking at the guards around the edge of the room. Raphael reached out and touched her arm. She pulled her hand away. 'I didn't do it. I just had to confess. I had to make it all end. It's hard to explain.'

'Try,' said Andrea. That one word conveyed a world of hurt and anger as though Raphael had slapped her face.

Raphael willed all his thoughts and feelings into the silence, begging her to understand what made sense to no one but him.

'Why, Raphael? Why?' she begged for an explanation.

'I …' He paused, struggling to formulate his thoughts. He hadn't envisioned having to explain this to anyone. It made perfect sense in his head, but … 'I don't think Josue did it …'

'But, Raph …'

He held up her hand to stop her. 'It's not about Josue. I think the closest we'll ever come to knowing what happened to Lola is that Lopez killed her, or paid someone to. Either way someone else was going down for it, either me or Josue. I have less to lose.'

'No you don't. What do you mean, less to … you've …'

'I've had enough Andrea. I can't do it anymore.' She looked confused. 'I lost my wife, my son, and now Lola. I was paranoid, scared, guilty. That was no life. Nothing more can happen to me in here. I'm free.'

'Free?' She shook her head. 'But you're locked up.'

'I thought somehow you might understand, but …' He sighed. 'It was my fault, I have to pay.'

'What was your fault?'

'If I'd taken better care of them, if I'd watched Benigno …'

'Oh Raphael.' She took his hands in hers. 'You can't think like that.'

'But I do.'

'The war killed them. The military killed them. There was nothing you could have done.'

They sat in silence for a minute. Raphael didn't think he'd ever make her understand.

'Did Lola ever tell you about how we met?' he said.

'What? What's that got to do with anything? What's wrong Raphael? Have they mistreated you? They've confused you, haven't they? So you don't know what you're saying anymore? I can get you help. I can get you a good lawyer. It's not over, we can get you out of here.'

'No. I'm not losing my mind, Andrea. I know exactly what I'm doing. Just tell me. What did Lola tell you about meeting me? You said once that she said she really loved me, that she wanted me to propose, and I didn't believe you. Tell me what she told you about me, please.'

Andrea shrugged, 'OK if it will help you in some way. She said she met you in a café and she thought you were attractive, no, interesting I think was the word. She seemed quite captivated from the start.'

'From the start? From the first time she met me?'

'Yes. Is that so incredible?'

Raphael raised one shoulder as though he wasn't sure whether it was credible or not. 'And then what? When did she start declaring her love for me?'

Andrea smiled. 'I don't know. It's not like we saw each other that often, and it was just gossip between sisters. She didn't tell me everything about your relationship.'

'But you clearly had the impression that you thought it was serious. You said she'd mentioned marriage.'

'Yes. Well, not as such. She said she wished you'd consider marriage, or something like that. That you were the one.'

'She said that?'

'Yes. What's all this about? She's gone Raphael. Just remember that she loved you and leave it at that. You'll drive yourself crazy with all this speculation.'

'It's not that simple.' Raphael wondered whether telling Andrea the truth about Lola was really a good idea, but what did he have to lose? 'I found a file. She was informing on me.'

'What do you mean, informing on you? To whom? What sort of file?'

'It was in my papers, my old files on stories I'd written. For the paper,' he clarified. 'It had photocopies of journals in Lola's handwriting, saying how she'd met me, and lots of details, and the most recent ones said she couldn't do it anymore, she couldn't carry on informing.'

'Are you sure?'

Raphael nodded.

'But there must be a logical explanation. Maybe someone planted it there.'

'But why?'

'Who knows why? Who knows why the security forces do anything?' Andrea sighed.

'But how did they get stuff written by her? It was definitely her handwriting. I checked.'

'You were pretty confused and exhausted then.'

'Are you saying I imagined it? Made it up?'

'No. Keep your voice down,' she warned, taking his hand again. 'I'm not suggesting that. I just can't believe Lola would do that. What would she gain?'

'I don't know. Money?'

'Lola wasn't that bothered about money, and anyway she had enough.'

'Blackmail? Could someone have been trying to blackmail her?'

'I suppose it's possible. She can't have led a blameless life. But there's nothing I know of that would cause great distress if it came out. That she'd go to such lengths to hide.'

They sat in silence for a while. Other people carried on conversations around them. Visiting time was not so long, most prisoners couldn't afford the luxury of silence. Andrea became aware of a guard walking behind her. 'I just can't believe she'd do that Raphael. I can't. Lola wasn't perfect, she never was, but not that. There has to be an explanation.' She paused. 'You don't really believe it, do you?'

'I don't know what to believe anymore. Everything is so unbelievable. The war, the death, and now Lola. But I did always have a feeling that our first meeting wasn't just random. I always felt like Lola had searched me out.'

'Maybe she did. That doesn't mean it was for a bad reason, Raphael. Maybe it was her destiny.'

'Ha. To love me?' Raphael said sarcastically.

'Why not?'

'So, was it destiny that my wife and son died?'

'I don't know, Raphael. Lots of people died.'

'But you can't believe that happened for a reason? That's too sick a joke, it can't be true. I can't believe that.'

'No, you're right,' she said, patting his hand, trying to calm him. 'But you said you were free now. Free of your guilt. Why not let it all go. Why not accept that Lola loved you? Maybe not how your wife did, maybe it was not how you wanted it to be, but in her own way she loved you.'

Raphael shrugged.

The bell rang, signalling that the visiting time was over. All along the row visitors began to stand up and make their goodbyes. Andrea reached across and took Raphael's hand again. 'I'll be back.'

'You do believe I'm innocent, don't you?'

'Of course, I do Raphael, how could I think otherwise? And I believe Lola was innocent too.'

Back in his cell, Raphael lay on his bunk. Was Andrea right? Or could she just not see any malice in her sister? He thought back over his relationship with Lola, how he'd always had the feeling that their first meeting hadn't just been by chance. But maybe that was just his own insecurity that he couldn't believe a woman like Lola could love him. He'd spent so much time convincing himself he didn't love her and that she couldn't love him – why? Because loving another woman felt like betraying Lidia? Because it felt wrong to have happiness? Why should he be allowed a second chance when Lidia and Benigno weren't? He took out a notebook and began to write. He didn't stop until the lights were turned out.

23

'You don't have to do this,' said Josue.

'Yes I do.'

'I mean I can't let you.'

'It's not up to you,' said Raphael.

'Wait let me finish. I'm not who you think I am.'

'Eh?'

'Lola and I were never lovers. I loved her, was crazy about her, but we were just friends.'

'So why did you let me think you were?'

'I don't know. It all just got out of hand, and then the police, and being beaten up, I didn't know whether I was coming or going. And you didn't seem bothered, you were still helping me, treating me as a friend. You were so good to me Raphael, and you had no reason to be.'

'But the woman at the hospital said. Everyone seemed to think you were her lover.'

'That part was true. The people at the hospital did find my flyer in Lola's bag, and they called me. I don't know why they didn't go through her address book, or try to find her family, they must do it all the time, but they called me. As soon as I heard Lola was at the hospital I had to go there. I didn't think they'd let me see her if I was just a friend, so I said the first thing I thought of, I said I was her fiancé. I didn't know she was dead. I thought she'd just had an accident or something. Then the police showed up and the receptionist must have told them I was the fiancé and I didn't contradict it. I'd just found out she was dead. I was in a complete daze, well you saw me, I didn't know what to say.'

Raphael nodded. He thought back to that night at the hospital when he'd first met Josue. How he'd thought he'd looked so young and innocent, so shocked. All of that had been true.

'Then the police wanted someone to identify her … I couldn't do that. I don't know what I'd have done if you hadn't been there.'

'But I don't understand. If you weren't her lover, why didn't you tell the police that?'

'Don't you think I tried?' Josue looked exasperated. 'I kept telling them I wasn't her boyfriend, that we'd never been lovers, that it was all a misunderstanding, but they wouldn't listen to me. I think that's why they beat me up; they thought I was lying to them. That one who interviewed me was a real nasty piece of work. I really thought I'd go down for it. Then just like that I was released. They said they had a signed confession and all charges were dropped. I never imagined it was you.' Josue looked down at his hands. 'I went looking for you, to tell you the good news and I couldn't find you at home or at work. Finally, someone at the paper told me you'd been arrested. I'm sorry it took so long to come and visit.'

Raphael shook that off, indicating it was no problem that Josue hadn't visited before. He shook his head and smiled to himself. 'Andrea told me not to trust you.'

'Who's Andrea?'

'Lola's sister. She said she'd never heard of you, that she was sure Lola didn't have another lover because she was too in love with me. I didn't believe her, but I was suspicious for a while, that's why I tried to check you out.'

'What do you mean, check me out?'

'I snooped around a bit, you know through my newspaper connections. You seemed to be who you said you were, you did give concerts and taught music.'

'I am who I said I was; I just wasn't Lola's lover. Ironic eh, living so close to you, and you being her real lover. What I wanted to be. And look where it got me. Just pretending to be her lover turned into a nightmare.' Josue laughed, then he became serious again. 'The friendship was real, Raphael. I needed you, and you were there for me. And now I want to help you.'

'But I don't know who you are Josue.'

'What do you mean? I was Lola's friend, that's all. And I'm your friend. I hope I am.'

'Tell me who you are. Who is Josue Chan? What's his story? Why are you so alone in the world?' Raphael had an anguished expression, his eyes large and dark, as though knowing the truth, all the truth about Josue was desperately important.

'OK, OK, I'll tell you. We lived in the Nebaj triangle.' As soon as Josue said that Raphael was pretty sure how the story would go, but he let him tell it. 'The village was razed and those of us who were left were taken to a model village. My parents and sisters died. I was the only one from our family. I didn't recognise anyone at the new village. There were people from all over, all speaking different languages, I hated it. I stayed a few months and then the army moved on and left the civil patrols in charge, it was still bad but a little easier, I managed to get away and to cut a long story short, I ended up in an orphanage, just outside the capital.'

'Which orphanage? I never could find a record of you at the orphanages I was familiar with.'

'They've changed the name since I was there. It was on the edge of the city, run by Presbyterians.'

'Presbyterians?'

'Yes, does that matter?'

'Probably not, carry on.'

'They gave us a basic education, taught us a skill, and one of the teachers played the guitar and though we didn't have proper lessons I picked it up, she said I had a natural talent. When I was too old to stay there, I worked with them as a teacher for about a year and then I came back to the city to try to make it on my own.'

'And you did.'

'Yeah I suppose I did.'

'But I was wary of people, didn't trust anyone too much. I had friends, but just the sort to have a beer with, or make some music with. Then I met Lola, and she was special, but she made it clear she had someone. I always hoped she might change her mind, but she didn't.'

A glimpse of a thought entered Raphael's head. 'Did she ever write you letters?' he asked.

Josue hesitated. 'Er yeah, quite a lot.'

'What sort of thing?'

Josue looked embarrassed. 'At first she used to drop me little notes about books to read or films to see. Sometimes a note to say how she'd enjoyed my playing. And well,' he paused, 'I suppose I got the wrong end of the stick a bit, I hoped for too much.'

'You wrote her love letters?' Raphael interrupted.

'Yeah. And I pestered her a bit, I suppose. She was always nice about it, but towards the end she started sending me letters saying it couldn't carry on, and maybe we shouldn't be friends. You're not mad, are you?'

Raphael shook his head. No, he wasn't angry, he was thinking. Could someone have copied Lola's letters to Josue? Was that what he'd found in his files and completely misunderstood? But what about the early ones, describing how she'd met him? Could someone have copied her writing and fabricated them? Just to ... just to what, drive him crazy?'

'How long did this go on?'

'What?'

'How long did you know Lola? How long had you been friends?'

'Ah, a little longer than I probably gave you to believe. A year or more I suppose.'

'And she wrote to you all that time?'

'Yeah, just the odd note here and there. Don't be angry Raphael. There was nothing going on, honestly. You can see them if you want.'

'No, it's OK. It's fine.' It was fine. Raphael had a plausible explanation at last. He didn't know what the truth was, he didn't know why anyone would want to put fake letters in his house, what they thought they could possibly gain, but stranger things had happened. He could have Lola back. He could re-create her memory. He could believe someone had made fakes out of notes she'd written to Josue. He could believe that they planted them in his house, for whatever reason. He could believe Lola had loved him. He smiled at Josue.

'What?'

Raphael shook his head.

'What are you going to do Raphael? You don't have to do this. Tell them the truth.'

'I can't. They won't believe me now. They have me all caught up in their net. They were going to frame someone for this. It's better it is me not you.'

'No Raphael.'

'Josue, you know as well as I do, the real killer will never be brought to justice. Take the chance. Get out of this place. Get out of this country. Go and live your life Josue.'

'But there must be some way out for you?'

'No Josue, this is the way out. The only way out. There is no death penalty anymore, I'll be better off in jail, safer. I've made my decision. That is one thing no one can take from me, not you or the police, my free will, my mind. I stay with my decision, end of story.'

'Is there anything I can do for you? I know I've not been much of a friend to you Raphael, but I care for you, you're the closest thing I've had to a ...'

Raphael was afraid Josue would start crying. He wasn't sure he could cope with that. 'Nothing, there's nothing I want you to do.' He paused. 'No wait, there is something. I'm going to write a book in prison, finally the novel I've been waiting all my life to write. I'll send it to you, try to get it published.'

'I will.' They sat in silence for a minute. '*Ai* Raphael, I don't understand you.'

'Neither do I. I don't understand anything. It doesn't matter. Look the guard is coming over; you'll have to go. Don't wait for the trial, go now, get away, start again, that's what you can do for me.'

They clasped hands like brothers. 'Thank you, Raphael.'

Raphael smiled.

Epilogue

On 1 November 2000, Day of the Dead, Raphael Sifuentes was sentenced to life imprisonment for the murder of Dolores Rodriguez. Andrea kept believing he was innocent and visited him regularly in prison.

Josue went into exile in Spain where he made a living by playing guitar in bars and found a publisher for Raphael's novel, *Dia de los Vivos* – Day of the Living, a love story in a time of war.

And Colonel Almendrez Lopez? He is still an officer in the Guatemala City police force and remains uncharged for any crime, during or after the civil war. But there still remains an incriminating photo of him somewhere, and one day his hour of punishment will come.

In 1995, 25 years ago, Manuel Saquic, a Presbyterian minister was murdered in Chimaltenango, Guatemala. His killer, believed to be a local military commissioner, was never arrested, despite a warrant having been issued for his arrest. This event partly inspired this novel, however all the characters and events here related are fictitious.

Que descanse en paz todas las victimas de la guerra civil en Guatemala.

May all the victims of the Guatemalan civil war rest in peace.

Rev. Manuel Saquic was a Presbyterian minister in Guatemala during the civil war. In 1995 he was abducted and was later found in an unmarked grave – he had been stabbed over 30 times. He was killed after speaking out against the country's military regime and injustices. He was a friend and colleague of the author, who was present at his exhumation and funeral.

An account of this real-life murder lies at the heart of *If It Falls*, the story of Raphael a former guerrilla turned journalist who, while working on the obituary for a fellow reporter killed in mysterious circumstances, stumbles across the story of Manuel Saquic.

Manuel Saquic at his ordination.

GUATEMALA Summary of Amnesty International's Concerns (January 1995-January 1996)

The body of evangelical pastor, Manuel Saquic Vásquez, was recovered from an unmarked grave on 7 July 1995. His throat had been slit and he had 33 stab wounds. Manuel Saquic, who was also coordinator of a Kaqchikel Maya Human Rights Committee (Comité de Derechos Humanos) in Panabajal, Chimaltenango Department, 'disappeared' following his abduction on 23 June. Residents of Panabajal said that the local military commissioner and his two sons, both army security agents, killed Pastor Saquic in reprisal for his human rights work and because he was the sole witness to the previous short-term abduction of another member of the Human Rights Committee in Panabajal. The authorities were widely criticised for withholding information about the body and for refusing to cooperate with the Presbyterian Church and MINUGUA.

In the following months, three members of the church, including the General Secretary of the Conference of Protestant Churches, Rev. Vitalino Similox, received death threats warning them against pursuing their investigations into Manuel Saquic's death. The death threats were signed by a group calling itself the Jaguar of Justice. Members of Manuel Saquic's family and colleagues were also reported to have received death threats. To Amnesty International's knowledge, there has been no progress in the investigations into the death of Manuel Saquic.

 Naomi Young-Rodas is now a minister in the United Reformed Church. At the time of publication (2008) she was an administrator at the University of Cambridge and finished this novel as part of an MA in Creative Writing from Manchester Metropolitan University. She lived and worked in Guatemala in the 1990s during the last years of the civil war; briefly teaching English and then working with the Presbyterian Church of Guatemala. She was involved in the search for Manuel Saquic and the appeals for justice.

Naomi Young-Rodas with children in Guatemala, circa 1994

Naomi has previously had poetry published in various anthologies including: *Singularities* Plain View Press, 2001, *Courage to Love: An Anthology of Inclusive Worship Material*, Darton, Longman and Todd, 2002 (winner of the LAMBDA Literary Award 2003), *Entertaining Angels*, Canterbury Press, 2005 and the prose anthology *Writers in the Crowd*, Treehouse Press, 2013. She published a collection of poems written during the COVID-19 crisis in July 2020 – *The Corona Poems* ©Naomi Young-Rodas

She will have two new novels published by TSL Publishing in 2021 – *Right to Possession* and *Detroit Debris*

www.ingramcontent.com/pod-product-compliance
Lightning Source LLC
Chambersburg PA
CBHW050400030726
47503CB00006B/1951